Prince Bonifacio

Prince Bonifacio
and Other Stories

by
Louis Ulbach

translated, annotated and introduced by
Brian Stableford

A Black Coat Press Book

ISBN 978-1-61227-228-3. First Printing. November 2013. Published by Black Coat Press, an imprint of Hollywood Comics.com, LLC, P.O. Box 17270, Encino, CA 91416. All rights reserved.
Printed in the United States of America.

TABLE OF CONTENTS

Introduction

"Le Prince Bonifacio" by Louis Ulbach, here translated as "Prince Bonifacio," was the title novella of a collection published by J. Hetzel and A. Lacroix in 1864, reprinted in 1869, and again by Calmann Lévy in 1875 and 1884. In that volume it was supplemented by "La Dame blanche de Baden," "Le Petit homme rouge" and "Le Démon du Lac", all of which are translated herein, as "The White Lady of Baden," "The Little Red Man" and "The Demon of the Loch," respectively. The three additional stories had all appeared previously in Ulbach's first collection of stories, *Les Secrets du diable* [The Devil's Secrets], published by Michel Lévy in 1858, which also contained, among other items, "Le Brelan," here translated as "The Brelan." "Le Prince Bonifacio" had previously appeared in a collection entitled *L'Île des rêves, aventures d'un Anglais qui s'ennuie* [The Island of Dreams: The Adventures of a Bored Englishman] (1860).

Louis Ulbach was born in Troyes in 1822 and published his first volume of poems, *Gloriana*, in 1844. The second poem in that collection, after the title-piece, was dedicated to Victor Hugo, under whose influence Ulbach's poetry was written, and the author was encouraged in his literary endeavors by Hugo, thus becoming an enthusiastic but somewhat belated member of the Romantic Movement, whose guiding light Hugo still was. He did not hit his stride as a writer, however, until the 1850s, when the visible Movement seemed to have passed beyond its initial brief and to have become political rather than literary. Many of its leading members were staunch Republicans, who involved themselves actively in protest against Louis-Philippe's government, agitating for the Revolution of 1848. Hugo was one of several stars of the Movement who accepted an office in the new government of the Second Republic, along with Edgar Quinet and Eugène Sue, and Alphonse de Lamartine as an unsuccessful candidate for its presidency.

That presidential election was won, in a landslide, by Louis-Napoléon Bonaparte, who followed his grandfather's example by transforming the nascent Republic into an Empire in the coup of 1851. Hugo, Quinet, Sue, Alexandre Dumas, Jules Hetzel and many other Romantic Republicans were exiled, and only some of them chose to take advantage of the amnesty offered a few years later to return; Hugo and Quinet stood on their dignity until the Second Empire eventually fell, in 1870, and Sue died in exile. Although that debacle forced the agitators in question to give complete priority in future to their writing, and the fiery resentment with which they charged it in consequence served to reignite the flames of Romanticism to some extent, the Movement, as such, seemed to many observers to be extinct, or at least to have been shattered; even the forefront of literary fashion had moved on, and those Romantic writers who continued to write and publish prolifically while resident in Paris, including Joseph Méry, Léon Gozlan and Ulbach, seemed to be settling into a popular groove, no longer revolutionary in their writing, even if, like Ulbach, they also devoted themselves to political agitation.

In political terms, at least Ulbach became one the fieriest of the belated Romantics, and that same fire was carried over into his literary criticism. He became notorious for pugnacious diatribes published in *Le Figaro* under the pseudonym of "Ferragus" (appropriated from the enigmatic antagonist of a novella by Honoré de Balzac), in which he launched attacks on the new trend of Naturalism—including an abusive attack on Émile Zola' *Thérèse Raquin* (1867)—as well as issuing scathingly sarcastic observations about the political order of the Second Empire that flirted dangerously with the tolerance of Louis-Napoléon's ever-vigilant censors.

Ulbach was the dramatic critic for *Le Temps* for a while, and he took over the editorship of a reincarnated version of the Romantic organ *La Revue de Paris* in its final years, until it ceased publication in 1858 when he finally tried the patience of the censors too far—a fate that subsequently befell his own short-lived periodical *La Cloche*, which took the form of a personal journal, founded in 1868. That earned him a period of imprisonment, and the fall of the Empire brought him no respite. His continued political sniping after his release got him into further trouble; the government of the Third Republic that imprisoned him again in 1871-72, and he had by no means endeared himself to the Communards in the interim, thus completing an unusually full spectrum of unpopularity. Of all the Romantic rebels, Ulbach was the one most likely, if asked exactly what he was rebelling against, to have offered the Brandoesque reply: "What have you got?" In 1878, however, he was appointed to Charles Nodier's old position as librarian of the Bibliothèque de l'Arsenal, and enjoyed a less turbulent existence thereafter, until his death in 1889.

Ulbach inevitably became more famous for his political agitation than his literary work, outshone by his *alter ego* Ferragus. When he took over the *Revue de Paris* his own work still seemed to have an element of daring about it, but the experimentation in style and method that he carried out in his early short fiction eventually gave way to a settled competence that was slicker but by no means as adventurous. His novels sold reasonably well, but it is arguable that they were all forgettable, and have, indeed been largely forgotten. They do not exhibit the same spirit of adventure that Méry and Gozlan, his most prominent contemporaries, retained even when they became thoroughly professionalized. Ulbach's early work, however, especially that collected in *Les Secrets du diable* and *L'Île des rêves*, most of whose contents were subsequently reshuffled in *Prince Bonifacio* and the complementary collection *Voyage autour de mon clocher* (1864), is considerably more enterprising in the methods with which it experiments and in its imaginative component—an imaginative component that was largely squeezed out once he had settled his narrative strategy. No matter how much he hated Émile Zola, Ulbach became something of a Naturalist himself, albeit a weak-kneed one, evasive of the seamier side of life that Zola was prepared to tackle head-on.

In much of his early work, most especially "Voyage autour de mon clocher" and the three stories from *Les Secrets du diable* that he reprinted in *Prince Bonifacio*, Ulbach seems to show the strong influence of Victor Hugo's close friend Paul Lacroix, who signed most of his work "P. L. Jacob, bibliophile," and who ended his career as Ulbach's immediate predecessor as librarian at the Bibliothèque de l'Arsenal. "Voyage autour de mon clocher" is a pseudo-autobiographical account of his research into the history of his home town of Troyes, and it was his reading of contemporary narrative histories that inspired him to write the triptych of stories that followed the novella in question in his first collection, and was reprinted (in reverse order) in *Prince Bonifacio*.

Although "Le Démon du lac" is not dated in the latter collection, it was probably written in 1850, the year in which the book acknowledged in its footnotes to have inspired it was published, in between "Le Petit homme rouge" (dated 1849) and "La Dame blanche de Baden" (dated 1854). At any rate, it seems likely that the first two stories were both written in the interim between the 1848 revolution and the 1851 coup, so their sentimental royalist sympathies—an aspect of Ulbach's work that never recurred—would have run directly contrary to the ideological grain of the day. It might be significant, in that context, that Ulbach chose to abridge "Le Petit homme rouge" when he reprinted it. (I have included the ending that he removed as an appendix to the version from *Prince Bonifacio*, for the purposes of comparison.)

Paul Lacroix's works show a consistent fascination, entirely expectable in a Romantic writer, with the role played in history by folklore and legends; he was perpetually fascinated by the past's fascination with the supernatural. An important aspect of his own fascination, however, was an insistence on standing back from such beliefs and refusing to endorse them. The whole point of being a historian, an antiquary and a bibliophile, from Lacroix's viewpoint, was to be able to look back on the past with a cool, clinical and skeptical eye, seeking to explain the force once exerted by beliefs that could now be appreciated, in a positivist era, as obsolete, killed off by the inevitable progressive evolution of ideas. That did not, of course, make the superstitious beliefs of the past and present any less interesting; if anything, it made them more interesting, by adding a curious element of perversity and paradoxicality to their contemplation and their literary representation.

That kind of perversity and paradoxicality is very obvious in the three Ulbach stories in question—perhaps more so than in anything Lacroix wrote himself, because Ulbach's clinical gaze and literary method are by no means as steady as his predecessor's. The effect is paradoxical, in that it aims simultaneously for philosophical distance and narrative intimacy, which raises considerable narrative difficulties in the tone and planning of the stories, and perverse, because the author is well aware of the fact that any dissent he manifests from the reality of legend is bound to undermine the narrative currency of his own endeavor, unless he can somehow change that currency into different esthetic coin.

Ulbach's narrative voice always seems uneasy in managing the convolutions of his stories forced by the necessity of inserting background material. Extra narrative distance is introduced into "La Dame blanche de Baden" by the employment of a frame narrative, allowing the nuclear story to be narrated by a credulous voice but filtered through a skeptical one. That was a device that Ulbach employed on a more lavish scale in *L'Île des rêves*, in which the stories making up the collection—including "Le Prince Bonifacio"—are embedded within a micro-Decameronesque frame in which they being told to one another by voluntary castaways on a desert island wryly thwarted in their quest for isolation by one another's inconvenient presence.

With or without that extra distancing move, "Le Prince Bonifacio" is one of the boldest of Ulbach's early experiments. It is a Voltairean *conte philosophique*, which sets out to satirize politics in the scathing fashion that Voltaire had borrowed himself from Jonathan Swift. In flippantly mimicking the form of fanciful folktales, however—as he often did—Voltaire had usually been content to borrow narrative devices from Antoine Galland's *Mille-et-une nuits*. That was something that the more positivistically-inclined Ulbach thought inappropriate, so he adapted a methodological twist that Swift and Voltaire had each used only once, Swift in the third part of *Gulliver's Travels* and Voltaire in *Micromegas*, substituting pseudoscientific speculation for magic in order to provide a crucial lever for his plot. Like Swift—but unlike Voltaire—Ulbach was as skeptical about orthodox science as he was about any other kind of political orthodoxy, so his invocation of scientific miracle-working confused the political satire with an element of satire directed against "mad scientists," but that only serves to add a little seasoning to the story.

Because Ulbach uses his pseudoscientific invention purely as a narrative device and not as a serious premise for logical extrapolation, it is doubtful whether "Le Prince Bonifacio" can quality full as an early exercise in *roman scientifique*, but the notion that it invokes eventually became ancestral to an entire subspecies of what ultimately came to be labeled "science fiction," and is therefore of considerable interest as a precursor. As in many Swiftian and Voltairean satires, the story's ironic slapstick has a nightmarish aspect that adds to its edge and makes it more interesting, from the modern viewpoint, than almost anything else that Ulbach wrote. It was, deservedly, one of his most widely-read endeavors in its second form as the title-story of his most oft-reprinted collection.

"Le Prince Bonifacio" was not, however, the first work in which Ulbach had experimented with the narrative move of substituting a pseudoscientific lever for a magical one in order to transform an apparently-traditional story into something new and strange. Although the two 1864 collections recycled almost all of the material from the 1858 and 1860 collections—some of which was further recycled in other volumes—one story that he never reprinted again was "Le

Brelan," although it is arguable the most interesting of all the stories in the first collection, because rather than in spite of its extraordinarily awkward narrative convolution.

Presumably, Ulbach did not reprint the story because he thought it less artful, and it is indeed rather clumsy in the manner in which it embeds two overlapping nuclear narratives within a third, and then embeds that in a frame narrative whose own narrative voice is rather confused. That mélange, however, is not the result of ineptitude, but of trying to do something very difficult and entirely new, and the story remains highly unusual, and perhaps unique, not only in the manner in which it attempts to remove the supernatural element from something resembling a traditional fantasy of diabolism, but also in the apparent moral thrust of the story, which has affinities with the "immoral tales" included in Pétrus Borel's *Champavert* (1833) and the *contes cruels* that became a central thread of the endeavors of the *fin-de-siècle* Decadent Movement. It is isolated from the *conte cruel* tradition, however, because it lacks the habitual steely cynicism of that format, and contrives instead a tone of exaggerated sentimentality that is distinctive and extremely unorthodox, although arguably perfectly fitted to a story whose implicit metaphysics is obliged to abolish divine mercy along with diabolical malice.

"Le Brelan" requires independent introduction, if only because its title needs explanation to modern readers for whom the word has become a dead letter. It is worth mentioning in this context that one of Paul Lacroix's fascinations was the history of card games, and that appears to have been an interest shared by Ulbach. The first story in *Les Secrets du diable* is "Argine Piquet" (previously published in the *Revue de Paris* in 1851 and as a booklet in 1853) whose eponymous character claims to be a descendant of the inventor of the game of piquet—the ancestor of modern whist games—and who spends her life trying unsuccessfully to devise a "perfect" card game, summarily symbolic of the contests of modern politics and personal affairs. The same line of thought, briefly but significantly echoed in "Le Prince Bonifacio," seems to have been one of the initiating factors of "Le Brelan."

Although invented considerably earlier, piquet became a very popular game in the seventeenth and eighteenth centuries, when it became a prominent feature of life at Versailles in the courts of Louis XIV and Louis XV. It was regarded as a game suitable for women and mixed company, played primarily for enjoyment rather than for money, but male poseurs often preferred an alternative game played by with the same 32-card "piquet deck," custom-designed for macho gambling, called brelan. Just as piquet was eventually elaborated into all the modern varieties of whist (without ever discovering Argine Piquet's perfect symbology), so brelan was eventually elaborated into the spectrum of modern gambling games including brag and poker. Brelan itself had numerous varieties, and it is not clear exactly which variety is played in "Le Brelan," but that is not really significant; what is significant is the fact that "a brelan" was a particular hand, of considerable but not necessarily unbeatable value.

The particular brelan featured in the story is three kings; the story does not specify exactly what the hand is that beats it every time, but there are several ways in which that might work, depending on the precise form of the game being played. The best-known version bore some resemblance to the kind of "Texas hold'em" nowadays standard in tournament poker, with each player holding three individual cards and a single card on the table being common to all the hands (in which case three kings could be beaten by any four-of-a-kind) but no mention is made in the story of the "flop card," and its beating is credited to "a superior brelan" so it is probably the case that the prial of kings is continually beaten by a prial of aces. In any case, the significant item in the story is the continual fall, or slaying, of the symbolic kings of hearts, diamonds and clubs, representing three aspects of aristocratic license. It is, however, also of some significance that the title is slightly ambiguous, "Le Brelan" potentially referring either to the particular hand featured, or to the game, or even, by extrapolation back to the old French root of *bretlenc*, to gambling in general. Translation inevitably narrows that range of meaning slightly, as translation often does.

Given that Ulbach chose not to include "Le Brelan" in *Prince Bonifacio*, it is arguable that it might have been diplomatic not to append it here, but by 1864—probably more than ten years after he wrote "Le Brelan"—Ulbach had cultivated particular notions of literary propriety that were a product of their era, with which a modern critic is not bound to agree. Although I sympathize with his decision to reverse the presumable chronological order of composition of the stories when setting them out in the 1864 collection, I think there is a good case to be made for extrapolating that process by one further step, and including what seems to me to be the most fascinating of all his literary endeavors. If nothing else, it introduces a kind of symmetry by framing the three historical stories that flirt with supernatural themes with a parenthetical pair of innovative endeavors on the margins of *roman scientifique*, which are surely Romantic in the most extreme and best sense of all.

The translations of material from *Prince Bonifacio* are reproduced from the version of the Hetzel and Lacroix edition reproduced on the Bibliothèque Nationale's *gallica* website. The translations of the supplementary ending to "Le Petit homme rouge" and "Le Brelan" are reproduced from the version of the Michel Lévy edition of *Les Secrets du diable* reproduced on the same website.

Brian Stableford

PRINCE BONIFACIO

I. In which it is proved that it is difficult for a prince
to satisfy everybody and his son

There was once a prince named Bonifacio, who was the best of men and the most detestable of princes.

I do not want to speak ill of humankind or of power, but it is certain that the private virtues of Prince Bonifacio were deleterious to his public virtues, and that, being endowed with a fabulous generosity, he did not want to force his subjects to pay taxes, thieves for whom prison might have been unhealthy to remain behind bars, or soldiers who had things to do at home to remain under arms, and that, in consequence of these concessions, the administration of finance, justice and the army were in a parlous state.

Now, everyone knows that, without money, Italian princes are not Swiss, and that all the princes in the world are not devoted servants. It is equally constant that justice needs to be administered, if only by the administration of violent beatings, and no one is unaware that an army is as indispensable to a ministry of war as a hare to jugged hare.[1]

The prince was not a rigorous observer or monarchical systems, however. He took things at his ease, and permitted others to act in the same fashion in his regard. His subjects did not quibble with regard to an old charter granted by one of his ancestors; and he, for his part, reproached himself bitterly for demanding of his apathetic administrators what he had every

---

[1] The famous first line of a recipe for jugged hare, "first catch your hare," associate in England with Mrs. Beaton, originated in the 18th century French *Cuisinière bourgeoise* [Everyday Cooking]

right to obtain from them. A mutual tolerance confounded duties, and the reins of government formed a rather confused tangle that no one thought of slicing through.

With such a system, Prince Bonifacio was deeply in debt, and he was obliged to have recourse to numerous loans to have the chimneys of his castle repaired. The people were scarcely any richer; money, which did not circulate, piled up in the coffers of a few financiers; the middle classes complained about the bad state of the roads that led from the capital to the surrounding drinking-dens, without making the reflection that beautiful roads are macadamized as much by good taxes as good gravel. That axiom was unknown in the principality; the bridges and highways had no representatives, and it was the trampling of passers-by that marked out the roads.

Prince Bonifacio XXIII believed, nevertheless, that he was the benefactor of his people, although he took no vanity from it. Every morning he asked his superintendent of police whether everyone was getting four square meals a day; for him, that was a scruple of conscience. The superintendent, whose table was well-provided, reassured the prince, and the latter, delighted to realize the utopia of a chicken in every pot at such low expense, suffered no indigestion and slept free of nightmares. One might have said of him, as his epitaph—the only veridical princely epitaph—that he never ceased dreaming about the happiness of his people. Sleep was, in fact, the prince's usual condition and dreams the only work of his intelligence; he only dreamed because he could not help dreaming, and the work in question was involuntary.

I have forgotten to tell you that Prince Bonifacio's State was effaced from the map of Italy a long time ago. It is, therefore, an old story that I am telling, and lovers of synchronism can place the reign of the sovereign in question in parallel with the story of the king of Yvetot.[2]

---

[2] The lord of the tiny seigneurie of Yvetot, near Rouen, was given the entitlement to call himself *roi* [king] in the 6th cen-

This, all went badly in the principality. That negligence, in making government careless, generated disorder in society: not a tumultuous disorder, the inhabitants being naturally placid, but a silent, peaceful disorder that inclined the principality gently and gradually toward bankruptcy.

A few minds, a little more vigorously tempered—sons who had been educated in the great capitals, such as Monaco, or had breathed the air of some powerful republic, like that of San Marino, tried hard to stir up an opposition. They tried to found a newspaper. No one stopped them, but, liberty being extended to its ultimate limits, and what can be written always being inferior to what can be said, no one felt the need to go out of his way to read a badly-printed rag. The founders of the paper had only one paying subscriber, Prince Bonifacio, and he was a slow payer; it was necessary to end him a bill twenty times over before obtaining settlement.

The party of the future had despaired. Fomenting a revolution was a very cruel means repugnant to the mild mores of those good folk; besides which, the principality had no National Guard. Then again, in order to have the appearance of serious combat, it would have been necessary to have recourse to the methods in use in military plays and to make use of the same actors to represent the prince's army and the revolutionary army. Now that means, excellent for the illusion of the gaze, is detestable in revolutionary practice.

They had even tried to recruit to the interest of progress the minister of the prince's kitchens, but that high functionary did not want a change of regime, and was apprehensive of the leaders of the opposition, as they would have been obliged to impose universal Spartan broth.

Boniface XXIII, warned about these murmurs on the part of some of his young subjects, took pleasure in these insurrectional whims; he missed the newspaper greatly when it was

---

tury, and "le roi d'Yvetot," mocked in a popular folk song, became a conventional phrase referring to individuals of great pretention but negligible worth.

forced to close down in order to satisfy the demands of its numerous shareholders, especially because of the charades that the organ of the future had felt obliged to publish at the end of every issue to stimulate the zeal of subscribers and patriots. It never occurred to the prince, however, that he might have to grant any satisfaction to the young people in question.

Bonifacio was a man of regular habits; he wanted to die in his routine. For twenty-five years he had had the same ministers and the same wardrobe. It was impossible for him to change his way of doing things.

"After me," he said, "my son can do as he likes." That was better than saying "After me, the Deluge," but Boniface said it in order to dispense with the need for all reflection, for he had, deep down, not the slightest intention of dying and making way for his son. He loved the latter far too much to want to inflict a mourning-dress on him as painful as that one dons for a father, and he slept far too well on his throne to think about going to sleep on the cold pillow of his ancestors.

When I speak of a throne, it is pure fiction. Boniface had loaned his classic throne a long time ago, in order to augment the accessories of the capital's theater, and the royal seat was a rhetorical figure, just like an academician's armchair.

Bonifacio, as I have just told you, had a son; he had only ever had the one. Heaven had respected the prince's apathy, and had not wanted to complicate the government of his States with a numerous family. Besides which, the Princess Mother had died a few days after the birth of the heir presumptive,[3] in consequence of her churching celebration, which had been too copious.

Bonifacio had wept for his wife like a man unaccustomed to weeping—which is to say, abundantly and loudly—and then had consoled himself completely, by virtue of that

---

[3] It is not obvious why the story persistently refers to Lorenzo as the heir presumptive when he is obviously the heir apparent, unless it is an ironic reference to Bonifacio's intention not to die.

law of dynamics that bring us promptly back to equilibrium when an abrupt accident had disturbed us, and which makes characters submissive to habit return invariably to their antecedents. The prince's habits being pleasant, he returned to them promptly.

Satisfied by having a son, and not having to fear that his scepter would fall to the distaff side of the family, the prince took pride in that legitimate heritage, and deviated from the dignity of his rank on that point, not wanting any bastards. Free of the companion that he had led with his right hand, he did not want to encumber his left, and put both hands in his pockets, or folded them over his chest, with the beatitude of the best of men in the best of terrestrial positions.

Lorenzo, the young prince, was twenty years old. He was as handsome as a prince in fairy tale; he was not at all the portrait of his father. Dressed to the age of twelve as a girl, in order to spare the civil list the expense of a tutor he had had a French governess who took pleasure in developing tender sentiments in him. She said nothing to him about the constitutional duties of a sovereign, and if she had read him *Télémaque*, the young heir would have been much less preoccupied with maxims of government than the story of the nymph Eucharis.[4]

---

[4] *Les Aventures de Télémaque* (1699; tr. as *The Adventures of Telemachus*) is a didactic novel by François de Fénelon, ostensibly offered for the education of an heir to the French throne, recounting the travels of Odysseus' son, accompanied and guided by his tutor Mentor, whose advice constitutes a stern attack on autocracy (as practised by Louis XIV), and a forceful argument for constitutional monarchy. It is obviously one of the models of "Le Prince Bonifacio," albeit in an ironic sense. In *Télémaque,* Eucharis, who has no mythological analogue, although her name translates as something like "lovely grace," is an attendant of the nymph Calypso; Télémaque falls in love with her, as his father had fallen in love with Calypso, but he is persuaded to leave her much more rapidly by Mentor's insistence that he put duty before love.

He was familiar with all the French romances, and asked nothing better than to act them out in his turn.

Lorenzo was as free as all his father's subjects, and the infinite leisure left to him by the absence of any social profession he employed in dreaming, strolling in a melancholy fashion and passing under a certain window in the city at certain times of day. I cannot affirm that Lorenzo did not commit little verses to paper in secret; I even suspect, speaking frankly, that he had a certain strength in the Apollonian art; but he dared not confide the essays of his muse to anyone—by which I meant anyone of his own sex. His Highness Bonifacio XXIII would have burst out laughing and made uproarious fun of those romantic tastes.

The young prince loved his father, but it must be admitted that he would have liked to love a father who was a little less fat, a little less comical, and a little less careless of celestial and terrestrial matters, more severe in his majesty and graver in his bounty.

Poor Lorenzo was an insufficient companion; he had no liking for dice or cards. As the Council on Ministers was held at table, and affairs of State were deliberated between the pears and the cheese, Lorenzo always wanted to dine alone, in private, out of respect for State secrets. Sometimes, Bonifacio sighed when he glanced at his heir presumptive's empty place and said, while having the Prime Minister fill his glass: "Lorenzo disappoints me; he doesn't understand politics at all!"

The prince's disappointment necessitated a few more glassfuls, and Lorenzo thus provided his father with regret and joy at the same time.

The party of the discontented, which met in a mediocre hostelry, and was, in consequence, paralyzed in its flight by the insufficiency of the menu and the poor quality of the wines, and could not rise as far as conspiracy, had tried to enlist Lorenzo and appoint him as him as a leader—which is to say, an instrument. Lorenzo had, however, declined that honor as a matter of duty, except that he that thought it appropriate to make a few attempt to excite some activity in his father's mind, and some desire for progress.

"Tut tut!" Bonifacio replied. "What did you want me to do? Create other needs for my subjects than those they can satisfy? That would be running the risk of making them unhappy. Do I tyrannize them?"

"No, Father, but solicitude..."

"Do you want me, on the other hand, to rack my brains to provide them with distraction? I let them be; let them do likewise with respect to me—and long live liberty!"

Discouraged, Lorenzo let his father be. The liberty of nonchalance that he heard so placidly evoked was ironic, a parody of the beautiful and strong liberty that has initiative and activity, and he blushed with shame in thinking that his country only played a ridiculous role in history, on seeing a void gradually form in the finances and disturbance in minds.

It was not, I repeat, that Lorenzo had the slightest idea of government, but he had a heart and there is always, in any kind of tenderness, a kind of illumination that imports foresight into happiness. The young prince would have found it very difficult to submit his plans for reform, but he sensed confusedly that there were other things to do than nothing, and that abandonment is not a principle.

Besides which, he had accessory ideas. Thus, although he was not bellicose, he wanted a small army.

"We can use it for tattoos," he said to the Minister of War, to exhort him to support his plans.

The minister, however, had no reason to prefer work to a sinecure, and he did not lend Lorenzo's proposals the slightest support.

"In that case, let's develop the arts of peace," the poet Lorenzo tried to say. "Let's create an Academy, and floral games."[5]

---

[5] The reference is to the *jocs florals* [the Occitan equivalent of the French *jeux florals*], the annual poetry competitions instituted by the *Consistori del Gay Saber* [Society of the Gay

But the Minister of Fine Arts and Letters was a jolly fellow who did not like boredom and who, under the pretext of a library, was making a collection of all the licentious books of Italy.

Finally, when he had failed in all proposals of the moral order, Lorenzo ended up asking his august father at least to have the streets swept and lighted—for, I am ashamed to say, the capital of the principality was an open sewer, and by night, people would have been forever bumping into walls if devout individuals had not had the idea of lighting little candles in front of statues of the blessed Virgin set up at all the street corners. Thanks to that system, which could also serve to refute the charge of obscurantism that faithless individuals still permitted themselves to level, people could go home without running the risk of spending more than an hour trying to find the door.

But Bonifacio XXIII did not want the filth to be swept away. It was, he said, necessary to think of everybody, and stray dogs did not deserve to be deprived of the ordure heaped up around boundary-markers. As for street-lights and lanterns, he considered them to be baleful inventions. This was his reasoning: "At night, all honest folk ought to be asleep in their homes; now, when one is asleep, one has no need of light. If I allowed the streets to be lit, I couldn't prevent people from walking in them; now, by walking in them, they might make a noise and wake the people who are asleep."

It seemed that sleep was the goal of life, and that Prince Bonifacio had no other objective than to make sure that no one was awake.

Lorenzo was saddened by this passive resistance, all the more so because he had that disposition of the soul in which one wants to do good, not only for the sake of doing good, but for the sake of beauty.

Science] in Toulouse, the oldest literary society in France (and the world).

Lorenzo had a weakness that does not always spare princes: he was in love.

II. In which we learn what a scholar never knows

It was neither a shepherdess nor a princess with whom Lorenzo was smitten. In that matter he was failing both his romantic education and his position as heir presumptive. I suppose that he only had to ask his divinity to put on the costume of a shepherdess—metamorphoses are no more difficult than that—but Lorenzo would not have dared to express that desire and Marta might not have agreed to it. It would have been even easier to become a princess, but I must declare that, in the sincerity of his worship, Lorenzo gave no thought either to the charm of inequality or the prestige of rank. He loved Marta because he loved her. That reason is peremptory in amorous matters. No subtlety can prevail against it.

One day, when he was walking in the fields, on the lookout for rhymes, he encountered a young woman collecting herbs. Lorenzo's fate was instantaneously fixed. The soft radiance of Marta's dark eyes, the chaste and proud fashion in which she curtsied in greeting her sovereign's heir, and the sympathetic little smile that she allowed the young man, a trifle pallid with ennui, to glimpse, all charmed and conquered Lorenzo.

To throw himself at Marta's feet, to declare his flame and threaten to run himself through with a dainty little épée that he wore for show at his side, was the advice given to him by his reading and memories of his French governess, but true love renders independence. Lorenzo was himself, to the point of expressing honest and sincere sentiments. He simply approached the young woman and was simply welcomed.

Botany betrothed them, without them having to confess that they loved one another, and when one of them wanted to tell the other and the other wanted to allow it to be divined, they found that the declaration was unnecessary. They looked at one another, blushed and exchanged their hearts in a squeeze of the hand.

Marta was the daughter of a scholar, Master Marforio.[6] She had lost her mother at the age when Lorenzo had lost his. The two orphans fund a connection in that loss, for which they were not yet consoled. They each felt as free as if they had been alone in the world, the scholar being as negligent of his paternal duties as Prince Bonifacio.

Marta and Lorenzo went for long walks, and God knows that no more innocent love was ever reflected in the azure of the heavens. At the end of a month, however, Lorenzo asked his fiancée for permission to visit the paternal house and swear solemnly, on the latest bunch of flowers that they had picked together, that he would rather renounce the throne than renounce the hope of having Marta for a wife.

The young woman was too ignorant of worldly things to appreciate Lorenzo's naïve oath at its full value and to tell herself that the prince might not be promising very much, the throne of his forefathers being extremely worm-eaten and somewhat precarious. She received that engagement of good faith and promised Lorenzo that she would obtain her father's consent.

I am beginning my story on the very day when Marta was due to raise that delicate question with the least delicate of confidants.

Master Marforio was considered, in the eyes of some people—especially his own, which he believed to be infallible—to be the greatest scholar in Italy. I shall not contradict his reputation, and I am disposed, after I have told you about

---

[6] Marforio is the name of one of the "talking statues" of Rome, on which satirical poems or comments were posted, thus becoming a kind of "bulletin board" and subtle forum for dissent. Marforio was often used to post replies to comments posted on Pasquino, the most famous of the set, who gave his name to the subgenre of satirical literature known as pasquinades.

his errors and follies, to admit that he was indeed a great scholar, one of those who had no doubt about anything and who only admitted the existence of God in order to have the pleasure of stealing his secrets.

Master Marforio had scrutinized everything, analyzed everything, passed everything through the alembic of his observatory and reduced everything in the retort of his intelligence. That abuse of investigation had not, however, brought him misfortune, like Dr. Faust. He was, fundamentally, a rather amiable character. Quite different from some of the scholars of our era and many of the scholars who came after him he was only pedantic and sententious at times, when he plunged himself into some difficult problem, and his good humor always shone through, like Noah's rainbow over the abyss. A mistake stimulated him without irritating him. Besides which, could he ever have admitted to making a mistake? His beard had turned white, but without his forehead being creased by overly profound wrinkles. Sedentary work had made him plump, but it is academically notorious that when a scholar grows rotund he is safe from hypochondria and all unhealthy influences.

Marforio was reputed to be a sorcerer, and, while laughing at that renown—which was not without danger in Italy, he was not far from believing that he had the gift of working miracles.

"Who knows?" he sometimes said. "I've never tried."

On that point, Master Marforio was mistaken; he had, in fact, wrought one miracle: Marta was by far the most prodigious achievement of that infallible scholar.

How could that lovely creature, so sweet, so simple, so charming in her figure and so candid in her soul, that harmonious statue of innocence, name him Father? That was a real conundrum—but it did not puzzle Master Marforio, who scarcely gave it a thought. Besides which, having found the secret of making roses bloom without rose-bushes he would have had no difficulty in laying claim to that flower-bed perfumed with all the virtues and blossoming with all the virtues.

In the series of his works, his daughter was classified somewhere between an experiment in chemistry or alchemy and a demonstration in physics.

Master Marforio's study would have delighted a painter and horrified an auctioneer. Everything there was piled up in confusion; it was chaos. Skeletons lay on books, like death on life; flowers were mingled pell-mell with stuffed monsters, spirit-lamps and telescopes, and in the midst of all that, those indefatigable shroud-weavers the spiders covered the books, the flowers, the instruments and all the rest of the debris with their cobwebs, like the irony of the progress that effaces and levels the instruments of the past.

Beside that official sanctuary, in which he granted his audiences, Dr. Marforio had a mysterious redoubt into which no one—I should say no living person—had ever entered. What happened in that laboratory, no one could say. It was, for the innocent Marta, like Bluebeard's closet. The young woman did not believe that there were women in it wickedly put to death by her father, but she knew that, for some strange and exotic endeavor, the secret of which had not been confided to her, Master Marforio had dealings with the gravedigger, and that the latter sometimes arrived and went away again with heavy burdens.

At any rate, the endeavor, whatever it was, caused the scholar no remorse; after each of these passably sinister visits, he was even conspicuously cheerful; he rubbed his hands together, patted his belly and tugged his beard.

"Bravo, bravo!" he murmured. "All's going well! Humankind is marching toward its cycle of renovation. Paracelsus was nothing but a simpleton; the philosopher's stone is nothing but a pebble. Isaac Hollandus, Basilius Valentinus and all those who have claimed to enable human beings to live beyond their natural span would want to come back to life to enjoy my discovery.[7] The homunculus was a chimera. Hu-

---

[7] Johannes Isaac Hollandus and Basilius Valentinus were pseudonyms attached to a number of apocryphal alchemical

28

mans can't be created, but they can be preserved; they can't be given life, but they can keep it. It's the sacred fire."

So, one day, in the middle of one of thee monologues, which he renewed on a daily basis, with a few variations, Dr. Marforio heard a knock on his study door.

"Come in," he said.

Marta appeared, with a smile on her lips and a slight blush on her cheeks, not daring to cross the threshold.

"Is that you, my daughter?" asked the scholar, with a veritable astonishment and a slight solemnity in his tone. "What's happened? Why so serious?"

"Father, first of all I wanted to embrace you. For some time now, you no longer look at me, you no longer think about me."

"I've been wrong, I confess," said the doctor, opening his white beard, to allow kisses to pass me by. The sight of innocence is a good counsel and a precious inspiration. I've been wrong, my little star! *Virgo virginea!* Albertus Magnus instructs humans to live far from men; he didn't say far from young women. I permit you to come and bid me good day every morning, mirror of the firmament, and every morning I will bless you."

While speaking thus, with his usual volubility, Dr. Marforio had drawn Marta toward him and solemnly gave her the most banal of paternal kisses on her lovely forehead, between the tresses of her long dark hair.

---

treatises. The former, who allegedly lived in the latter part of the 16th century, is most famously credited with a volume known in French as *L'Oeuvre de Saturne* (tr. as *A Work of Saturn*), while the latter, allegedly active a century previously, appeared on a number of works in both Latin and German, including *Duodecim claves philosophicae* [The Twelve Philosophical Keys] and *De microcosmo deque mango mundi mysterio et medicina hominis* [On the Microcosm, the Great Secret of the World and Human Mediine]..

"Well, my girl, are you content?" he asked, after granting her this favor, as if to send her away.

Marta hesitated to speak. It seemed to her to be sacrilegious to surrender the pure and dear secret of her soul, which would doubtless be greeted by a burst of laughter. She stood in the middle of the study, motionless, her head bowed, tracing bizarre and impossible lines with her finger in the dust that covered a stout book placed on a shelf close at hand.

Fortunately, Dr. Marforio, although he did not know very much about the art of provoking consequences, was possessed of a loquacity convenient for timid listeners; it gave them time to arrange and organize their ideas. Scholars sometimes have these fortuitous utilities.

"What do you want from me?" he said to his daughter. "You're not yet at an age when one needs to remake nature's jewel-case. Do you need an elixir to preserve and maintain your hair? Scholars to come, French and German chemists, will exhaust themselves in vain efforts to find the solution or ointment that will stop hair turning gray and falling out. I shall take that secret with me to the grave. Do you need an enamel for your teeth? Rouge for your cheeks? I would rather demand them of you, charm of my life. Speak! I can open infinity for you, for I can dispense eternal, immutable beauty!"

The doctor paused, pensively, and then continued: "Oh, I confess that it would cost me to try that operation on you. My hand might perhaps tremble. Do you have confidence in your father, Marta. Are you convinced, as you ought to be, that he is the greatest scholar in the principality, one of the greatest scholars in Italy, and, in consequence, one of the greatest scholars in the world? If I said to you, 'My darling, I'm going, with a little instrument of which it's unnecessary to be afraid, to make a light incision in your forehead, about which it's unnecessary to worry, and make a few little cuts in your lovely skull with a pretty little saw,' tell me, my little star, would you be scared?"

Marta opened her eyes wide and stared at her father; she really was afraid, but of being obliged to recognize that her illustrious father was mad. The poor child had no understanding at all of science or scientists.

"But that's not what it's about," she stammered.

"What is it about, then? It's true, *Primavera*, I was wrong! To offer youth to you is to desire zephyrs for the spring and roses for the month of May. What do you want? Is your heart sighing after some impossible dream? If that's all it is, you shall have it. Or have you, daughter of a mortal woman, merely requiring the love of a mortal man, come to me, poor modest flower invisible to the gaze, to ask me for a philter, to render you visible and beloved?"

Marta could not help smiling; her father had skirted her secret; but the young woman had not come in search of a philter; her gaze was a sufficient powerful alchemist, and had already carried out the task.

"Aha!" said Dr. Marforio, who had seen his child's smile. "I've guessed it! Eureka! Nothing escapes a scholar! You want a philter, Marta. It's a great imprudence; it's necessary not to toy with philters. Fortunately, I'll always be here to cure you, to save you, and it wouldn't displease me if you were in some danger, in order to provide more proof how infallible I am."

"But Father, I no longer need a philter."

And the young woman, laughing and blushing at the same time, emphasized the phrase *no longer*, to assist her secret to escape.

Although he was a scholar, Dr. Marforio was not a complete stranger to worldly matters. He had lucid moments; it was a residue of inferiority. Who among us can flatter himself on being perfect, alas? In addition, he might have been young himself once. At an age when science was a muse and not yet a shrewish and exclusive spouse, he might have experimented with something analogous to amour. He understood, therefore, what his daughter was implying, and made a movement of surprise that did not testify to a profound amazement.

"Aha! You've permitted yourself…in fact, why not? Have I forbidden you to? Explain to me, then, what you're asking of me."

Significantly reassured by these reactions, which she thought paternal, Marta confessed Lorenzo's name and explained the heir presumptive's desire.

"A prince!" exclaimed the doctor, with laughing out loud. "He's only a prince! I was afraid he might be Apollo in person. You deserve better than that, my daughter—although I know how difficult it would have been to find anything better in the principality."

"You're making fun of me, Father," the young woman murmured, with an imploring gesture.

"Well, let's not laugh anymore," the joyful scholar went on. "What do you want to do with your little prince, my dear daughter, and what do you want me to do to him? Perhaps he's fearful of humiliating his dynasty, vowed by tradition to uselessness, if he plies the bellows at my furnaces. In any case, Albertus Magnus, in his eighth precept, says expressly: 'The man who dreams of the Great Work will avoid any relationship with princes and lords.' Do you want to make me run aground so close to port?"

Marta was scarcely thinking about that; she had a strong desire to interrupt her father to tell him that this was not about him, but only about her; that Lorenzo did not worship the scholar, but the scholar's daughter; and that she had not come to ask for the role of bellows-operator on her hero's behalf. Without being able to admit that scholars in general are implacable in their egotism, however, the young woman knew from filial experience that Dr. Marforio had a very particular fashion of evaluating everyday events, and that it was a waste of time to try to interest him in anything other than his laboratory for very long. So she sighed, and continued to listen.

"He's genteel, isn't he, my love, your bird of romance? Well, he'd cut a sorry figure in the midst of my stuffed owls. Release the thread that retains his wings; let him fly away, Marta, and I'll find you a handsome scholar, who will be my pupil, and who will espouse my doctrine as well as my daughter."

Mata was unsure whether to laugh or cry. She was very emotional.

"I love Lorenzo and will never love anyone but him," she said, finally.

"The words of a young woman—light leaves that the wind bears away, as Ovid says."

"Lorenzo loves me too, Father. Anyway, just because he's a prince, that doesn't mean he's ignorant."

Love is the school of diplomacy; the last French Republic proved that conclusively by creating a School of Administration. Marta was becoming clever.

"What does he know, your handsome prince?" asked the doctor, with a mockery that as not exempt from curiosity.

"Oh, we haven't talked about science," Marta replied, "but we've talked about you, Father, and Lorenzo admires you."

Incense never loses its perfume. Dr. Marforio smiled— but he had not yet been flattered enough.

"Well, if he admires your father, I can't say that I admire his. His Excellency Bonifacio XXIII is a brute, for whom furnaces only serve as ovens in his kitchen. Oh, if he had understood scholars! What a prince! What a principality? With him, I would have been able to experiment with my system on a large scale. And you expect the son of such a prince, of a buffoon who pays no heed to me, you expect the heir to that stupidity to be anything other than an idiot? A pretty idiot, if you wish, but an idiot."

"I don't expect anything, Father," said Marta, who had been momentarily reassured and was glimpsing triumph. "I don't know anything about politics, but I'm certain that Lorenzo has intelligence, and that he loves science sufficiently to make his father love scientists, if he wanted to take the trouble."

"I'm not saying that it would take a Cicero to appreciate my worth," said the doctor, shrugging his shoulders, "but do you seriously believe, my daughter, that your prince, if he wanted to..."

"He's irresistible, Father."

"For young women, maybe—but for Prince Bonifacio?"

"Good fathers don't refuse their children anything," said Marta, slyly placing her forehead on the doctor's shoulder.

"So Bonifacio is a good father, is he?" said Marforio, laughing. "Well then, that's the only virtue he's forgotten to lose. You can tell Lorenzo that my house is open to him."

"Thank you, Father," said Marta, effusively.

"You'll be a princess, on condition that your prince is or becomes a scientist. Perhaps it's the great Alchemist of Hearts who has prepared this little sentimental romance, in order that I might put myself in a position to preside over the destiny of the principality. There's a women at the beginning of all great things; but it would be lacking regard for fortune not to lay down one condition. You'll only be a princess on the day that I become Bonifacio's prime minister."

"You're scaring me, Father!"

"That's a good sign. So much the worse for you, my darling, if you're making me ambitious. I have my reckless love too; you have your prince, I want to have mine."

Marta sighed, and smiled. Lorenzo could come; that was what delighted her—but these burlesque conditions, these pretensions on the scientist's part, appeared likely to spoil or compromise the lovely poem that she sensed stirring and singing in her heart.

As for the doctor, he was possessed by a joy that might have caused an alienist to tremble. He could distinctly see his star rising on the horizon—and although it would be painful only to be the prime minister of a microscopic principality, he was impatient to hear the hour chime when the principality, paltry as it was, would become a gigantic laboratory, whose inhabitants would be his subjects of analysis, the ministry his spirit-lamp, and Prince Bonifacio his bellows-operator.

As for the ambition of having the hereditary prince as a son-in-law, he scarcely thought about that, and to the pure and simple happiness of his daughter, he gave no thought at all. Dr. Marforio was too great a scientist to lower himself to such vulgar sentiments.

III. The Politics of Sentiment and the Sentiment of Politics

Lorenzo was informed of the doctor's favorable disposition. As emotional as if he were about to enter parliament, booted and spurred, with whip in hand, to say to it: "Gentlemen, the State is you!" he put on his best suit, had himself powdered and perfumed, robbed the crown jewels in order to find a passable tie-pin and studied himself for an hour, spoiling his natural charms.

I have often noticed that the necessity of social relationships, when they intervene in a poem, expose the best-intentioned heroes to ridicule.

It is as well that Lorenzo was a fine young man, full of heart and spirit. If Heaven instead of condemning him to be born a hereditary prince of a compromised crown, had permitted him a useful and productive position, there is no doubt that he would have made his way in life. In his sentimental strolls, when no one had been watching him, he had acted with all desirable delicacy, and Marta had been unable to imagine any him in more beautiful costume than the slightly worn pearl-gray suit in which she saw him during their everyday encounters. But the inspiration and the sentiment of exterior harmony that are never lacking in a prince, in amorous roles, seemed to abandon him when he had to premeditate his interview with the doctor. He came out of his shell.

As he was about to measure himself against the pretentions of stupidity—sorry, I mean science—he thought it necessary to import vanity into his exterior appearance. He wanted to make himself exceedingly handsome, and consequently made himself exceedingly ugly. The seraph travestied himself in threadbare elegance. He borrowed ruffles for his collar and cuffs from his father's wardrobe and put on coronation garters to seduce Master Marforio.

That absence is taste is fairly commonplace among people of imagination and fine sentiments; I can offer no better proof than the grotesque apparel of all contemporary muses. Fundamentally, however, it was not as untimely as one might think. If Marta was to suffer the travesty of her lover, the doctor was to experience a keen surge of pride; and as he was acting to seduce the father rather than the daughter, it could be reckoned that Lorenzo was a good judge of the human soul, instead of simply a naïve lover naively putting on his Sunday best.

What a fine dissertation I might begin here on the dignity, opportunity and eloquence of costume—even the ugliest of costumes! One cannot emphasize enough how much prestige there is in ceremonial dress. Would a general win a battle in a dressing-gown? Would plaintiffs think themselves properly judged by a judge without his robe, or a Minos wearing his nightcap?

Proverbs, which are to the truth what old wives' remedies are to great medicine, are specious lies. The falsest of all of them, however, is surely the one that claims that the habit does not make the monk. The inventor of that axiom did not know Italy, in particular, or humankind in general. What difference is there between a functionary and a supplicant if not the costume? And how many diplomats would be recognized to be incapable if they were refused a braided jacket for the crowd and good cooks for their colleagues?

Master Marforio was not very rigorous with regard to etiquette, but he was too much of an Academician not to require a certain artificial pomp. When he saw Lorenzo bow three times and appear before him with an abdomen laden with lace, hands charged with jewels and his back bowed down by a gala jacket, the scholar blossomed; he almost had a yen for some coquetry of his own—but as he knew full well that his genius was his finest adornment, and that his glory would cast a gleam over his costume, he only took the trouble to adjust the disorder of his dress, and took three paces toward the prince in order to welcome him.

Marta, the poor child, had fled. Her lover did not please her that day. He resembled Prince Bonifacio, and she no longer found within his heavy cravat the charming lines of the lovely flexible neck that inclined sideways so gracefully when they walked together on their own along the green pathways of the countryside. Lorenzo's hands, so dainty and so limp-wristed, of which she sometimes made fun because she found them so pretty, disappeared gauchely beneath gross masses of lace, and the wretch, who had not had any self-respect at all that day, had slipped the large rings of a prelate on to his fingers, which complete their deformation.

Only his mouth, being uncovered, had not changed, and still retained, in the sinuosity of two slightly fleshy but irreproachably designed lips, the faint and adorable smile that pursued Marta in her daydreams, and more especially in her dreams. Without that mouth, she would have been horrified by him, but how could she hold anything against that smile, which begged for forgiveness and which she would have forgiven anything?

Lorenzo had displayed so much respect in his Gothic official costume, and was so emotional in approaching the doctor, that the later completely forgot the reason for the meeting and treated the heir presumptive as a mere student who had come to solicit the favor of a university grade or an examination. He did not give him time to stammer the few words of introduction and excuse that the prince had rehearsed repeatedly on the way, in order to get thoroughly used to them and not to mangle their effect, and questioned him *ex abrupto* about his knowledge of physics and his predispositions to chemistry, not to mention astronomy.

Lorenzo scarcely expected that ordeal, but I believe that, if he had expected it, would have been no less of an ordeal. The little that the young prince had learned about physics was scarcely worth the trouble of remembering, and the little that he remembered of chemistry and astronomy was not worth the trouble of repeating. His science, his true science, was that which begins with invocations and ecstasies, which talks about thing but does not interrogate them, which says to flowers, plants, horizons and stars, "I love you," but not "Who are you?" or "Where do you come from?" Lorenzo had come, his heart swollen with love inside his old ceremonial costume, to say to the doctor: "Let me worship Marta!" and here was the doctor asking him for his opinion about the transmutation of metals, the Rosicrucian Brotherhood, the microcosm, and everything—except the condition of his heart.

Lorenzo modestly admitted that he knew nothing; that, being destined for power, it had been thought best to preserve him from theories, dogmas and prejudices, rendering him inaccessible to error by prohibiting him from seeking the truth, but that he would like nothing better than to run the danger of learning.

"Oh, young man," said the doctor, in a familiar manner, "how that step honors you! The sciences are not ungrateful. People think them surly and ill-tempered, but they are like the old witches of legend, who want to be tamed by force and then to deliver to the conqueror a young and virginal bride."

At the word "bride," Lorenzo blushed. Perhaps that was an allusion to the object of his visit. He made an effort to pronounce Marta's name—but Marforio was astride his hippogriff, and continued galloping.

"You will reign one day, young man; you will be in charge of souls; it will be necessary for you to combine thousands of wills—and you have no idea how to combine to inert elements! You will have finances in a parlous state to administer, and you don't know how to make gold! Perhaps you will send men to war; at least once in your reign you will have brave men killed who would like nothing better to live, in order to satisfy the temperament of a few bilious counselors or amuse children who like drums and drill, and you don't know how to prevent death or to create mortal fear! Derision, derision! What is a prince who can disturb the moral order but has no rights over the physical order? Who takes responsibility for the happiness of a people but has no idea how to predict a famine or prevent a tempest? Oh, young man, young man, why are you a prince?"

Lorenzo could have replied: "Because my father is a prince and his name is Boniface XXIII." He had no better reason than that, but legitimate sons do have the principle and guarantees of legitimacy. Lorenzo was, however, all the less inclined to reply because the doctor, who was still interrogating him, did not give him time to get a word in.

After an hour of that conversation, Marta, who was awaiting, full of troubled anxiety, the outcome of the discussion, and who thought she ought, out of a sentiment of respect and modesty, abstain from witnessing it, and even from listening to it, and who had not found Lorenzo so ugly that she had renounced the hope of finding him beautiful the next day, decided to go and knock boldly on the laboratory door. As no one replied and she could hear her father speaking, she turned the key in the lock and came in, in order to be able to hear more clearly.

The doctor, his head tilted backwards and his mouth open, with one foot on a stool, holding a bottle in his hand in which horrible monstrosities were agitating, was explaining to poor Lorenzo, who dared not yawn, that the vessel might perhaps contain the veritable homunculus, the familiar spirit of Giuseppe Francesco Borri, the Milanese, who had once been arrested by the Holy Inquisition in Rome for having made the philosopher's stone, and who had died in prison for having refused to use it to the profit of his judges.[8]

---

[8] Giuseppe Francesco Borri (1627-1695) was a pupil of Athanasius Kircher who developed messianic pretentions, and travelled widely throughout Europe, harassed by creditors and heresy-hunters. He did die in prison in the Castel Sant'Angelo, where he had earlier had a laboratory; the legends of his gold-making, as is usual with alchemists, were considerably amplified after his death.

Sadly, as if her were listening to the reading of an elegiac poem, Lorenzo was leaning back in his armchair, gazing at the doctor and wondering silently when he would be able to talk about his love.

Fortunately for him, his incarnate love gave the door a vigorous shove, and the young woman, laughing impishly, suddenly hurtled into the laboratory.

"Have you reached an agreement?" he asked.

"Agreement!" exclaimed Marforio. "Do you, by any chance, want to raise or encourage some opposition, some conspiracy, against my grand theory? Speak—what is it?"

"Me?" murmured Lorenzo. "I've come to ask you for the right to love Marta."

"Oh! That's right!" replied Dr. Marforio, putting down the bottle in order to take the young woman's hand. "I'd forgotten. You're talking to me about rights? It seems to me that you've usurped that one somewhat, my prince. No offense, but the daughter of Dr. Marforio can't be the wife of Prince Lorenzo."

"Oh, I don't care about the prejudices of my birth," said Lorenzo, with a slightly revolutionary expression.

"Of course! Me neither," replied the scholar, "but I mean that Marta must be the recompense of a man of genius who understands me and will assist me in applying my system to the government of States."

Lorenzo went pale; the handsome young man had scruples. He believed that his father's subjects did belong to him unconditionally, and that he might well be failing in his duties as heir presumptive by promising to surrender them. As is evident, Lorenzo had been badly brought up and did not know his rights, while exaggerating his duties.

"Doctor," he replied, gravely, "let's not make a question of intimate happiness into a question of politics. The destiny of the principality is dear to me, but we aren't its only arbiters. Let's settle what interests us personally; later, we'll see."

"No, no, I won't allow myself to be enticed," the doctor replied. "Marta is every bit as dear to me as your principality might well be to you. Besides which, your affairs aren't going to well, and I don't see what great sacrifice you'd have to make in making me agreeable to His Highness Bonifacio. Don't worry—things couldn't be any worse than they already are."

"Monsieur!"

"What! Isn't it common knowledge that you're paying your functionaries with little images that represent money, but don't produce any of it; that half your army has to stay in bed to permit the other half to appear in uniform; that you're having to sell off crown property cheap to buy gloves? If I wanted to play the prophet, I'd predict the imminent collapse of a monarchy devoid of money, or vigor and of talent, which can't afford a police force for its criminals or spectacles for its honest folk."

"But once again, Monsieur, what had common opinion to do with my love?"

"What! Don't you understand, young man," the doctor retorted, majestically, "that I can't give my daughter to just any prince that comes along? I want a solid son-in-law who can offer me guarantees—and then again, when all is said and done, I only have this one opportunity, this one superb, unique opportunity, to try out my marvelous discovery on a large scale, and you want me to renounce it! Oh, you're nothing but an egotist!"

Lorenzo looked at the doctor's daughter with a heartbroken expression. He was suffering from this ridiculous discussion, as she had already suffered; but his dolor was mingled with remorse. He thought that behind these grotesque reproaches, there were real truths, and that he was in truth a very paltry prince, the son of a very imprudent father.

Suddenly, another idea diverted his attention from that one. As if in a flash, Lorenzo saw Dr. Marforio as Prince Bonifacio's prime minister, and in spite of the respect that his title of prince of the blood obliged him to maintain for the head of his household, he knew his father very well, and judged that he would be so well suited by a companion like

Master Marforio, that he could not help a smile brushing his lips: an ironic smile that was also dolorous—and sensed that he was defeated, and ready to make any concessions for the sake of his love.

After all, so much the worse for the inhabitants of the principality! People always have the governments they deserve, and if they allowed themselves to be badly administered by Bonifacio XXIII, it was because they did not want to be any better administered. To give them Marforio as a prime minister would therefore be to endorse their wishes and complete the power.

Lorenzo had left his happiness hanging in the balance for at least five minutes with the happiness of his future subjects; that was more than any ordinary prince would have attempted, and he had now acquired the right to lean on the side that pleased him. Besides which, people wanted reforms in the principality; Dr. Marforio seemed to be in a humor to provide them, of every shade and caliber. It might be worth a try. The party of youth might perhaps be satisfied. In spite of his follies, the scholar was certainly not ignorant. He had proffered one opinion whose justice had made a considerable impact on Lorenzo. "Don't worry," he had said, "things couldn't be any worse than they already are."

That consideration, which is not always admissible in human projects, was reassuring for the young prince. It is the reasoning that makes people try old wives' remedies. The fellow's utopia might be worthy trying.

And then again, after all, Marta was worth more than any crown, any principality. To be the husband of the doctor's daughter, Prince Lorenzo would have given all the glory to which he might lay claim. Who can tell whether, in the utmost depths of his soul, a little voice might have been singing the song that consoles all troubles and losses in advance: the song that advises one to be happy rather than rich and powerful?

What did an old throne with gilded nails, which was falling apart and no longer gave shelter to anything but worms, matter, as long as he, the tender poet and Prince Charming, could sit down with impunity beside his beloved on the moss in the great wood, and say to her: "Let's forget the world, if the world will forget us?" What did it matter if he could not put the heraldic crown on his head, as long as no one stopped him picking wild flowers, sniffing them and putting them in his buttonhole?

Lorenzo was a born troubadour. Nowadays, there are very few princes who have that vocation, but before Metternich, European display-cases offered numerous varieties of the species.

Lorenzo did not try to struggle any longer. He promised everything that was asked of him, and risked the happiness of his people in order to have the right to come every day to tell Marta how much he loved her. Every day, there are princes who commit the same imprudence without having the same pretext.

In return, the doctor promised his blessing. Marta did not promise anything, but she allowed a kiss to be taken that was worth as much as a province.

When the heir presumptive had made his three bows, and when the door of the house has closed behind him, Master Marforio uttered a sigh of triumph.

"Well," he said to his daughter, "are you content?"

Marta fell into her father's arms.

"He's good, your little prince," the doctor went on, "and he's certainly very elegant. What a beautiful outfit! On the other hand, though, he doesn't know anything. You deceived me—he's as ignorant as a sheep."

Marta did not want to contradict her father twice over, but she thought that Lorenzo knew enough and that his outfit did not suit him at all. The latter point, in particular, she felt keenly. She sighed.

"Never mind!" said her father, who had taken the wrong inference once again by that sigh. "I'll give him lessons."

Marta promised herself firmly, however, to protect her fiancé from paternal lessons. She would suffice to instruct him in what he did not know—which is to say, the best way to wear lace and to arrange his hair; after that, her prince would be perfect.

Oh, if peoples were no more demanding than the doctor's daughter, one would have no need to reason with them except with the aid of iron—by which I mean, of course, curling tongs!

IV. A Ministerial Crisis

Prince Bonifacio XXIII had no suspicion of the madrigal that awaited him, or of the ambitious aims of Dr. Marforio. I realize that, if he had been paying someone to watch his son, he would have had every chance of being fully informed, but he was not. Even so, one day, one of his chamberlains chanced to remark, one day, that he thought that Prince Lorenzo was in love.

"So much the better!" exclaimed Bonifacio, with the contentment of a good father and a good king. "The art of love informs the art of kingship!"

That remark deserved to be reprinted, with a commentary, by the official newspaper of the principality, and one day taking its place in a collection of His Highness's witty remarks and famous rejoinders, but Bonifacio did not like to entertain the public with his intimate affairs, with the quips escaped from his good humor any more than the state of his health, and when he had indigestion, he did not make it a point of honor to inform his subjects. Posterity would therefore remain in ignorance of the jokes His Highness made and the medicines he took. The history of the principality would have been difficult to write, by virtue of the reticence of the official news outlets, if the young people's party of which I have already made mention had not substituted for the negligence, modesty or calculation of the prince by means of secret notes, articles and pamphlets.

Bonifacio, as an economical prince, would have much preferred a trivial love affair for the distraction of his heir to some other passion that might demand money. He knew that one of the privileges of princes is to make or promise such a great gift in their person that they are subsequently dispensed of making others, and he was not anxious at all to discover the objective and motive of Lorenzo's quotidian strolls.

One day, His Highness had retired to his apartment to work in secret with his prime minister when Lorenzo, resolved to make good on his promises to the doctor, decided to obtain an audience.

It will be readily understood, in accordance with the details I have given regarding the finances and the lack of formality customary in the court, that the antechambers were unencumbered by lackeys, and that if one happened to find ushers there, they were there to seize crown property,[9] not to introduce visitors. Lorenzo did not see anyone who could announce him. After having knocked discreetly on several doors and visited several rooms, however, he happened upon the council chamber to which Boniface XXIII, in order not to allow any State secrets to escape, had retired with his prime minister, taking care to remove the key from the lock.

These excessive precautions have their imprudence, however. Through the keyhole, deprived of its key, Lorenzo perceived his august father laying out cards on the council table, the dimensions of which might well have sufficed to contain the topography of the principality,[10] but were in fact playing cards.

Instead of admiring the infinite delicacy of the good prince, who locked himself away rather than provide a bad example, Lorenzo felt himself go pale with shame and sadness on surprising his father in that recreation. I know that Père Daniel[11] assures us that card-games are a school of diplomacy,

---

[9] The French word *huissier* [usher] can also mean "bailiff."

[10] Similarly, *carte* [card] can also mean "map."

[11] The historian and philosopher Gabriel Daniel (1649-1728) in his *Histoire de France* (1713), subsequently expanded by other hands for use as a textbook; it was the kind of history of which Ulbach would have disapproved, consisting of a long

and that the game of piquet, among others, informs the art of governing men, but Lorenzo had probably never read Père Daniel, and then again, it was not piquet that his father was playing. At any rate, Lorenzo judged the theory by the practice, and did not hold it in high esteem. He sighed sadly, and told himself, in the depths of his heart, that he had doubtless come to propose another folly to cure his father of this one. Dr. Marforio would certain play another game than one of cards, and Lorenzo was not without apprehension with regard to the effects of the doctor's grand theory.

Bonifacio was not simply indulging himself in forgetfulness of his terrestrial grandeurs in consenting to gamble with his minister; we shall see that he had his reasons. In the evening, gambling is an elegance; by day it is a abandonment. We shall not be astonished, therefore, that His Highness allowed himself, in the absolute secrecy of the locked room, a certain casualness of costume and appearance that the terrible party of the young would have criticized in energetic terms had they known about it. Thus far, however, the secret had not come out, and no one knew that Bonifacio XXIII, in the very room where his ancestors had so profoundly raised their heads and maintained their status, was dressed in a simple dimity waistcoat, devoid of powder or cravat, in order to give and audience to kings named David, Alexander, Caesar and Charles, and queens named Judith, Argine, Rachel and Pallas.[12]

I repeat, however, that gambling was not merely a debauchery for the prince; it was also a principle of political

---

catalogue of military actions. Daniel also wrote a precursory item of *roman scientifique, Voyage au monde de Cartesius* (1690), attacking Descartes' theory of vortices and the heliocentric model of the solar system.

[12] These are the individual names given by French gamblers to the four kings and four queens in a pack of cards. English and American gamblers do not like to be on such intimate terms with the instruments of their vice, although that does not prevent their occasional ruination by reckless and perverse love.

economy, and his dream, in view of the penury of the treasury, was to win back from his ministers the meager salaries that he was constrained to pay them, when he could no longer limit himself to making promises. This financial system, which I record for what it may be worth, did not succeed in application, and at the precise moment when Lorenzo was looking through the keyhole, Bonifacio was becoming privately alarmed by the enormous charges that his minister was imposing on the budget, and wondering if he might not be able to get rid of his ministers, those functionaries being a luxury item designed for official display, and the work that they did being just as easy to neglect without them.

The prime minister was enjoying an extremely disrespectful lucky streak, and the prince was not far from believing that he possessed a chief of cabinet expert in the art of giving good eyes to blind chance. To accuse the functionary of high trickery was, however, an extremity to which the prince dared not descend without having proof. In the meantime, and although he was not a descendant of Henri IV, he was making vain efforts himself to introduce some intelligence into the distribution of trumps, but as his methods were naïve and unpracticed, the prime minister was able to detect them and thwart them without appearing to have noticed them—which annoyed Bonifacio even more.

Through the keyhole, Lorenzo could read the sentiments imprinted on the paternal physiognomy distinctly. His Highness was no longer Serene; stormy creases were amassing above his bushy eyebrows, and, in order that the tempestuous image should not lack anything, enormous drops of sweat were raining down his forehead.

Bonifacio XXIII was losing with an incredible persistence; his prime minister was costing him more than all the others put together, so the blood had never risen with a more apoplectic fury to the sovereign's head. He beat[13] the cards in

---

[13] The French *bat* [beat] cards, whereas English and American gamblers are content to "shuffle" them, although it probably

the true sense of the term, subjecting them to an angry frottage that was equivalent to a spanking. As he invoked to his aid all the resources of cunning and chance, His Highness lent artificial excitations to his snuff-taking that did not work to the advantage of his play, his nose or his shirt-front.

Lorenzo judged the moment opportune. His august father would not dare, for reasons of dignity, to hurl the cards in his minister's face, but he ought to be delighted by a distraction. In consequence, the hereditary price proffered several respectful raps.

The gamblers stopped dead, as if marionette strings retained them by the wrist. Bonifacio, who was in the process of dealing the cards, remained open-mouthed, his hand raised; the minister, after some hesitation, pushed back his armchair and came to enquire through the keyhole who was permitting himself to disturb the deliberations of an intimate council.

I must confess that, during the interrogation in question, Prince Bonifacio, with a briskness that denoted a certain political aptitude, attempted to stack the deck, but while speaking, the prime minister glanced at his sovereign and the compromising gesture was perceived. Bonifacio swore that he would never forgive that sly glance, and conceived a violent hatred against his adversary, who ruination was resolved.

Lorenzo gave his name and asked for permission to come in. The moment was decidedly well-chosen. On learning that the importunate individual was his son, Bonifacio swiftly gathered up the cards and the stakes and slipped them into his bosom.

"Shh! Not a word," he said to his minister. "You'll answer to me for your silence with your head!"

The threat was obviously exaggerated. Bonifacio had no more leverage on the head of his prime minister than the char-

---

does not add any extra measure of sado-masochism to the foreplay in question, in spite of the lewd terminology with which the present sentence progresses.

acter in a certain comedy had on the churchwarden's nose.[14] Capital punishment had been abolished in the principality a long time ago, without anyone—not even among the thieves—coming to any harm as a result and demanding its restoration. But there are banal formulas of exaggeration that have existed since the beginning of the world, and which are at the disposal of princes and their subjects alike. It is for that reason that people are frequently asked to swear on their heads, and they swear of their own accord on their honor. It proves nothing and pledges nothing; it seems that perjury is rendered easier by the exaggeration or the inanity of the caution of the oath.

The minister therefore took the threat for what it was worth. He put his finger to his lips and promised silence.

"I hope that Your Highness will be luckier another time," the courtier murmured, bowing to his master.

That compliment of condolence was a final drop of vinegar. Bonifacio raised his head and dismissed his minister in a loud voice, saying: "That's good that's good. We'll discuss it another time. I'll think about it, and I'll let you know my decision."

The minister smiled and withdrew, walking backwards to the door. When he was outside, he dared to burst out laughing, covering his mouth to conceal his seditious gaiety. In every country in the world palace walls have ears; in Italy, even in the most relaxed principality, they can also have eyes.

"All's well," said the eminent functionary. "He'll never be able to catch up. If this goes on, I'll win half a century of the ministry. Was he scared when his simpleton of a son

---

[14] Jean-François Regnard's *Les Ménechmes, ou es jumeaux* (1705) includes a line in which one character asks another what he is doing with "*le nez d'un marguillier*" [a churchwarden's nose]. It was considered funny enough, in context, to be echoed in later comedies, including Pierre-Louis Roederer's *Le Marguiller de Saint-Eustache* (1819), and was even quoted by Voltaire.

walked in! There's another one who doesn't understand cards, for whom power will be devoid of profit!"

And on that reflection, which consolidated his devotion to the reigning prince, the minister went home, where his secretary was waiting for him with dice, to resume a game analogous to the one that had just been interrupted. The chief of the cabinet applied to his subordinates the system that the prince applied in his regard, and paid them in the manner that he was paid by the latter. It was perhaps one of those occasions when the spirit of justice found its easiest satisfaction.

In the meantime, Prince Bonifacio, wiping away the sweat that had put a fluvial crown on his head, pulled himself together and interrogated his son. "What has happened, Lorenzo, so serious that you've come to interrupt me in the middle of my most serious occupations?"

Lorenzo did not flinch; he neither blushed nor sighed, and apologized for having had the temerity to interrupt his father's work.

"Oh, it's not that I'll have any difficulty postponing that business until tomorrow, and many others," said Prince Bonifacio, smiling, "but when one's in the swing of things..."

"Father," said Lorenzo, gravely, taking the armchair left vacant by the minister, I need to talk to you about two things that are dear to you: my happiness and the happiness of your subjects."

"Damn! The conversation won't be cheerful. Go on, my son, speak: you have debts and you need money, but I don't have any. I was just explaining to Colbertini a new banking system designed to furnish me with some."

"I'm not asking you for money, Father," Lorenzo continued, with a certain embarrassment. "I don't want to be a burden on the treasury."

"A burden! What burden? Oh, my word you're a good boy," said the prince, in a fit of gaiety. "You're preserving the treasury. It won't count it to your credit, and won't obtain much profit from your good intentions. You only have futile virtues, my dear Lorenzo: the fine merit of being economical with an empty chest. So, you don't have petty debts? Even if there were…gambling debts, you could confess them to me. I'm not stern, you know!"

Lorenzo knew perfectly well that his father was not stern. As if to add a commentary to those encouraging words, however, the prince pulled his hand out of his bosom and extended it to his son. That violent and quite unnecessary gesture—since it did not tell Lorenzo anything he did not know already—had the effect of shifting the cards and chips in their hiding-place, and Bonifacio was alarmed to see a cascade of spades, hearts, clubs and diamonds tumble from inside his waistcoat on to the table. That was more effusion than he had wanted to display.

The joyful prince was not a man to remain downcast, however, or to be disconcerted for so little.

"You can see, my son," he said, with a certain solemnity, "the very items that I was using in my economic demonstration a little while ago. Don't think for a moment that these instruments of pleasure…"

"Father," Lorenzo interrupted, almost reluctantly and in a tone of gentle reproach, "I'm not asking you for State secrets."

There was an irony tempered by respect in those words that went straight to Prince Bonifacio's heart. He launched himself from his armchair like a balloon taking off.

"To hell with reticence and decorum!" he cried. "I have the right to show myself as I am to my child, my heir, since I already do that honor to strangers—that Colbertini, for example, whom I detest. That man has been my prime minister for many years; people think he's the chief of my cabinet. Well, between us, he an ass. He annoys me, not to mention that I think he's something of a cheat. Can you imagine that just now, to cheer ourselves up and settle a petty account, we were playing cards. Don't tell anyone! The rascal won with a relentlessness, a persistence…there are times, Lorenzo, when I regret not being a cruel prince. I'd take pleasure in making that Colbertini suffer, in using pincers on him till he bled. But one can't remake one's character. I'm placid and good, and it would give me pain to find pleasure in such cruelties—that's why I contain myself. But if I could do that insupportable minister a bad turn..."

"I've come to see you precisely to ask for his position."

"For yourself? That's impossible! You can't be my minister. It would be more economical, I agree, but it would be contrary to custom and I think that would offend the constitution. You'll understand that I have no intention of violating a constitution that I've never laid a finger on."

"I have no political ambitions," said Lorenzo. "It's not for myself that I'm soliciting it."

"It's not for yourself? So much the better. You have a minister to propose to me? So be it, I accept. I'll appoint him. Look, here's paper, and a pen. Colbertini sharpened the quill himself. I'm writing: *I, Bonifacio XXIII, etc., etc, appoint by these presents Lord*...what's the name of my future minister?"

"Marforio."

"A fine name. I only have ministers whose names end in *i*. This will make a change. I sign, I apply my seal, the business is done; he's appointed. What a fine thing omnipotence is! A sheet of paper, a quill plucked from a goose, a drop of ink, and one has a minister. It's not as easy to obtain a good cook. By the way, what does this Statesman do?"

"What, Father—you don't know the celebrated Marforio, the glory of your reign, the finest decoration in your crown?"

"My word, no, I don't know him. One sometimes has wealth without suspecting it. I didn't know that I had the marvel in question. Is he a singer, a dancer or a horseman?"

"He's a scholar, Father—the greatest scientist..."

"In the principality? Thank you. That's not saying very much—but I don't want your scholar. He's bound to be boring. I prefer my imbecile Colbertini. Give me back my piece of paper; I'm revoking my nomination. A scholar in my Council! That would be discordant."

"However, Father, if you knew Dr. Marforio..."

"I don't want to know him! A scholar! He'd get me into trouble with my clergy, and my minister of education. Then again, he'd want money, wouldn't he? Endowments, trinkets, sashes of every shade? Scholars don't live like anchorites, and you're not unaware, my poor boy, that the finances are a trifle dilapidated. Unless your scientist knows how to forge currency!"

"He knows better that that, Father; he'll serve you gratis. He'll only ask you for the right to experiment on a few of your subjects with a system of moral and physical improvement from which he expects great results. In any case, Dr. Marforio is amusing. He's not a pedant—on the contrary, he's an amiable fellow, witty and candid, an old man with style."

"Then you're mistaken—he's no scholar. But one point appeals to me: he'll serve me for nothing. Those are the good servants, the true ones, the ones for whom one can't pay too dear! A minister without a salary! There's a marvel! Besides which, you know, it would give me a certain luster in history; and although I care very little, fundamentally, for that loquacious muse, I wouldn't be sorry to know that she might one day say of me: 'The great Prince Bonifacio XXIII was able to solve the problem of reigning with very few taxes and being served for nothing.' Just between us, it's hardly worth the trouble, but since it would be stingy to deprive oneself of ministers, and it's fashionable to have some, I resign myself to putting up with a few, provided that they don't cost much and look the part. Does he look the part, your scholar?"

"You'll see, Father."

"Oh well, after all, I'd rather have a few handsome ministers and not to have to pay them. Oh, Lorenzo, Lorenzo, may you not learn for a long time—may you never learn—what worries supreme power brings! With your Dr. Mar...Marfur..."

"Marforio, Father."

"A fine name! With Dr. Marforio, I've solved at a stroke the famous economic problem that I was exhausting myself trying to find with that traitor Colbertini. Since I won't be paying him, I won't have to play cards with him for his salary. It's quite simple. I've made up my mind. Go and fetch my new minister."

"Yes, Father, I'll bring him right away," said Lorenzo, delighted by the outcome of his approach.

"By the way," said the prince, "how did you make the acquaintance of your Dr. Marforio?"

Lorenzo, who was about to leave the room, stopped and blushed. "That, Father, is the second part of my secret—the one that pertains to my personal happiness. Since the interests of the State have been dealt with, I can talk to you about my own. The doctor has a charming daughter. When you've seen Marta, Father..."

"I'm stupider than Colbertini!" exclaimed the worthy prince, falling back in his armchair with a loud burst of laughter. "What! I didn't guess right away that you were setting out a lover's trap for me! Oh, you're great politician, my lad! Well, is she as pretty as her father is wise, the beautiful Marta?"

"You'll see, Father, and I have no doubt that when you've admired her candor, the ingenuous grace..."

"Enough, enough! I know the vocabulary. It was the just same in my day. But it's not a minister you're proposing to me—it's an entire family!"

"If you don't mind, Father, let's only talk about the minister today."

"On the contrary—let's not talk about that any more, since it's done and dusted. After all, I have a good opinion of your scholar, since he has the intelligence to have a lovely daughter. Take him his appointment, and call in at the servant' parlor on the way. I'm giving a big dinner. The budget can make me that little gift, in view of the savings I'm making for it."

Lorenzo left, and ran in great haste to take the good news to Dr. Marforio.

In the meantime, Prince Bonifacio continued mopping his brow and muttering: "What a day! So much work! And people think I don't do anything! A ministry changed, public encouragement given to science in its most eminent person-age, Colbertini struck down, an economy realized, my gambling losses gloriously avenged! So many things in one day! If the opposition isn't content, it will be in the wrong."

Prince Bonifacio was right. The day's events might have made the opposition rejoice for more than one reason.

"However," the Prince said, after a few minutes, "Colbertini isn't aware of his disgrace. Let's make haste to inform him."

In consequence of that resolution, which was not exempt from malice, the best of men and the most ungrateful of princes wrote to that morning's adversary:

My dear Count,

I have had nothing but praise for your services thus far, and I experience a very real satisfaction in giving you this testimony, at the moment when grave considerations force me to allow you to go into the retirement that your age and labors imperiously demand.

I shall never forget that you have been the confidant of my most intimate thoughts. Remember that yourself.

P.S. It is the misfortune of princes to remain insolvent with regard to those who have served them best. I cannot pay you, my dear Count, but I would like the weight of my debt to ensure that you will always be in my thoughts.

Yours, etc., etc.
BONIFACIO XXIII

"Will he fully understand that postscript?" Prince Bonifacio asked himself, with a certain anxiety that resembled remorse. I can't ask him to let me off the sum that I've lost. I'll pay him, certainly, out of my economies, when I've made them—but if he takes it into his head to demand them, I'll have him indicted. Under the terms of the constitution, he's responsible for my mistakes; I'll easily find a few solid enough to get him hanged. That's a card-game that will begin a treasury of charge-sheets."

Fully reassured by these reasons of State, in which he did not sense any improbity, His Highness had the fatal message sent, and went into his dressing-room to get ready to welcome the greatest scientist in the principality in a worthy manner.

V. Dr. Marforio's Utopia

The meeting between the doctor and the prince merited the honors of comedy. Bonifacio, in spite of the sentiment of his personal and official dignity, was a trifle excited by the thought of having a scholar—a true scientist—for a minister. Those diabolical individuals who argue with Heaven and Earth sometimes treat the powers of this base world with a familiarity and a disdain of which the prince was fearful. What if his prime minister were to become his master! I am sure, however, that the question of emoluments weighed very heavily in His Highness' mind, and that the prospect of being served gratis gave the appearance of Dr. Marforio the charm of a liberation. No salary! Those two words resonated like "no dowry" in the eyes of a miser.

For his part, Marforio had the emotion of an artisan of the Great Work nearing the supreme goal, who has no more to do but draw a light curtain in order to receive the full blinding light of the truth. The ministry was only a means; science was his only ambition. It mattered little to him to be called Excellency and to climb into His Highness' rickety old carriage. For him, the essential thing was the possibility of finding experimental subjects, of making a mockery of prejudice and stamping his foot on the brazen face of ignorance.

Never had the pride and joy of participating in divine things put more of a gleam in the eyes and on the brow of a mortal. The perspective of triumph had tenderized the doctor's heart; he had become almost sentimental. When Lorenzo had left him, recommending him to hasten to the palace, Marforio felt his legs turn to jelly. He sat down.

"Marta, my daughter, come and kiss me," he said to his child, and he gave her a truly paternal kiss.

"Come on, Father, let's think about what you're going to wear," Marta replied, her heart beating very forcefully.

The doctor put on his best clothes, and regretted for a few moments having thus far neglected the care of his personal appearance.

I ought to have a sky blue coat embroidered with silver, he said to himself, *a coat the color of the firmament. From today onwards, I'm entering the service of the Supreme Being, and costume is symbolic.*

Marta feared that honors might render her father little crazy. The poor child was indulgent toward the past. She wanted to arrange the ceremonial wig on her father's fine gray hair personally. She stitched lace ruffles on his collar and his sleeves, while accumulating recommendations.

"Do you know how to address a prince?" she asked, dusting the doctor's hat.

"Of course! I'll salute him in Latin, Greek, Hebrew and all languages past, present and, I dare say, future."

"That's not it, Father. You have to bow."

"Do you want me to hire a dancing instructor?"

"Be patient and prudent, Father. Prince Bonifacio has never received scholars at court. He might not know how much he owes you—don't offend him."

"Don't worry, child. I know what indulgences one had to make to the grandees of the world. I'll spare him all the more because he's no eagle, the worthy Bonifacio!"

"Above all, Father, don't repeat that opinion at court!"

"Oh, I imagine that it must be widespread there, and that even Bonifacio can't be blind in that regard."

"But if he does happen to be blind, Father, don't open his eyes."

"Have no fear. Have you any more recommendations, my little precious?"

"Don't be too distracted. You sometimes take more from your interlocutor's snuff-box than the latter would wish—watch out for that. And finally, don't forget me, and once you're installed, remember that you've left your child all alone in your house."

"And my laboratory too. Have no fear; if Bonifacio understands me, I'll install all my instruments tomorrow, and you can come to join me."

"Oh, no, Father, I won't come," he young woman relied, swiftly, blushing deeply. "I shouldn't go to court,"

"You don't want to go there yet, sly one? But when you're a princess, you won't be able to refuse to come."

"Princess!" the young woman repeated, fearfully. "That word scares me. As long as I'm always loved, I'll bless God."

"And your father, of course, who will have won you a crown with his genius? Let's go—adieu! I'll tell you all about it, and I promise to bring you back some bonbons from the court, for they must eat them at every meal."

When His Highness Bonifacio was informed that Dr. Marforio was waiting, the prince drew himself up to his full height, had the door of the audience chamber opened wide, and advanced majestically, lifting up his foot and stretching his leg.

The doctor did not want to seem intimidated in the presence of a sovereign whose public and private capacities he had criticized severely, but the very effort that he made to remain calm gave his countenance a rigidity and embarrassment that Bonifacio interpreted as the result of exactly such emotion.

The prince wanted to show courtesy toward such a modest scholar. "I'm delighted to see you, Doctor, and to make your acquaintance. My son tells me that you've been agreeable enough to bear a share of the heavy burden of power. I can't refuse my son anything; you're a minister. Let's sit down and chat like old friends."

"I confess, Prince, that in thinking about the ministry," Marforio replied, "I did not feel the puerile pride of governing men so much as the ambition of endowing the world with my system."

"Oh, yes, you have a system, an obsession. We'll talk about that later. I never oppose my ministers; I leave them free to act and do as they wish, on the sole condition that they don't annoy me anymore. Carve, gnaw, amuse yourself—but don't ask me for money. As for the government of men, between ourselves, there's not much to it. With two or three lessons you'll know as much as Machiavelli. Oh, if the people had time to reflect, they'd be tempted to do without us. Look, I, whom am talking to you, am merely the son of my father, Bonifacio XXII; well, if I wanted to take the trouble, I could play the role of a great man like anyone else—it's not a matter of drinking the sea. Except that, I confess, it's tiresome; then again, it's so unrewarding to the artist and spectator that I prefer the placid gleam of my reign. It's not dazzling, but it's sufficient for illumination."

"You're a philosopher," said Marforio.

"And you, my dear Minister, are a flatterer, which is proof of a first-rate aptitude for the profession of courtier; you have my compliments. It's said that you have a pretty daughter?"

"And you, Prince, have an amiable son."

"Yes, he's polite, but a trifle timid. It's the fault of his governess. Fortunately, I don't need him. He's been making eyes at your heiress, my heir."

"Prince, believe that I knew nothing about it..."

"Of course! You're a scholar! You doubtless gaze at the stars with a big telescope and don't see what's happening under your nose. It's always the same."

"Would Your Highness deign to instruct me in the duties of my position?" suggested the doctor, slightly put out by the Prince's persiflage.

"Your duties? To initial the ordinances that I sign—but don't worry; I'm economizing on paper, so I don't sign very many. To sit beside me at table and always to support my opinion—except when I'm supporting yours, for then it's necessary to seem to be resigning yourself and bowing down, vanquished, to the weight of my reasoning. Then, there's...my word, I've forgotten the rest. But the head clerk in the ministry office will tell you all that. As a general rule, only one condition is indispensable to be my minister, the appointment. Since you have that in your pocket, you're a minister as perfect as your colleagues. You only lack the costume. I'll reclaim Colbertini's. Although he's been serving for twenty-five years, I think it's still presentable. Now that we're bound together, my dear doctor, tell me, just between the two of us, frankly, what science is."

"What science is, my lord?" exclaimed the doctor, thinking that he had found an opportunity to ride his hobby-horse.

"Yes, I can guess what you're going to tell me. Big words, grandiose phrases! But those of us whose profession is to learn and recite aren't duped by that rhetoric. I imagine that science is, like power, the art of living on the respect of others and making oneself a jolly little niche. But truly, what do you know that I don't, for example?"

"It will be necessary for Your Highness to tell me what he had studied."

"Me, I haven't studied anything, and I'm proud of it. I used to play the viola quite nicely at one time; I'm not without skill at cup-and-ball, and I can handle a deck of cards without too much disadvantage—except when people cheat." Bonifacio added the final remark in a bitter tone.

"I don't know anything about all that, myself," said the poor doctor, proudly, who found his prince inferior even to the poor opinion he had had of him, "but I know the origin of the world, I know how to decompose the elements and combine unknown forces."

"So what? Do you know a better way to brew coffee, or to make the hours that follow a meal less melancholy? Have you found the elixir of youth? So long as science can't prolong the pleasure of life for an hour, nor add a single enjoyment to the sun of so-called terrestrial felicities, it will be, like power, a last resort of the ignorant."

"Well, my lord," said Dr. Marforio, stiffening himself, trying to make himself taller in order to be more imposing, "I, your minister, am bringing you exactly that enjoyment you regret. The elixir of youth that pretty women desire even more than ugly ones, and which many men would like to drink, I can cause to well up, and I offer it to you; it will be the reward for my welcome."

"You can rejuvenate people?" asked Bonifacio, with a curiosity that was not disinterested.

"I can't efface wrinkles from the brow, and I can't make roses flower again in the snow," replied Dr. Marforio, "but I know the art—or, rather, the science—of lightening the flight of the years, of preventing any destructive action of mind on the body. I can prolong life and preserve it. I can prevent the flame that burns within us from burning us up."

"Indeed!" Bonifacio interjected. "I'd be curious to see that." He did not understand it very well, and rendered himself the justice that thought had never wearied his own body.

"The problem of life is the only interesting one," the doctor continued. "Everyone has tackled it. Some have invented philters, others have pretended to rejuvenate by means of evocations and spells. My science is less empirical; it rests upon the most judicious philosophy; it has drawn its elements from the knowledge of the body and the study of the soul. One of my colleagues, one of those demi-scholars that Germany offers as a model to France, Dr. Flourentius, claims that it is sufficient to drink fresh water, to eat discerningly and to do everything in moderation to live for two hundred years, as an extraordinary term, and a hundred and fifty on average."

"Two hundred years—that's nice!" murmured Bonifacio.

"Bah!" retorted Marforio. "What's that, if I can give you eternity?"

"I'll accept," said the Prince, laughing, "but only on the condition that it's still gratis."

"What if I suppress, at a stroke, the quarrels, disputes and wars that are the agents of destruction?"

"Bravo! That would be an economy for my budget and a great subject of joy for my Minister of War, who has a very peaceful character. But my dear Marforio, if people don't die any more, will they still continue to multiply? I fear encumbrance; the earth is small."

"I've foreseen the circumstance," the doctor continued, gravely. "There are minds so ill-formed that they're never content with anything. They begin to weary of life at the age of ninety-nine and kill themselves at a hundred and twenty. Anyway, I provide the possibility of living forever, but I don't impose it."

"Yes, I understand; people are always at liberty not to drink the elixir. As for me, my dear doctor, have no fear; I have a very well-formed character, and a robust soul. I've accommodated myself to the paltry and limited existence that I already lead. I won't weary of the boundless and limitless existence you're promising me. When do we uncork the benevolent phial?"

"The incomparable merit of my system consist precisely of the fact," Marforio continued, "that I do not make use of any phial, lotion or philter. I only employ the resources of banal humanity. It will be sufficient that I live long enough to leave pupils behind, and that I find someone to give me in my turn the benefit that I will have given. That is the price of the world's salvation."

"*Per Bacco!* You're going to be a precious minister!"

"I have noticed," the doctor went on, "that sleep, which generally passes for the repose of the body and the soul, is very often a fatigue for the latter that exercises the most dangerous influence on the former—the most treacherous of all fatigues, since we are unconscious of it at the time, and can neither obtain diversion from it or its suspension."

"I've always suspected as much," said Bonifacio. "I often wake up with a heavy head and an upset stomach! Dreams trouble the digestion. Oh, if one could only sleep without dreaming!"

"You've touched upon the delicate point, the pivot of my system."

"My dear minister, that penetration is habitual to me. Give me the pleasure of no longer being astonished by it."

"To suppress dreams," Marforio continued, "to make sleep into what it really ought to be—repose, the annihilation of thought—would be to double or triple human existence. How many times have poor sleepers gone to bed with dark hair and woken up with white hair? They've aged twenty years in a dream. Take note, too, that dreams are reflections of thoughts of the previous day, or projections of thoughts of the day to come. Ordinarily, they're useless to the past and the future alike, and one regards as miraculous, as celestial visitations, all dreams that have a meaning, which contain a logical warning. Humankind, therefore, has everything to gain from no longer dreaming."

"I'd no longer see, as in a nightmare, that scoundrel Colbertini incessantly winning against me," sighed Bonifacio. "But dreams are often remorse. Will you suppress the conscience, my dear Marforio?"

"To begin with, that would be rather convenient for Statesmen, and I suggest that they wouldn't companion about it," riposted Marforio. "Then again, what does remorse matter, if I suppress criminals?"

"You're right—remorse would be superfluous. But how would you do that?"

"It's quite simple. Humans no longer living in continual excitation, resting the humanity that weighs upon them by day, would no longer experience wicked temptations. To suppress the obstinacy and relentlessness of thought is to suppress deviance, excess, intoxication and the vertigo of the imagination."

"Hmmm!" said the price, breathing deeply, like a man constrained for the first time to take a dive and striving for air. "I don't see what you're proposing to do, exactly."

"The brain is the instrument of intellectual and moral life," the doctor continued. "I've discovered that it's not the principal agent of physical life."

"I've always suspected as much," Bonifacio put in, folding his arms over his stomach.

"In consequence of that discovery," Marforio continued, "I believe that, if one were temporarily to refuse the brain the instruments that it causes to act, it would no longer toil, and would leave the body in an immobility profitable to the entire organism and the brain itself. Armed with that conviction, I've carried out experiments, and this is the result. By means of a delicate instrument, which cuts through iron like a fruit, I make a circular incision in the bones of the skull, in such a fashion that the top of the cranium can be lifted off like a lid."

"Like opening a snuff-box," said the prince, taking a pinch of tobacco from a tortoiseshell box.

"Your Highness understands perfectly. With a spoon made of a metal of my own composition, after I've paralyzed the resistance of the will with a narcotic, I carefully remove the cerebrum; I leave the cerebellum, which is sufficient for bestial life, and I deposit the poor cerebrum in the most limpid water, where it bathes entirely at its ease and is penetrated with freshness."

"That's how farmers refresh butter," said High Highness, who had a weakness for analogies.

"Undoubtedly," Marforio replied. "I leave the cerebrum to repose in that fashion all night. In the meantime, the body only lives a vegetal existence. In the morning, at cock-crow, I fish the cerebrum out of the crystal bowl in which I've deposited it; I replace it in the skull; I close the lid again—and the individual wakes up and acts, thinks, works, completely relaxed, rejuvenated, without aggravation, without the baneful influences that bad dreams and troubled sleep leave behind."

"That's prodigious!" exclaimed Bonifacio. "But do you think the method is infallible?"

"Infallible."

"I thought that one couldn't touch the cerebrum with impunity."

"Once, perhaps, because one took hold of it clumsily; but now the means has been found of manipulating and kneading brains as one wishes."

"What a precious minister I have here!" said Bonifacio, laughing.

"You understand that, with such a system, I lengthen life by the entire quantity that is lost in sleep. It's a light that I blow out every evening and relight every morning."

"Instead of putting people in prison," asked the prince, "couldn't one be content to remove their cerebrum for a day or two?"

"Indeed."

"It's fabulous! It's fabulous! My dear friend, your system delights me. Perhaps it's absurd, but it ought to be amusing. We shall see whether it offers any difficulty in application. But on whom have you carried out our experiments?"

"Thus far, I've contented myself with the dead..."

"Ah!" exclaimed High Highness, jumping in his seat. "But in that case, you can't answer for the living?"

"On the contrary, my lord, the latter have a complaisance that will facilitate the experiments. Besides which, I was about to add that I've also experimented in lunatic asylums, and the results obtained have surpassed all the anticipations of science. It's enough to confound understanding."

"You've cured madmen?"

"Oh, no my lord. If I'd cured them, I'd have been defeated, since I'd have changed the conditions of the mental life of their cerebrum. I observed that not only were they as mad the next day as they had been the day before, but that there was even a small recrudescence, a progress."

"That's utterly peremptory," said the prince. "You must show me these fortunate lunatics, wise enough not to be cured. But on whom are we going to operate?"

"I thought that my lord would be delighted to sleep without bad dreams and to set a good example for his subjects."

"Of course, of course—but I wouldn't be sorry, either, to have seen the operation succeed on my ministers first. I'll abandon them to you."

"My lord will be content."

"Well, my dear Marforio, I never suspected that the last word in progress and the last word in science would be cracking skulls! I'm curious to see you at work. When shall we begin?"

"Whenever Your Highness pleases."

"I need to prepare my ministry for the operation; those fellows are bound to want to keep their cerebrums intact."

"Oh, my lord, don't think that they'll be deterred something so trivial. Give them a title, an honor, and you'll have all the cerebrums in the principality at your disposal."

"What a man you are! You leap over all the steps of politics in a single bound!"

"And you, my lord, all the abysms of science."

"We were made to understand one another, my dear Marforio."

"I had that hope, my lord."

"It only remains for me to judge your capacity at table—but I'm confident of that."

"I shall justify it, my lord," said Marforio, who did not feel calm, and who, in spite of the gravity of the undertakings he had made, would have danced a saraband in the middle of the room if he had dared. After all, Richelieu was a good dancer.

Bonifacio went into the dining room, and introduced his new minister to his colleagues.

Marforio understood at the first glance that he would easily be able to reason with those excellent individuals. They had not resisted twenty years of power, and a few were flourishing in the physical and mental plumpness that was, in a sense, the objective and the recompense of the high functions exercised in the principality.

"What fine heads, eh?" Bonifacio whispered to his prime minister.

The doctor ate with a good appetite, but on seeing him handle his knife with vivacity, which was throwing off sparks, the prince wondered whether the amiable doctor was thinking about his system, or the sumptuous dinner that the budget was providing for him.

VI. How Dr. Marforio Yielded his Secret

The dinner was merry. The doctor, as I have said, was only pedantic at times, and the time had passed for that day. He held his own with Prince Bonifacio and the entire ministry. Now, Marforio's colleagues were not incapable men. The Minister of War, notably, who believed that he was obliged to represent the entire military force of the principality by himself, was a kind of colossus, as red as a poppy, ornamented with a terrible moustache, who drank with a superior intrepidity. He did not hide his disdain for the scholar, and after having searched laboriously for a pleasantry, ended up asking him whether he had invented gunpowder.

That joke was produced with frightful gales of laughter, continually renewed. But Marforio was admirably mild-mannered, and from the corner of his eye he took the measure of his colleague's skull, and said to himself silently: *What if, instead of floating his cerebrum in water, I were to plunge it into wine? It would be in its element!*

The Minister of Education was the most modest. He was afraid of letting his ignorance show, and did not say a word.

The Minister of Finance was calculating, as each new dish was brought forth, the expenses of the feast, and thinking about bankruptcy.

There was no Minister of Public Works, the pretext for that post having always been lacking.

The Minister of Justice was a poor ruined gentleman, who had taken possession of the blade of the law, with Bonifacio's agreement, in order not to be struck down by it, and who had found no other means of escaping the debt-collectors and bailiffs than becoming their commander-in-chief. He was inviolable, and did not render those who did not pursue him destitute.

Thus, there was in all the branches of government a small system of compensation and equilibrium, which caused the machine, without really working, to appear to be moving.

Marforio slipped a few words about his system into the conversation. All Their Excellencies opened their eyes wide. They all put their hands on their foreheads, but none of them offered his head.

Bonifacio was outraged by that egotism. "I don't say that they're heads devoid of brains," he whispered to the doctor, "because, in that case, they'd be useless and they'd be right to refuse, but I assure you that they're ingrates. And people are astonished that, with instruments like them, I can't work miracles!"

"Let's get them drunk," Marforio replied, laconically.

"That will be difficult, They're all practiced, like Mithridates, and have no fear of the poison."

Marforio kept filling the glasses. Perhaps he even found a means to mix some auxiliary beverage with the wines he poured. At any rate, by the end of the meal, the Minister of War was leaning his powerful head on his plate and snoring like a cannon. The other ministers submitted to the contagion in their turn, and soon no one except the prince and the doctor.

"Finally, the moment has come!" exclaimed His Highness, in a low voice, wiping his forehead with his napkin.

Marforio sharpened his instrument. He set up a mysterious box, which he had taken care to bring along when taking possession of the ministry, and, after bolting the doors, he made his final preparations.

The scene was strange. Bonifacio went pale. "I ought to have requested the experiment before dinner," he murmured.

Calm, solemn and as radiant as a prophet, Marforio poured water into large crystal bowls and attached little labels to them, in order to be able to recognize them.

"This is the Minister of War," he said. "Here's His Excellency of Education. This bowl is for the Finance Minister."

"Hurry up! Hurry up!" said Bonifacio, feeling a serious disturbance. His halting voice demonstrated sufficiently that the dinner had been an imprudence on His Highness' part.

"There! I'm ready!" Marforio replied, making the famous instrument that open skulls sparkle in the candle-light. "Which one should I start with?"

"I don't know," Bonifacio replied, whose benevolent soul suddenly experienced scruples. "Suppose you were about to do them harm, my friend?"

"I reply in the negative, my lord."

"It'll be a fine time to contradict you when you've killed them or rendered them idiots!"

Marforio smiled; he found the slightest dread excessively chimerical. "I offer my life as a pledge, as a guarantee," he said, proudly.

"Go on, then! I did promise," the prince replied, resignedly.

"Who does You Highness want to indicate to me?"

Bonifacio paraded a melancholy gaze over his ministry. Deep down, he cared as little about any of them as any other, and he held them all in very low esteem; even so, he did not want to sacrifice them lightly. "Start with the Minister of Finance," he stammered. "I value him the least and could replace him very easily."

Marforio advanced toward his subject, but as he was about to make the circular incision, and which Bonifacio, veritably trembling, covered his eyes in order not to see that action of the utmost temerity, the doctor paused.

"We haven't made our conditions, Prince. I'm giving you the secret of life. Do you think that the stupid pride of being a minister is sufficient recompense for me?"

What does he want from me? the Prince wondered. "I thought, my dear Marforio," he said, aloud, "that all of this was offered gratis?"

"So it's not for me that I'm stipulating, my lord. If I succeed, permit Prince Lorenzo to marry my daughter."

"Is that all?" exclaimed Bonifacio, expelling the air from his lungs. "I was afraid. I give you my word, my dear doctor, that Lorenzo is free; besides which, I'll reign for such a long time that he'll never reign, and I won't be offending my ancestors by permitting the misalliance."

"I accept your word," said Marforio, briskly removing the wig from his colleague in finance, and tracing a line along the forehead with the tip of his instrument.

Trembling and agitated, Bonifacio plunged his head into his napkin. After a few seconds, not hearing any noise, he dared to peep, and remained dumbfounded by the strange spectacle offered to him. The Minister of Finance, smiling and sleeping the most profound slumber, was lying back in his armchair. His skull was open and a removed portion permitted a void to be seen therein.

With the utmost care, Marforio deposited his colleague's brain in the bottom of the crystal bowl destined to receive it.

A frisson of admiration, in which fear was also a participant, ran through High Highness from head to toe. "It's extraordinary, extraordinary!" he repeated, several times. "If I hadn't seen, I wouldn't have believed it."

"Your Highness can be assured that his minister is intact, and that when his skull is closed, absolutely nothing will have changed externally."

Marforio gave the skull a light tap, and the lid fell back with a slight click.

"He's still alive?" asked Bonifacio.

"Feel his pulse! Listen to his respiration! You can see that his face has been embellished. Since I removed the thought therefrom, it's no longer grimacing. I'm convinced, my lord, that your minister was chagrined."

"Poor Madredi! Is that possible? Can he have taken my interests to heart to that extent? It's necessary to relieve him of that chagrin, my dear Marforio."

"Have no fear! He'll leave it at the bottom of the bowl of water."

"Suppose we leave it there for today?"

"Impossible my lord. My colleagues might perhaps hesitate tomorrow before eating and drinking. I'm in haste to convince you completely."

The same operation was carried out on the Minister of War, the Minister of Justice and the Minister of Education. Marforio showed the prince that life had not been affected, and that the eminent functionaries, relieved of the burden of their thoughts, had taken on an expression of incredible bliss in their sleep.

Bonifacio was genuinely jealous of the calmness and the pleasant appearance they had in their repose, all the more so because he was not tranquil himself. If he had dared, he would have offered himself for the experiment right away, but he reflected that the experiment would only be complete and decisive in his eyes when he had witnessed the awakening. First, he had a great need to know how they would feel the day after such a major operation.

"My dear Marforio," he said, "you're a great man. You add luster to my reign, and I desire to learn your method of putting people to sleep as quickly as possible, in order that I might render you in my turn the service that you have rendered today to my poor ministers, and will render to me tomorrow.

"When will our children be married, my lord?" asked Marforio.

"Whenever you wish. Arrange that with Lorenzo."

Marforio bowed. He was modestly triumphant. He was fearful of manifesting the immense pride dilating his bosom before the ignorant prince.

It was agreed that the ministerial cerebrums would be locked in the Treasury Room. It was unused; no one ever went into it. There was, however, a great honor in that assimilation of the objects steeped in water with the crown jewels. The key to the precious retreat was carefully removed. The bodies were put to bed.

None of the servants in the castle worried about the precautions Bonifacio XXIII took with regard to his ministers. It was not the first time that they had fallen asleep at table, although it was the first time, in such circumstances, that they had slept anywhere else but under the table.

Bonifacio, when he saw the doctor depart, renewed the expression of his sincere admiration for him. He was impatient to be rejuvenated in his turn, to have an appearance as fresh and as reposed as that of his ministers.

Marforio, for his part, was so swollen with pride that he was as light as a balloon. He went home on foot; it was a final concession that he made to humanity before raising himself definitively to a higher level.

Marta was waiting for him on the doorstep. I must admit that she was not waiting alone, and that Lorenzo was keeping her company.

"Rejoice, my children," said the worthy Marforio, kissing his daughter. "Marta, you shall be a princess whenever it pleases this handsome prince. As for me, from this happy moment onwards, I'm the greatest scientist in the world."

"What! My father didn't put up any resistance?" asked Lorenzo, who was not at all anxious to know whether the doctor's theory had been put to the test, and whether the experiment has succeeded.

"Him, resist me!" retorted Marforio, who thought too much of his recent success to perceive that they were not thinking about that. "Come to the castle tomorrow, Lorenzo, my friend, and you shall see how science acquires titles of nobility."

With that, Marforio, who had made a sufficient sacrifice to family emotions and domestic details, went into his laboratory in order to savor his overflowing joy at his ease. I shall respect that flood, which is of no relevant to my story, and we shall remain, if you have no objection, in the company of the two lovers.

"Is it a dream, Marta?" asked the sentimental Lorenzo.

"I'm very happy," murmured the young woman, thanking the moon and the stars with her gaze.

"Oh, Marta, I love you! And I would have sacrificed the hope of a crown for the hope of being your husband."

"No, my lord, you have a duty to the happiness of the principality, and God does not want me to have to be egotistical in order to love you."

"If you knew, Marta, how nearly ridiculous the title of prince seems to me, with its derisory authority in the midst of those faded trinkets! Instead of taking you to court, I'd rather run away with you."

"I don't have those fears, just as I have no ambition," Marta answered, with a smile that lit up in the depths of her heart. "I want to be a princess, since you're a prince, and I want to support you and give you confidence. Come on, my love, let's not be afraid of happiness. Since it has arrived, let's seize it!"

"Marta, you are wisdom, just as you are beauty," said Lorenzo, applying his lips to the young woman's hands.

"Adieu, my prince," she replied, slipping away. "Be sure that when I'm a princess, I'll resist flatterers."

Lorenzo did not protest. He smiled and went back to the paternal palace, to which he always had a key about his person.

In consequence of the more than tolerant dispositions that I mentioned when I began, His Highness Bonifacio XXIII has no guards to keep watch on the gates of his palace. He slept tranquilly, without any need for sentries at his door, and as he wanted everyone in his household to conform to that habit, as soon as the prince had blown out his candle, obscurity blacked out all the windows on every floor; from the attics to the porter's lodge, everyone was in the process of going to sleep. The people who had, by way of exception, the right to enter or exit from the narcotized palace were obliged constantly to carry their own key.

This detail, as you will see, is not irrelevant to my story; for, at the moment when Lorenzo introduced his pass key into the lock, he felt another pass-key entering from the other side collide with his own. Someone was trying to get out in the same way that he was trying to get in. As he result sought by these two contradictory actions was the same for both, and it was a matter, in sum, of going in and going out, and because, in order for that to happen, the opening of the door was necessary, the door opened.

A shadow, albeit sufficiently robust for its passage to be sensible, tried to glide between the wall and Prince Lorenzo.

"Who's that?" demanded our hero, resolutely. He knew that thieves had no more business being in the palace by night than by day.

The shadow, held back by the slender but muscular hand of the prince, seemed determined to remain silent.

"Beware," said the latter. "I'll call for help, and have a light brought, and then I'll see who you are whether you like it or not...."

"Don't make any noise, my lord," the shadow in question finally hazarded, in response.

"What! Is that you, Colbertini?"

"Alas, yes, my lord, it's me," replied the voice of the dispossessed President of the Council, with a sigh. "It's me."

"What are you doing here at this hour?" asked the prince.

"You see, my lord, I'm like a servant who's been sacked. Ah, that's the price of twenty-five years of loyal service. Princes are ingrates."

Lorenzo smiled and was tempted to reply: "What about ministers, then? People have always done more for them than they've done for the prince or the State"—but the hereditary prince did not want to embark on a discussion of political philosophy. "It seems to me, Count," he said to Colbertini, "that you're going home very late. Everyone in the castle is asleep. Of whom have you been taking your leave at this hour?"

"I'd forgotten a few small items," murmured Colbertini.

Lorenzo was struck by the ex-prime minister's embarrassment. He scented a mystery. Although Bonifacio XXIII's palace had no chance of ever becoming a volcano, and although Colbertini, a trifle Machiavellian when he was playing cards, was scarcely so when it was merely a matter of ideas, Lorenzo feared a conspiracy, or at least an intrigue. "Something's going on," he said, sharply, to the former minister, trying to look him in the face—a maneuver that the darkness rendered very difficult, but which succeeded very well because of Colbertini's lack of heroism.

"Undoubtedly, my lord, frightful follies have been committed in the castle, and I've been very much afraid that His Serene Highness will require a Council of Regency before long.

"Count!" said Lorenzo, severely.

"Excuse me, my lord, but, in truth, it's enough to make one doubt reason in general, and that of the one presiding over the destiny of the State in particular. If you knew the horrors, the sorceries, that were being practiced! Oh, I was very wrong, when I was a minister, to refuse the establishment of an Inquisition in the principality. I'd have the means of avenging myself."

"Avenging yourself on whom?" demanded Lorenzo, ominously.

"Oh, I'm not accusing His Highness," Colbertini hastened to reply, his initial emotion having dissipated somewhat. He failed to recognize my services, but that was his right. But I have the right in my turn to hate that false scientist, that sorcerer, who has replaced me by means of intrigue, and who would have killed half the principality within a fortnight if he'd been allowed to."

Lorenzo smiled and shrugged his shoulders. As he was ignorant of the first principles of Marforio's famous system, he could not admit the ferocious intentions attributed to him.

"You're unjust," he said. "The doctor had replaced you, but he didn't supplant you. I have to confess to you that it was me, without nurturing any hostile sentiment against you, who solicited in his favor. As for his pretended cruelties..."

"Oh, it was you, my lord, was it? Colbertini retorted, in a bitter one. "I hope you don't repent one day of the imprudence you've committed, but as I don't want you to accuse me of calumny, come with me, and I'll show you the first actions of your new minister."

Lorenzo did not understand Colbertini's excitement at all—by which I mean that, while admitting the rancor and resentment that the minister was exhibiting, he had no suspicion of the pretexts that the latter was putting forward to color his vengeance.

Everyone in the palace, as I have said, was asleep. Lorenzo and the ex-minister groped around for some time; then the heir presumptive found a hidey-hole where his domestic took the precaution every evening of placing a tinder-box and a candle, and the two interlocutors were able to look at one another at their ease,

"How pale you are!" Lorenzo said to Colbertini.

"My lord will be just as pale as me," replied the minister, with a taut expression.

They went up toward the solemn apartments. When they arrived at the Treasury Room, Colbertini took a little key from his pocket, which he introduced rapidly into the lock.

"Go in, my lord," he said.

Lorenzo wondered whether he was about to observe a deficit in the crown jewels, but the presence of a treasure would have been much more astonishing than its absence. He looked, and saw nothing except crystal bowls full on water.

"Well?" he said.

"Well, my lord, this is all that remains of my former colleagues." And Colbertini pointed at the cerebrums soaking in the liquid.

Lorenzo brought his candle closer and read the labels that Marforio had placed at the bottom of each jar.

"What does this mean?"

"It means, my lord," retorted the former President of the Council, in a lamentably hypocritical tone, "that you have delivered the fate of the principality to a madman and a demoniac, and that his first action has been this sacrilegious murder."

"That's impossible."

"Impossible, you say! I merely invoke the evidence of my eyes. Justly alarmed by the public destitution that had struck me, I came to present to His Highness the humble supplications of the civil servants who know me, when I learned that my lord Bonifacio had withdrawn and shut himself away with his minister. A curiosity—entirely disinterested, I assure you, as I was only thinking of the happiness of all—suggested to me the idea of looking through the keyhole.

"Well," said Lorenzo, "it appears that that's how one observes ministers. It was through the keyhole that I saw you this morning, you know, working with my father."

Colbertini blushed slightly. "Our occupations were inoffensive, at least," he continued, with a gesture of pride. "My lord knows full well that if ministers were never locked away with their sovereign, the vulgar would have no confidence in the power. It's part of the art of reigning. But imagine my terror when I saw, as clearly as I see you, my lord, that abominable scientist mutilating the heads of my former colleagues, opening their skulls and removing these brains, which he has doubtless destined for some diabolical work."

Lorenzo looked at Colbertini and the bowls, alternately, feeling extremely anxious. There was a mixture of the grotesque and the horrible in the mystery that was repugnant to reason, but which was not incompatible with the doctor's extravagances.

"Where are the bodies?" asked the prince.

"You're still in doubt?" conducting Lorenzo to the beds on which the members of the council were lying.

"Look at that bloody line around the head," said Colbertini. "That's the trace of the murder."

Lorenzo felt dizzy. Even so, he plucked up the courage to touch one of the empty skulls and open it up. Colbertini was triumphant: a crime unprecedented in the annals of the principality had been committed by his father and his future father-in-law, acting in complicity. Honor, love and power all collapsed at the same time—and it was him, in his egotistical passion, who had facilitated this murder!

The poor young man, who was twenty years old, under the sway of romantic ideas, and who imagined that the inviolability of human life is the first and most sacred duty of a sovereign, burst into heartfelt sobs. He let himself fall into an armchair.

"All is lost!" he murmured. "Oh, Colbertini, what have I done?"

It is necessary to be just to the former President of the Council; that dolor disarmed him completely, and he no longer had any firm desire but to get the prince and the principality out of the difficulty into which this savage experiment had put them. As his re-entry into government would naturally be one of the most efficacious means, it is not surprising that he thought of it immediately.

"No, all is not lost…yet, my lord," he said to Lorenzo, in a tone of humble compassion. "There are only few people strictly essential to the equilibrium of the State. The death of these good men is doubtless a misfortune, but a misfortune of which they are the first—and I ought to say, the only—victims. Let the secret remain between us, and let the public be told that they were struck by apoplexy at table; the public will believe it. We'll make your father understand that card games are the most inoffensive games; we'll put Marforio in a lunatic asylum, and if you wish, prince, we'll persuade High Highness Bonifacio XXIII to abdicate in your favor. We'll then administer the principality for the greater glory of Lorenzo, and this accident will be the departure-point of an era of renovation."

Lorenzo nodded his head and appeared to approve, but he had not heard—or, in consequence, understood—a single word of the minister's speech. He was thinking about his compromised love and weeping quietly for the loss of his fiancée, much more than for the loss of the high functionaries.

"I await your orders, my lord," said Colbertini, finally.

"My orders?" replied the prince, emerging from his reverie. "What do you expect me to order? Bury these cadavers and make these horrible vestiges disappear. At least the darkness is protecting us. Wake up some devoted servant in the castle, have him help you, and tomorrow, I'll take responsibility for everything with regard to my father. You're a devoted servant of the dynasty, Count; swear that you'll keep the secret."

Colbertini hesitated momentarily before swearing, but as his was a deceptive mind, he thought that a political oath only binds those who receive it, and not the man who makes it. In consequence, he promised out loud to bury the night's mysteries in his memory, while he promised silently to reveal them at an opportune moment, if his portfolio were not returned to him swiftly, with an invitation to form a government.

Lorenzo was honest; he received the oath and believed it, He was in a hurry to get away from the vile spectacle that the Treasury Room offered to him at that moment. He withdrew, extremely sad, inconsolable and full of remorse, accusing himself of all these sorceries and seeing Marta's sweet face drawing away and disappearing into bloody clouds.

I can affirm that the hereditary prince served a cruel apprenticeship in supreme rank that night. He did not go to bed. He stayed up until dawn, leaning on his window-sill, allowing tears to fall on the street below and lamenting, as a son, as a prince, as a lover, with an ardor that would have provoked the enthusiasm of the party of the future if they had been able to see that pious and saintly dolor.

What will people say tomorrow when they find out that the entire ministry is dead and buried? The poor prince asked himself, twenty times an hour. *Will they believe in that fake apoplexy? How could my father, so gentle, so human, consent to this butchery? How could the doctor have demanded it of him? Poor Marta! What will become of her? What have I done in claiming the ministry for Marforio? So this is his system! Superstitious practices that recall the most barbaric epochs. Oh, science! It isn't worth as much as a simple impulse of the heart and the everyday inspiration of conscience. What luck that Colbertini was there just in time to warn me! But why was he there? There's a mystery in that, which I ought to elucidate. As long as he finds someone discreet to help him! I didn't dare to stay there; I was afraid of those cadavers, which had served as playthings. In a few hours, they'll be buried; I'll fund an expiatory mass. I'll go to find my father. But Marta! What will become of her?*

Underlying all his remorse, his agitations, it was always the name of his fiancée that he found, as the most pointed spur of all, the sharpest blade to pierce his breast.

Toward daybreak, worn out by that night of insomnia, Lorenzo looked at himself in a mirror and was afraid of himself, so pale did he seem.

"Colbertini was right, I'm paler than he was; I'll put on my princely face. Oh, the happiness of others—what a heavy burden!"

The young and charming egotist forgot to add to that reflection that the happiness of others is an especially difficult task when individual happiness is mingled with it, and in a contrary sense. Let us add that the happiness of the principality, and even the salvation of the souls that Lorenzo believed to have been put to death by Marforio's procedure, preoccupied him considerably less than the question of knowing whether his marriage to the doctor's daughter was permanently compromised. One can always find ministers anywhere, by paying the price, but what can replace love?

"Fortunately," Lorenzo said, sighing, in order to sum up his mediations and all his nocturnal anguish, "the dead are buried, Colbertini is discreet, and I've repaired all the damage!"

Without anticipating events, I can assure you that the prince was wrong on at least two of these points. He had aggravated everything and not repaired anything; as for Colbertini, his discretion was more than problematic, and perhaps, even while swearing to keep silent, he had followed the advice of Père Sanchez,[15] which assures us that one can dispense oneself from keeping an oath by mangling the words when one swears—saying, for instance, *uro*, I burn, instead of *juro*, I swear. It is beyond doubt that if he had said that he was

---

[15] The Spanish Jesuit Tomas Sanchez (1550-1610), an expert in casuistry.

burning, Colbertini was telling the exact truth, because he was burning to get his hands on power again. As regards the burial of the dead, we shall see how he had carried out that task.

In the meantime, I can assure you that the presence of the minister in the prince's palace at a rather advanced hour of the evening, stemmed from an immoderate desire on Colbertini's part to know exactly what he had only learned in part through the keyhole, and when hazard brought him into contact with Lorenzo he was leaving to ruminate a frightful vengeance, which nothing, evidently, could have led him to renounce.

VI. In which Dr. Marforio's fortune attains its apogee

During the night, Lorenzo had been tempted several times to escape from the palace, run to the doctor's house and say to him: "Flee; disappear with your blood-stained hands; don't touch your daughter and leave her to me."

To talk to the doctor before he got up, however, it would have been necessary to wake him, to make a noise, perhaps to cause the scandal that he wanted to prevent. Lorenzo was timid in the face of scandal, so he remained decently at home until the time when Bonifacio permitted people to stir and give signs of life in the palace. As soon as he heard that His Highness had asked for his first breakfast, however—he had more than one—Lorenzo went down in all haste and ran to the scientist's domicile.

He met him half way radiant and superb, more sumptuously dressed than ever, with the particular illumination in his face that is peculiar to lunatics and men of genius, which often leads to confusion between the two. Benevento Cellini recounts in his *Memoirs* that when he arrived at the culminating point of his career, he had an aureole about his face that was perfectly distinct in the dark. He was sure that his friends were not mistaken about it; his enemies, of course, could not see anything at all. Doctor Marforio's aureole could even have dazzled his enemies. Lorenzo was far from reckoning himself among the scholar's detractors, even though his faith had been considerably shaken. He saw that gleam, and sighed.

Marforio extended his arms to the young prince. He would have liked to be able to embrace the entire universe, so triumphantly was his soul distended.

"Ah, young man!" he said, "the day that is commencing will go down in the annals of the principality."

"Alas," sighed Lorenzo, who did not know how to embark upon the series of his reproaches and recommendations.

"I haven't closed an eye all night," the doctor continued. "Such a great emotion, at my age!"

"I haven't slept either," said Lorenzo.

"Indeed, my lord, the moonlight has discolored your face. A sweet insomnia, that of lovers! Go and tell my daughter about your sighs; for myself, I'm in a hurry."

"Where are you going?"

"To the palace, of course."

"In the name of your honor, and Marta's, I implore you not to go there."

"Why not?"

"You ask me that, Doctor, after the strange follies into which you've dragged my father? Oh, the primary guilty party is me, who listened to you, who recommended you; but we'll repent, we'll expiate our sin together, won't we, Doctor?"

"Expiate? What sin? Repent? Of what?"

"Oh, Doctor! You—a man so good, so gentle, so inoffensive!"

"Aren't you going to add *so stupid*? Come on, what crime have I committed?"

"What about yesterday evening's murder?" said Lorenzo, in a vibrant whisper, in the doctor's ear.

The latter shrugged his shoulders. That insouciance was a sign of madness. Even so, Lorenzo tried to cause remorse to enter into Marforio's sanguinary heart.

"Is it possible that science extends to scorn for the holiest laws of nature? You doctor, killing so coldly!"

"Who have I killed, then?" asked the doctor, smiling, and continuing to move forward in spite of Lorenzo's efforts to retain him gently by the arm.

"Who have you killed? What about my father's ministers?"

"Ah! You think I've killed them? Well, come with me, my young friend, and you shall see marvels!"

"Doctor, I implore you, don't go to the palace. Flee; leave the city. Public rumor will be quick to accuse you; I fear that the secret might not have been kept as religiously as I'd hoped. Spare yourself the dolor of being accused and convicted of murder."

"Oh, how amusing you are, my prince, with your fearful expression! I was right to say that you're ignorant! But know that your precious ministers aren't running any risk."

"Alas, I know that; unfortunately, they have none to run."

"How you say that! Come and see them in their peaceful sleep, and you can tell me what you think."

"Once again, Doctor, it's futile to go to the palace. You'll no longer find anything there."

"What?"

"I've cause the evidence of your sinister errors to disappear."

"What! What do you mean?"

"That I've had the ministers respectfully buried..."

"Is it possible?" cried Marforio, leaping on the spot with a fury of which one would never have thought him capable. "Triple fool that I was to put my trust in princes! But the murderer is you! The murderer is you! Oh, my God! You're right—I'm doomed! Such a beautiful experiment!"

And Marforio, waving his arms and tugging his beard, surrendered to a disorder of gestures suggestive of a tempest, and set off at a run for the palace. Lorenzo strove to follow him, trying to calm him down and bring him back to less barbaric sentiments.

"Aren't you ashamed, Doctor, not to regret the experiment, when you have killed..."

"But I haven't killed anyone! They were alive, they were asleep; you've buried them all alive."

"But those open skulls!" said Lorenzo, astonished but undisturbed by this assurance. "Those removed brains!"

"Is that supposed to be proof? Is one dead because one's head is split? Were their cerebrums indispensable? For all the use they were making of them!"

"You dare to laugh, Doctor?"

"Me! Do I look s if I'm laughing?" Marforio replied, abruptly, forcing Lorenzo to look him in the face and to see his eyes, flashing and full of tears. "You have dishonored me, Prince, and you have killed the men I was about to save."

"But I saw..." the prince stammered, feeling close to terror. "And Colbertini, for his part..."

"Ah! Colbertini! It's him, the traitor, who has done it all to avenge himself! His poor colleagues! Buried! What can I do? No one will want to believe me!"

Lorenzo was marching breathlessly beside Marforio, who had resumed his course. Finally, unable to keep up any longer, and completely out of breath, the prince stopped—but the Doctor's lungs and legs were not exhausted. The dread of seeing his experiment fail, and, on the other hand, a hope all the more ardent because it was illusory and insensate, precipitated him toward the castle. He was holding his hat in one hand, loosening his cravat with the other, and running flat out.

Suddenly, he stopped at turned toward Lorenzo.

"If only you had taken their pulse!" he shouted, in a strangled voice.

Lorenzo sighed, and could not help admitting to himself that he had indeed forgotten to take the pulse of the ministers in question—but how could one not suppose that it was superfluous to take the pulse of people whose brains one had just seen floating in water?

The doctor's indignation, and the singular assurance he had put into protesting the innocence of his system to the end, impressed Lorenzo. "My God!" the young man said to himself, all of a sudden, "what if I have been the murderer? What if, by some improbable but possible phenomenon, that operation had not had the consequences that Colbertini made me see? And now they're underground! What a horrible punishment Heaven is inflicting on my egotism! It's because I wanted to put the interests of my love before the interests of the State, it's because I wanted Marforio to be a minister, that all this disorder is in the principality. Oh Marta, angel of innocence! How will you be able to look at me without horror?"

Lorenzo as exaggerating slightly, for his imprudence, in his view, was a consequence of the most generous and most religious impulse of his heart. He had only made the error of having had men who were veritably exposed buried a little too soon. The only guilty party was still the doctor. Colbertini, who had not felt their pulses, was not beyond reproach. But what could he, Lorenzo, have on his conscience? The responsibility of an excessively precipitate burial, at the most. But, in addition to the fact that the principality probably did not have any regulation regarding the legal delay accorded to sepulchers, the matter of deferring the interment was like the precaution of taking the pulse—a superfluous concern, a derisory precaution!

For a prince, therefore, Lorenzo was attaching too much importance to secondary details. He was praiseworthy on one point, praiseworthy without restriction or reserve: he did not experience a single joy or chagrin that did not prompt, immediately, an invocation of Marta. His love was the immutable pole toward which his thoughts turned, and it was impossible to obey more completely the exigencies of his amorous dignity.

But if his love satisfied his conscience, it had never had, in the social and political context, the value of a principle. It is understandable, of course, that in the interests of ambition or pride, a prince might break the moral law; that can be reckoned a vigorous action that is applauded if it succeeds and criticized if it fails—the people are easily enthused by events engendered by cupidity and the thirst for honors—but if a handsome prince like Lorenzo takes love for his inspiration and guide; if he subordinates his conduct to that natural, human, sublime sentiment, no one will understand, because it is widely accepted that the heart has nothing to see and nothing to say in the management of men, and that the art of reigning, whatever the worthy Bonifacio, who knew hardly anything about it, might say, has nothing at all in common with the art of love.

Lorenzo, therefore, had a great weight upon his heart, and felt that all the earth piled up on the poor ministers was pressing upon him. What would be said in the principality when the strange events of the previous night became known? To whom could he appeal? Who would defend his father, Marforio and himself?

The prince had sat down on a stone bench in a deserted street, and there he meditated dolorously. He was half way between the palace and the doctor's house, somewhat akin to the biblical ass between the two piles of oats. It was not—good God!—as if, in normal circumstances, the attraction would have been equal on both sides, but if Marta's soft eyes were calling to him from the left, the side of the heart, honor and duty were calling him to the right. What should he do? There was a third way, the cowards' way, that great politicians would have recommended to the prince: that was to go neither to the right nor the left but straight ahead, and to go at hazard, but Lorenzo, an honest and candid soul, found that course repugnant. After many sighs, many alases, much faintness and confusion, he resolved to march straight toward the danger, to confront all the perils, and also to go lend a little support to his father and the doctor, whom Colbertini's escapade had put into a very embarrassing situation.

Lorenzo dared not look at the paternal palace from afar, being in horror of it. He was quite surprised when he was only a few steps away not to hear any rumor. A cook, who was plucking a chicken on the threshold of the main gate was singing as he caused his victim's feathers to fly. I have no idea why, but the sight of the chicken's white flesh gave Lorenzo gooseflesh. Was it reminding him of the ministers? Or was it simply that the preparations for a feast—plucking was not an everyday occurrence in the house of Bonifacio XXIII—were not in accord with the prince's mourning? At any rate, Lorenzo, as white as his shirt-cuffs, crossed the threshold with his heart hammering terribly, and held on to the wall as he climbed the staircase.

As he reached the first floor he heard a cry, then a second, and the a third; then a door opened violently in the gallery at the top of the stairs, and Dr. Marforio, his clothes in disorder and his wig tipped backwards, passed in front of Lorenzo and went into His Highness' apartment.

He's gone mad! thought the prince. *Despair has finished him.*

At the same time, a man emerged from the door through which Marforio had just passed. Was it a man or a ghost? Lorenzo could not say—but all his blood congealed in his veins; he thought he had been transformed into a statue.

The Minister of War, or the shade of the Minister of War, advanced solely and gravely, as if marking his steps. Behind him came his colleagues; not one was missing; all of them, fresh-faced, with a smile on their lips and a little red lines in the middle of their forehead, filed past and went into Bonifacio's apartment.

Lorenzo dared not say a word to the ministerial apparitions, and when they had disappeared, he wiped his face, sighed, raised his eyes to the heavens, searched the air for a solution—some indication that would permit him to decide who was mad, him or Marforio.

He had not emerged from his stupor when a voice whispered in his ear: "Be careful not to say anything, my lord. All is for the best!"

It was Colbertini, who had also witnessed the procession, and who, without being any less surprised by Lorenzo, was hiding it better.

"Oh, it's you," replied the prince, with a sigh of relief. "Explain that vision to me—last night's cadavers!"

"Not cadavers, my lord. I noticed that at the last moment. I haven't abused the facility given to me to avenge myself. I could have taken advantage of the pretext and had my former colleagues buried in the condition in which I found them."

"What horror!"

"Oh, Prince! In politics one often kills for less than that, and in a crueler fashion. But I reflected. If this is some sorcery, why should I not assist it to reveal itself? Master Marforio is trespassing on the rights of Providence. Much good may it do him! It isn't me who'll hold him back, and I'm curious to see how far he'll go."

Colbertini rubbed his hands with paltry satisfaction, which proved that, in the Statesman in question, passions never rose to impersonal levels.

"So they really are alive?" asked Lorenzo, amazed.

"Undoubtedly, my lord. I've talked to them, and I can attest that they haven't changed in the slightest—unfortunately for them, I might add."

"It's strange," murmured the hereditary prince, thrown into utter confusion by that phenomenon, not knowing what to say or think.

Colbertini bowed, and hastened to descend the palace staircase. He thought himself sufficiently disengaged from his oath of discretion. He had promised not to reveal the death of the ministers, but he had not sworn to keep quiet about the singular state in which he found them, and in order to help his vengeance germinate he had no hesitation in sowing news of the prodigies accomplished by his successor throughout the city. That would both provide apparent evidence of his generosity and create future impossibilities for poor Marforio. A minister obliged to govern by continual miracles cannot remain in power for long; if he is not crucified, he is ridiculed—and either alternative would please Colbertini.

"Well," said Lorenzo, finally, when he was alone, "let's not think about it. Let's live in the midst of these miracles, let's not argue about them. Reason is exposed to the risk of great errors. The heart alone is infallible. Let us only listen to and follow my heart. Oh, Marta, in the ocean of doubts into which such bizarre and inexplicable events have hurled me, you are my saving beacon, my star!"

And after that invocation, which always summarized and completed the various operations of his intelligence, Lorenzo wanted to give himself the complete spectacle of the resuscitated ministers—he preferred to call them that, believing in the miracle of resurrection rather than that of life without a brain.

There was laughter and loud conversation in Bonifacio's apartments. When Lorenzo went in, Marforio was in his sovereign's arms, but as those two obesities could not easily embrace one another, their upper bodies were close together while their lower extremities were at a distance.

"Come in, my son," said the excellent prince. "Salute in your father the happiest monarch in Italy, and in your father-in-law the most infallible scientist."

Lorenzo shivered as he thought about Colbertini and at the idea of burying the ministers.

The latter, a trifle bewildered by the astonishment of which they were the object, were having great difficulty understanding what had happened, about which they had been told repeatedly, not knowing whether to be annoyed or to rejoice, were standing there, open-mouthed and blissful, turning their heads from time to time to make sure that they were fully secure.

The Minister of War, less calm than the others, was shaking slightly.

"It's nothing, it's nothing," Marforio said to him, to reassure him. "A little water might have got into the skull; I'll be more careful tomorrow." The doctor moved closer to Lorenzo and added, in a whisper: "Colbertini had taken their pulses. Shh! Don't mention our terrors—it would frighten them." And straightening himself up, as if he had no fear of bumping into the firmament, Marforio exhaled a pride resplendent with a joy that defied all analysis.

Bonifacio searched for formulas and exclamations. "A toppling of all human laws! A glorious usurpation of the rights of Providence! Marforio, my friend, I authorize you to be addressed by me in the informal manner; you are more than my minister, you are my shadow, my satellite, my *alter ego*, the superintendent of my cerebrum. I'm going to create a new order right away, a decoration, and you'll be the first and only one decorated. I want the people of my principality to have a sense of the great event that has just been accomplished. Let them ask of me what they will, and I'll give it to them immediately. If a constitution can give them pleasure, I'll give them one or two more. I want to be lavish, to signal such a stunning phenomenon. My dear Marforio, you can open my skull whenever you wish, and Lorenzo's."

"I have no ambition, Father," said Lorenzo, who did not care much about sleeping better, and valued his daydreams too much not to want to hold on to his dreams as well.

"At Lorenzo's age, and when one is in love," replied Marforio, with a hint of compassion, "one scarcely thinks of economizing life and repose. He'll think about it later."

The ministers listened to this overflow of expansion on the part of their sovereign and their colleague, without joining in with anything but faint smiles. They did not have any very firm conviction, and, I repeat, kept passing their fingers over their foreheads with little furtive gestures, to assure themselves that the closure was hermetic.

"Oh, it's solid," said Marforio.

"Do you recall the conversations we had yesterday?" asked Bonifacio, to assure himself that their memories had not changed. And the obliging ministers, responding immediately, repeated, in the same terms, the opinions that they had expressed the day before.

"It's marvelous! Marvelous!" Bonifacio never ceased saying.

"And will that happen again every evening?" asked the Minister of War.

"Certainly," said Marforio. "Do you feel any ill effects?"

"Thus far, no; I slept as if I were fifteen, but I feel some slight embarrassment."

"Yes, yes, I know—a little water. It's nothing. The first time, you understand, one doesn't take every precaution."

That judicious remark made the entire ministry tremble. Indeed, one does not take every precaution in a first attempt, and they might have been running serious risks.

In sum, the doctor's system was judged worthy of acclaim. There was celebration in the palace, but no one wanted to proclaim the reason for the celebration too loudly. Marforio was afraid of inept imitators, and it would have been dangerous to put within the range of anyone a means of inducing sleep that would simultaneously furnish better means of preventing reawakening.

They drank to the health of the ministers. The latter, reserving their brains and exciting their cerebellums, welcomed the ovations. I shall spare you the jokes that lightened the tone of the meal. Marforio was stifled by embraces. Even Lorenzo, constrained to yield to the evidence, put in his little word of praise and his grain of incense.

Colbertini, who had no reason to be discreet, had gone to spread the news of the prodigious event everywhere. By nightfall, everyone knew that Marforio had stolen the secrets of God. A popular manifestation inclined to the honor of science was immediately organized. The party of the young, irritated against Colbertini for a long time, was delighted to extol his successor. Besides which, at first glance, the application of science and physiology to the government of States seemed to be the realization of a great idea. It was no longer the influence of a name or the preponderance of a fortune that would determine aptitude for administration, it was science, in its most elevated expression. And what science! Science that touched the instrument of intelligence itself, modified its springs, and took pity on the fatigues and consumptions of the mind.

A few good folk, habituated by custom to see everything in dark shades, shook their heads and cried materialism. They were allowed to cry, but the miracle was compared to the miracle of Saint Janvier.[16] No one doubted the possibility of displacing cerebrums. The famous party of the young decided that the implausible was the true; that progress manifested itself in such coups; that there was no room for doubt—and, I repeat, no one doubted it. Fanaticism was taken to the extent of declaring that the ministers were a credit to the fatherland. Poets composed cantatas without being paid, which one only sees in Italy. Singers sang without being forced to do it. It was a fine day for the Estates of Bonifacio XXIII.

Who can tell what moral authority Marforio might have obtained, if he could have consented not to have positive authority? A man who had wrought such a great revolution in physiology and given such a furious twist to routine might, with a little effort, have been able to discover aerial navigation and a means of landing on the moon—but the delights of Capua awaited Marforio, and progress was not accelerated in its march as much as one might have hoped or dreaded.

The marriage of young Lorenzo and the beautiful Marta was such a natural consequence of the complete success of the famous system that there was no more to do than order the candles and the violins. Bonifacio placed a much higher priority on marriage than birth. He had no fear of humiliating his ancestors by giving his blessing to the daughter of an academician as his daughter-in-law. He thought that the misalliance in question would please his people.

I have to admit that it did not displease them, for they thought it sufficiently appropriate to watch the procession go

---

[16] The legend of Janvier de Bénévent [Januarius of Beneventum in English terminology], the patron saint of Naples, had been recently popularized by an account offered by Alexandre Dumas in his travel book *Le Corricolo* (1843). The miracle in question is the liquefaction of his blood, preserved after his death and kept in two ampoules kept in a vault in Naples Cathedral but removed one a year and taken to a nearby monastery in order that the liquefaction can be observed.

past and to admire the grace and dazzling youth of the young couple. The ministers with the movable cerebrums were the object of public attention and examination; people never wearied of commenting on how good they looked. They talked like normal people; the imaginative even claimed that they had gained in intelligence, although even Marforio did not go as far as that in his enthusiasm.

"Unless," he said, "pure water has qualities as yet unsuspected, for it's impossible that those gentlemen have acquired, by reflecting less, intellectual virtues that they always lacked when they had the free exercise of their faculties night and day."

Three days after the wedding of the heir presumptive, Bonifacio XXIII, who saw his ministers growing fatter and younger, and not experiencing any annoyance, consented to entrust his august forehead to the doctor's scalpel.

"Above all," he said to him before swallowing the necessary narcotic, "don't be too emotional; forget the dignity of my forehead, and tell yourself that your sovereign is no longer anything but your subject."

Marforio was not emotional. He scalped with incredible dexterity. His Highness' cerebrum went into the water like all the rest; the only distinction that the doctor accorded him was a slightly more ornate bowl—but in terms of dimension, color and weight, the cerebrum of Bonifacio XXIII had absolutely nothing about it that could distinguish it from one taken from any other skull.

"O equality!" said Marforio on seeing the prince's instrument of thought bathing in the water.

The day after his first slumber, Bonifacio was delighted, and went for a stroll through his capital to show his subjects that he was an illustrious example of the superiority of his prime minister's system, and that he did not recoil before anything to encourage the sciences, accelerate progress and add to the principality's elements of happiness and civilization.

On the last point, however, doubt was beginning to creep in, and the party of the young, perfidiously excited by

Colbertini, who had become its soul after having been its terror and bête noire for so long, began to murmur and to wonder whether, of all utopias, science might not be the most vain, and whether there were better empirical means to increase the happiness of peoples than leaving them free and loving them intelligently.

I shall show you by what maneuvers Colbertini wanted to take his revenge and make Marforio expiate his glory and his ambition.

VIII. In which it is demonstrated that even the greatest scientists cannot anticipate everything

Bonifacio's ministers, and Bonifacio himself, found great benefits in the operation to which they submitted; they woke up without fatigue, and only the occasional slight infiltration of air into an incompletely sealed skull caused them to remember the fissure. Marforio took infinite precautions to make sure that not a single drop of water remained in the interstices of the cerebral mass. The Treasury Room was a sanctuary that preserved the sacred bowls admirably; no one except Colbertini had a key to that retreat. We shall see that the exception was unfortunate, and how Lorenzo was to repent of not having reclaimed that key during his first encounter with the former prime minister.

One day, a veritable and serious danger menaced the government; a cat was surreptitiously introduced into the palace, and was found mewling and scratching at the door of the Treasury room. Marforio shivered at the thought of the peril to which the august cerebrums might have been exposed. Precautions were taken in consequence, without it being possible to explain the reason. Evil passions would not have failed to take advantage of the information, and regicide, brought within the scope of cats, might have become a formidable instrument of opposition. The police were ordered to distribute poison pellets in all the corners of the palace, and bars were put on the windows of the Treasury Room.

Those violent dangers were not, moreover, the only or the greatest inconvenience of the system. It was not long before a singular phenomenon was observed.

The brain, abruptly interrupted in the petty labor of reflection by a few hours of apparent death, returned, on resuming its functions, to the previous day's departure-point. Memory did not suffer from that violent interruption, but only memory survived: sterile memory, without further acquisition. It was gradually perceived—when I say this, I am thinking of Lorenzo, as a benevolent observer, and Colbertini, as a spy—that the ministers and the prince, while gaining in repose, had lost the common privilege of discovering instantly on awakening an idea sought in vain the night before.

That Marforio had suppressed fatigue was incontestable, but he had also suppressed labor.

On the day on which he had been subjected to the operation, the Minister of Education had been in the process of drafting a circular to his subordinates recommending a primer that had just been published, after fifteen years of preparation, by a neighboring academy. The unfortunate minister had paused, before going to dinner, at a very difficult sentence, which sought to explain something that he had never really understood—the utility of reading. The next day, when His Excellency, rested, calm and refreshed, wanted to continue his sentence, he found it impossible to find anything therein other than what he had already found. There had been a pause in his intelligence.

The incessant circulation of the intellectual sap that accumulates in sleep the forces that activity expends in wakefulness had been interrupted, and could not be reestablished. He recommenced the same task every day, and every day he quit it in the same fashion, in the same place, with the same word.

The Minister of War provided a similar example. With a view to furnishing the army with music he was examining a very ingenious wind instrument. But the intractable minister did not want authorize the instrument until he had learned to play it himself. Previously, it appears, he had made moderately rapid progress, but after the operation in question He persisted in playing the same tune, without being able to finish it.

The other ministers, and Bonifacio XXIII himself, experienced the same effect of the voluntary lacuna created in their mental existence. The slightest effort of intelligence became useless to them. One might have thought their schemes attachments to Penelope's weaving; every night some goblin unraveled the design traced by day, and required it to begin again.

Lorenzo, troubled by this result, asked Marforio for a remedy, but his father-in-law burst out laughing. The latter had declared himself to be infallible, and the best proof he could offer of his infallibility was that of not consenting to recognize an error.

"What are you talking about, young man?" he said to his son-in-law. "Have I ever claimed that they would have more intelligence after the operation than they had before? They were stupid, and they've remained so. Respect prevents me from telling you that your father is scarcely any better. Find me a man of intelligence willing to undergo the operation, and if he becomes stupid, your objection will have some weight.

That response was peremptory. Where, in fact, could an intelligent man be found who would allow his cerebrum to be manhandled?

The heir presumptive, who had never had much enthusiasm for his father-in-law's utopia, though it his duty to maintain the most absolute secrecy regarding the critical observations themselves, and simultaneously to make sure that the insufficiency of the men in government did not become too obvious externally. He attended the rare Council meetings; if there was any decree to issue or measure to take, he strove to extract a decision from the groping of the ministers and the sovereign.

The public would never have perceived the intellectual immobility that resulted from the famous system if Colbertini had not pointed it out to the party of the young, waxing indignant about it. The crowd, which saw Bonifacio's flourishing appearance, did not feel any more inconvenienced than before, admired Marforio's skill and made no protest. The organized paralysis was of little significance; it did not increase taxes, and although nothing was done for them, they did not demand anything.

As you know, public opinion would never be manifested forcefully if there were not far-sighted people to alert it, set it on the road to protest and find a formulaic slogan for it. That was precisely what the party of the young set out to do. They set about stimulating the apathy of the inhabitants by demonstrating to them that, instead of being happy, they were very miserable, because they were badly governed.

That useful propaganda was a little slow to take effect, and perhaps it would never have done so without a singular reinforcement that came from France, in the person of an innkeeper. He established a new tavern, in which wine and good food, by accelerating the life in young cerebrums, gave more emphasis and more fire to remonstrations. The ill-humor that was conceived there against the old restaurants extended all the way to the government.

It is the fatality of absolute governments, even when they are paternal, as Bonifacio XXIII's government was believed to be, to be held responsible for everything, bad weather and epidemics as well and poverty and moral afflictions. Substituting for the role of Providence, it assumes its charges in wishing to reap its profits. Not exciting or encouraging individual initiative, those charges are accountable to each individual for his share of activity and free will. It is unjust, according to eternal law, to blame them for hail, rain or plague, but it is logical to demand a reckoning from them for the modicum of moral or material aid that everyone finds internally to resist a scourge or to be consoled for it.

I beg your pardon for that little sally, which is a little solemn for the principality in question, but history has immutable principles, and it is in telling stories, in particular, that it is necessary to invoke them.

So, the party of the young indulged in superb diners and eloquent protests. It fulminated against the centuries-long stagnation of the country and spoke irreverently about Marforio's famous system, which it had initially acclaimed, and the cracked heads of the ministers, of whom it made fun. The walls were covered in caricatures in which the cerebrum operation was criticized and harshly treated.

I leave it to you to imagine how saddened Lorenzo was by that opposition, which increased every day. Let us grant him the justice that his marriage had not rendered him egotistical. Retired to a corner of the paternal palace, he lived in quotidian ecstasy, and never stopped reciting to Marta the sweetest names and loveliest verses that he could imagine, in order to hug her tenderly to his heart, thanking God for having blessed him, but a sharp dolor was mingled with that intoxication.

Lorenzo sometimes thought that his happiness was the recompense and result of Marforio's utopian ideas, and lived in perpetual fear of some catastrophe. So, even though he did not have the slightest appetite for power, especially impotent and ridiculous power, he tried, as I said just now, to take some interest in business matters in which no one else was occupied, and every evening, with Marta—who was not a bad adviser—he chatted to the lovely star on a terrace of the castle about the irreparable misfortune of being the heir presumptive of an imminent revolution.

His worthy father and sovereign thought himself the happiest of monarchs, and experienced an unusual contentment when Marforio put his cerebrum back in place in the morning. Lorenzo tried in vain to get an idea, or the shadow of an idea, into that poor head. The intelligence that resumed its clockwork movement every day like a mill stopped for the night, no longer had any impetus, and force. It no longer had the befit of the mysterious nocturnal labor that is perhaps the only true and profitable one.

Lorenzo realized that sleep is not a repairer but a solemn and omnipotent initiator, and he begged Marforio and the cracked heads to renounce the baths of cold water. The scientist did not want to let go, however, and the experimental subjects were too comfortable in their inactivity to give it up.

One day, the opposition sent a delegation to solicit an audience with Bonifacio XXIII and explain its grievances to him respectfully. The prince received the deputation with the most charming of smiles; he was surrounded by his ministers, and bliss had never had fresher, rosier and more committed representatives.

Bonifacio did not understand a word of what was said to him. With his unalterable good humor he took the piece of paper that was handed to him, which, having been drafted in the famous French hostelry I mentioned a little while ago, had the menu for the opposition's last dinner on one side and the most urgent demands of the party of the young on the other.

Lighting, street-cleaning, the restoration of vigor to a somewhat out-of-date constitution and a few ideas of reform, as simple as they were moderate, constituted the whole program. Bonifacio promised to discuss it in Council, and did indeed discuss it—but, by virtue of a perfectly excusable error, he had looked at the wrong side, and it was the dinner menu that he debated in a desultory manner with his ministers, without reaching any agreement.

I ought to add that Marforio was never present at Council meetings—he had too much studying to do for that—and Lorenzo, hoping that grievances as plausible and easy to satisfy might be discussed even by cracked brains, and still wanting to make sure one last time of what he could expect from his father and his ministers, abstained from the deliberation.

The following day, and on the days thereafter, the deputation reappeared; it was greeted with the same smile and made the same promises in the same terms; the same deliberations were resumed, only to arrive at the same lack of result. That was that; the opposition became disposed to energetic action, and Lorenzo realized that if he did not intervene his father's crown would be under threat.

The young prince had no interest in power for power's sake, but, if he had modest tastes, he also had the sentiment of a double duty. The innocent troubadour would have been very happy to leave the palace hand in hand with the charming Marta and go into the country with his gentle companion, in order to forget, in some poetic retreat, the wickedness and stupidity off governments. He did not know the formula that the philosophers of romance had yet to invent: a cottage is a heart; but he had the sentiment, or rather the presentiment, of it. Oh, if, by some miracle for which he would have been grateful to Marforio, the principality had been able vanish into thin air like fairy castles; if he had been able to be alone with his dear Marta in the shade of some retreat like those painted by Ariosto, how poetic life would have been, what a madrigal in duet! But his dream was to remain buried in his soul, like a butterfly that has no flowers, and it was necessary for him to occupy himself with those grotesque individuals, Marforio and the ministers, without forgetting that his father was not sufficiently separated from his entourage in the caricatures.

Lorenzo had a meeting with the leader of the party of the young. He promised to use all his influence to see that hopes of progress were not perpetually disappointed. He promised, in the name of the government, to produce some innovations that would satisfy public curiosity and would make the patriots' long wait worthwhile. Lorenzo was aware of the temerity of his promises, but ever since the fatal day when, listening only to his love, he had introduced Marta into his father's household, he had felt partly responsible for the good and evil committed within the principality. On the other hand, petty prince as he was, he was still too much of one to fall into the error of princes, and to promise more than he could and dared to deliver.

An extraordinary event seemed to remove his anxiety and give ample satisfaction to the party of the young.

Every morning, Marforio came very punctually to visit the bowls confided to his care, extract the cerebrums of His Highness and Their Excellencies as carefully as he could and replace them all in their respective housings. It was the only opportunity he wished to conserve of being in the company of his colleagues.

One day, the doctor had complete his task with the customary attention, and after having hermetically sealed the heads of the eminent functionaries whose intellectual movements he was regulating, had gone back to his laboratory to continue a series of very curious experiments, when Lorenzo ran after him breathlessly and knocked on his door.

"Well, what is it now?" demanded the scientist, surprised by his son-in-law's excitement.

"Oh, don't worry," Lorenzo murmured, naively, "Marta's not ill." The poor prince imagined that a father's first alarmed thought was for his daughter; he had forgotten that his father was a scientist.

"It not a matter of my daughter. Has someone wanted you to bury my subjects again?"

"No," Lorenzo replied, "but are you quite sure, Doctor, that you were not mistaken this morning when putting each brain back in its box?"

"Quite sure; the precautions I take guarantee that there will be no surprises."

"In that case, an inexplicable phenomenon is occurring, and I implore you to come and see. The ministers have entirely new ideas and tastes quite different from their usual tastes."

"It's quite simple," Marforio put in, blushing with pride. "The progress is complete. You doubted that renovation of intelligence, but I knew perfectly well that, at a given point, the reposed instrument would take on inclinations different from those it had previously exhibited."

"It's not possible, Doctor, that a flute will play you the tunes of a violin because it has been asleep for a fortnight!"

"Indeed! You've become a joker, my son-in-law! It ill behooves you to mock what you don't understand."

"Oh, I'm not mocking, I swear," Lorenzo said. "I'm too frightened."

"Of what?"

"Of this activity that is succeeding inertia."

"Bah! I'll demonstrate to you that it's all perfectly logical."

Lorenzo shook his head and returned to the palace with Marforio.

There was, in fact, a very strange scene manifest in the palace, which all the doctor's science might perhaps find it impossible to explain.

IX. In which the ministers begin to work

When I mentioned the sinecures constituted to the advantage of each of Bonifacio's ministers, I was not exaggerating, but it is evident that the inaction in question did not prevent each of them having an organization, offices, employees, paper and pens, and each minister receiving his subordinates' compliments on his birthday, or reprimanding them from time to time in order to put on a show of working. Bonifacio would have liked nothing better, as this story has illustrated, than to sack all the ministers and all the ministerial employees. The equilibrium of the budget was an insufficient goal for him; he was in pursuit of its absolute alleviation—its volatilization, so to speak. Disposed as he was to economies and the simplification of government, however, the prince was constrained by an official decorum toward his neighbors. Human respect—or rather, sovereign respect—obliged him to expensive complications about which he moaned.

It is one of the idiosyncrasies of Italy that each of its states can aspire individually to liberty, but cannot free itself from the obligation of rendering accounts to neighborly curiosity. The land where orange-trees flourish is constrained to the humiliation of putting their blossom under the noses of foreigners in order that the latter may regulate their good humor according to how much perfume is exhaled. No one has ever known why, but these enchanted lands are continually exposed to the accidents that befall Prince Charmings in fairy tales; whenever they want to sit down, four or five hands grab their seat under the pretext of making sure of its solidity. When they wants to eat, before they have lifted a morsel of food to their lips, four or five hands reach out and hold the mouthful back on the pretext that Europe is interested in the guest's good digestion. It is doubtless in order that Italy should be her own mistress that societies of *carbonari* are formed; everyone knows that charcoal-burners in general do not like to be ordered around in their own homes.

In the time of Bonifacio XXIII, *carbonari* were not yet blackening the horizon, but neighborly curiosity was already excessive, and eager to be satisfied that Lorenzo's father was protecting his ministers. He would have been forced to do as other petty potentates did and have German ministers if he had not had Italian ones. Forms and formulas are one of the great principles of European equilibrium. Bridoison[17] understood something of that. As for sentiment, there is never any to be seen. Bonifacio could carve, corrode and scalp his ministers and his subjects, but he had to have ministers. It was already quite enough that people turned a blind eye to his joviality, tolerance and good humor. For a long time he would have been constrained to sadness if a judicious prelate, in a diplomatic conference in the principality had not remarked that Bonifacio's bonhomie, rather than profiting liberty, as might have been feared, gave business license, which was quite different.

In fact, liberty, among all its other inconveniences, has that of setting a bad example; it no longer justifies an intervention in itself. License, on the other hand, has the advantage that it puts the States in which it has been attained at the disposal for the first righter of wrongs in the vicinity who has a taste for conquest. Bonifacio's amiable qualities, therefore, did not frighten neighboring tyrants; order by virtue of work and

---

[17] A character (a corrupt judge based on a real individual) in Pierre Beaumarchais' play *La Folle Journée, ou Le Mariage de Figaro* (1778). He becomes Don Curzio in Mozart's opera based on the play.

activity by virtue of liberty had given them other dispositions in his regard.

I am only elaborating these considerations, which are holding up the denouement of my story, in order to help you understand that Bonifacio, obliged to have ministers, had, in consequence, ministerial employees, and why the latter were very surprised on day by the changes that had taken place in the ideas of each of their ministers.

The Minister of War, who began his pretended endeavors every morning by performing exercises on the famous musical instrument, demanded to know that day why the primers had not been distributed. There was profound amazement in the offices. Distribute primers to the army! To want soldiers to be able to read, and probably write! What an innovation! What progress! To create intelligent bayonets! What a bold, but imprudent, idea!

A quarter of an hour later, the rumor had spread through the city that the stout Minister of War concealed a strong and alert mind within his thick envelope, and was deploying a prodigious activity.

A phenomenon of an inverse kind, but equally extraordinary, had taken place in the Ministry of Education. The minister had arrived intoning the gallant couplets that constituted the principality's national anthem, and had asked the inspectors what condition the musical instruments were in. There was no longer any question of primers there, but of curious wind instruments that ought to be giving a pleasant and economical music to the principality.

The employees looked at one another, opening their eyes immeasurably wide; they thought that music as doubtless about to acquire an importance within the curriculum that it had not previously had, and a zealous head clerk immediately sent a circular to all the schools in the principality instructing top priority to be given to the study of musical instruments, His Excellency's wishes being express in that regard.

The Minister of Justice talked about nothing but sums of money available, which initially alarmed and scandalized his employees slightly, fearful that ministerial venality might be revealed by these financial plans. They ended up thinking, however, that it might instead be a matter of salary increases, and that new way of looking at the question changed the initial suspicion into enthusiasm. Another minister whose dispositions were published, commented upon, and, when the opportunity arose, energetically extolled!

For his part, the Minister of Finance, ordinarily so saddened by the insoluble problem of his budget, was charmingly cheerful. He sent for his treasurer and spoke to him for an hour, with laughter on his lips, about the rope, hanging, prison and gendarmes, to the extent that the treasurer imagined that all the tax-collectors and financiers who profited from the prince's distress and the embarrassment of the people were about to have their necks wrung—and, as that rumor spread rapidly, although it made a few tax-farmers grow pale, it excited an explosion of cheers from the masses.

The party of the young, which was very young, allowed itself to be taken in by these rumors.

"Finally!" it said. "The government's on the move; and not for want of urging. The opposition always attains its goals. Marforio is definitely a great scientist!"

Lorenzo was not the last to hear talk of new resolutions on the part of his father's ministers. He went in search of the latter. As usual Bonifacio was fresh, pink and smiling, standing at a window busy watching goldfish frolicking in a bowl of water. By virtue of a singular affinity he had been smitten for some time with a fine passion for bowls and clear water.

Lorenzo questioned him, but the prince did not know anything. A ministerial Council was immediately convened. Their Excellencies arrived with an allure that was suggestive of intoxication. They were all fidgeting and shaking their heads, as if beehive had had been enclosed with the cerebrum in each skull.

"Why, what's the matter?" asked Bonifacio. "You're behaving strangely today, my dear friends. Calm down and let's talk."

Lorenzo, by special favor, was often given the honor of admission to Council meetings. All the ministers began speaking at once; the confusion displayed by the meeting was very strange and very comical, and simultaneously rather frightening. The Minister of War thought he was in charge of the Ministry of Education, the Minister of Education was talking about war, the Minister of Finance only wanted to talk about justice, and the Minister of Justice tried to pick a quarrel with Bonifacio about his culinary expenses. Not only did the roles seem inverted and the personalities interchanged, but none of the ministers had abdicated his former character to the extent that no vestige of his original estate remained, either in his gestures, his posture, or his speech. Those residues of habit added to the disorder and the cacophony.

"What's got into them all?" Bonifacio wondered, finding it difficult to maintain his placidity in the midst of all that chaos.

"I fear something must have happened during the night," said Lorenzo, who did not want to alarm his father excessively about the inconveniences of Marforio's system.

"I've a good mind to render the lot of them destitute," His Highness continued. "It's annoying to have all this buzz and their insistence on trespassing on one another's duties."

"Wait until the doctor arrives, Father; he's the only one who can explain and cure the fever that's agitating them."

We know how Lorenzo, more emotional than he wanted to let on to his father, went in search of Marforio and how the latter went with him, mocking the young prince's fears—but we ought to add that even the scientist was somewhat bewildered by the tumult into the midst of which he fell.

The ministers were stamping their feet and moving around, and never shutting up; there was an ever-increasing flood of words. Like clocks with broken springs whose mechanisms were unwinding noisily, all those broken-down cerebrums were possessed by a rapid, noisy movement that had ended up being communicated to the body. Their faces were red; sweat was pearling on their brows. Evidently, madness was marking and claiming its victims.

In spite of his confidence, Marforio felt some dread. I am saying that he was afraid, not that he felt the slightest shadow of remorse. He took the pulse of the various ministers, and tried to understand something of their interminable and confused speech.

"Someone has been into the Treasury Room," he said, eventually, after due reflection.

"No one," said Bonifacio.

"Personally, I agree with the doctor," said Lorenzo. "I believe, in fact, that some imprudent and treacherous individual has dared to tamper with the bowls."

"If I knew his name…!" thundered His Highness.

Out of prudence, or a residue of pity, Lorenzo dared not give up the name of Colbertini.

"What has been done to them?" demanded Bonifacio, seriously disturbed, burying his head in his hands.

"Someone has switched the labels, of course, and caused me to exchange the minister's cerebrums."

"How horrible!" cried the prince. "And this misfortune could have happened to me!"

"Fortunately, there was no one with whom Your Highness's cerebrum could be exchanged."

That response, which Bonifacio interpreted as flattery, calmed him down slightly. "We need to make enquiries," he said.

"Undoubtedly," replied Marforio. "Although, all things considered, on thinking about it, I'm not totally displeased by the new experiment that has been offered to me."

"Hmm! You experiment too much, my dear prime minister."

"Let things take their course, my lord. There's no danger. The essential thing, after all, is that they're alive."

"Undoubtedly."

"Well, they seem to me to be in robust health."

"Yes, but what about this fever?"

"Bah! What if they talk a little too much? They've kept silent for so many years."

"Indeed—but this racket!?"

"Block your ears. In any case, is Your Highness in the habit of listening to them?"

"I don't know—they've never said anything. But how can I not hear them? And what will the public think?"

"What the public thinks!" retorted Marforio, who sometimes had fits of penetration. "It will be delighted; it has accused you of governing with mutes; it certainly won't be able to say that now. The public takes tumult for toil, words for deeds; fundamentally, it doesn't like change and cares very little for progress, provided that its posters and programs are renewed from time to time. It's a maniac whose stomach can only eat one kind of food, but likes the plate to be changed frequently."

"What a Statesman your father-in-law is, eh, Lorenzo!" said the prince, delighted by that aphorism.

"What do you expect to happen?" asked Lorenzo, who was not as prompt as his father to regain confidence and be distracted from his anxiety.

"I don't know," Marforio replied, "but I'm optimistic. My system seems to be taking on a development that I hadn't anticipated initially. Hazard is the great initiator, just as it is often the great secret of triumphs. Do you think that it would be impossible for me to give one man several intelligences at the same time? As soon as the cerebrum consents no longer to have the exclusive importance that the ignorance of scientists once attributed to it, why should it not, in traveling through different skulls, acquire ideas? That's a conjecture, but a conjecture based on experiment..."

"For my part," said Bonifacio, "I don't want to learn anything."

"But how can the cerebrum acquire ideas by occupying empty spaces?" Lorenzo objected.

"I expected that remark," said Marforio. "My dear boy, intelligence is modified in accordance with the volume, the atmosphere and the configuration of the box that encloses it. The cranium is a study, and everyone knows that, depending on whether one can stretch out, yawn, move to the right or the left, a study can be more or less inspiring. There are, moreover, bodily habits, dispositions of the cerebellum that influence the cerebrum in their turn."

"But what if they're going mad?" said Lorenzo, indicating the entire ministry, which was muttering, agitating frantically and talking at cross-purposes.

"There'll always be time to calm them down if they go too far," said Marforio.

"So, my dear fellow," said the prince, "Your opinion is…?"

"My opinion is that they're all right as they are, that we should leave them that way; that Providence, in permitting this confusion, has undoubtedly put me on the track of a new discovery; and that I shall have a new opportunity to add to the glory of your reign and the prestige of the principality."

Seeing that his father was going to consent to the prolongation of the dangerous comedy, Lorenzo tried to intervene, but Bonifacio did not let him speak.

"Since the experiment has begun, we might as well let it run its course," he said. "Be careful, Marforio. Don't give my ministers too many ideas. They're rather amusing in this intoxication that had gripped them, but they're making a lot of noise."

"They'll calm down," Marforio replied, authoritatively. "They're not used to the change of cerebrum yet."

Lorenzo made his escape. The unfortunate prince was afraid of losing his head. "Oh, in what padded cell am I living?" he murmured. "Oh Marta, can it be that the purest and most honest love has consequences so odious and so grotesque?"

We already know that Lorenzo made Marta's name his first and last invocation in embarrassment, but, faithful to the sentiments that had made him aspire to the hand of the doctor's daughter, the most delicate of princes and the most unfortunate of heirs presumptive had not thought of regretting his love. He was only deploring the fact that the happiness of the principality was not a consequence of his intimate happiness, and that his pastoral was having such a tragic denouement.

He also had a strong suspicion that his ordeals were not over yet. Marforio was indefatigable and intractable. The doctor would always find confirmation of his infallibility, even in setbacks. To what extreme might Lorenzo see sovereign majesty, in the person of his father, descend? And it was him, Lorenzo, and him alone, who had wanted a ministry to be given to Marforio! He was the indirect cause of all this disorder! He could not blame anyone else, and did not, alas, have anyone on which he could avenge himself.

However, after a little reflection, Lorenzo told himself that Colbertini, if it really was him who had switched the labels on the jars, had a terrible responsibility to assume, and, as it was necessary that someone should pay for everything, Lorenzo eventually convinced himself, by means of a logic common enough in all walks of life but particularly fitting for the use of princes, that Colbertini ought to receive an exemplary punishment.

Colbertini, who had been a minister for twenty-five years, was not unaware of the manner in which sovereigns reason; he had foreseen that Lorenzo, although relatively perfect, would not renounce the pleasure of making him expiate the sins—which is to say, the imprudences—of the castle. In consequence, having done Marforio the bad turn whose consequences we have just witnessed, he had prudently gone into hiding and had put the famous key to the Treasury Room, which the prince had been careless enough not to reclaim from him, in a safe place.

I am well aware that Lorenzo could have advised his father have the lock of the room in question changed, but one cannot always think of everything, and if princes were infallible, dynasties would never be in peril of catastrophe, revolution and restoration, and the world would be a very boring place.

Colbertini invented to reveal himself at the critical moment. He hoped fervently that Marforio's sorceries would not always prevail against traditional politics. His intrigues had rendered the party of the young very demanding, and he thought that the minister, and Bonifacio himself, could not resist the demands of that opposition indefinitely. As for the opposition itself, Colbertini planned to offer it the old programs, in the guise of novelties, and lull it to sleep with the same old stories, rejuvenated for the occasion. Besides which, nothing calms and disarms a party like triumph, and not a single one has ever been seen that has persisted in the inflexibility of its line after being admitted to participation in government.

Such were Colbertini's calculations. Although lacking in grandeur and generosity, he did not lack a certain amount of luck, but, by means of an inexplicable illusion of the country, one of those mirages that delight people, and one of those utopias that surpass all probability, the trap laid for Marforio served the cause of his glory, and the famous switching of cerebrums provoked and explosion of hope and enthusiasm by which Colbertini was amazed.

The distinctions between genius and madness are difficult to establish at all times, in all latitudes and with all characters, but in a principality like Bonifacio's, it was impossible; standards of comparison were lacking for genius, and were too frequent for madness; people no longer paid any attention to them. That is why the minister's extravagances, instead of frightening the party of the young, gave it confidence. There was no talk of anything but the innovations and ameliorations introduced by the various ministers.

All the soldiers were wandering around with notebooks in hand, spelling out their letters. Sentry duties, already so rare, had been definitively replaced by study-periods; and when the defenders of the fatherland stopped at the door of a tavern, it was only for the purely intellectual pleasure of deciphering its sign.

The professors of the university (did I mention that there was a university? I can't remember, and in any case, you'll be glad to hear it) got haircuts and began to strut like the most bellicose conquerors in the world. Soon, one only encountered students arranged in platoons and marching with gigantic musical instruments; the fife had become the instrument of Apollo. The Minister of Education had invented a rifled fife whose piping could be heard at enormous distances.

The financiers, since their Minister's cerebrum had been swapped with that of the Minister of Justice, were being encouraged to study the law, and that disposition caused great excitement in the population. Some claimed that the money men would discover means of augmenting their perfidies and resources in the legislative arsenal; others, on the contrary, were sure that the study of laws was the most moral and most useful kind of education. That debate was itself a symptom of progress; if usury had declined, the advantage would have been incontestable, but it was already a great deal, in real terms, that people could contest it.

As for the Ministry of Justice, it was only preoccupied with financial questions. It did not want lawyers to be paid refresher fees, and it constrained them to indemnify their clients for the time they made them waste, the annoyances they occasioned them, and the evil that they caused to be thought of them by talking too much. The people applauded this system, although the prosecutors were furious. One rather comical eccentricity, which really was a trifle excessive, was that every time a magistrate denounced and harassed a delinquent, he was obliged to deposit a large sum of money, in order that, in cases where individuals were unjustly harassed, or victims of slanderous denunciations or misdirected zeal, they could be generously compensated.

The people, of course, clapped their hands at this system of precaution and responsibility, but old jurisconsults shook their heads and claimed that the profession would become impossible, and that justice would cease to exist as soon as the obligation of never being unjust was imposed.

The critical murmurs were drowned out, however, in the general chorus. Because many questions were raised, it seemed that many were being resolved. The party of the young was overwhelmed. It had great difficulty coordinating its ideas and forming a precise opinion about all the reforms that were taking effect at the same time—for I am only mentioning the principal points here, and it is perfectly evident that the ministers were involving themselves in everything.

Bonifacio was amused; he did not weary his head with understanding and anticipating; he looked on, laughing at the discontented and smiling at the flatterers, ate all his meals with the customary punctuality, abolished the Council of Ministers because it was impossible to reach any kind of understanding and agreement, and seemed in the eyes of his subjects to be working hard, since he was doing no work at all.

Marforio studied the new experiment, congratulating himself every day. "Why didn't I foresee it?" he said to himself every morning, as he replaced the cerebrums in the skulls designated by Colbertini.

After a few days, when it was firmly established that the changes of domicile were free of danger for the brains, and when the ministers' fever had to some extent evened out, the doctor took pleasure in shuffling the labels—or, rather, getting rid of them—and leaving the distribution of the organs that he was removing and replacing to chance.

That was the apogee of the triumph for the scientist, and the signal for an incendiary recrudescence for the activity of the ministers—and, in consequence, for the civilization of the principality. Decrees, measures and changes multiplied, succeeding one another and contradicting one another with a vertiginous rapidity.

"We're going too fast," Bonifacio sometimes said.

"This is only the beginning," Marforio replied, drunk with enthusiasm.

The entire principality seemed to have been bitten by a tarantula. As the ministers' brains were only transporting the ideas with which they were already impregnated, but not augmenting them, the movement was, in essence, merely a perpetual displacement. Thus, the musical instruments, after having been inflicted on professors, were inflicted on magistrates, who rendered justice to the tunes of traditional folk songs. Then tax collectors were required in their turn to fill the public purse to the accompaniment of the melodious instruments in question.

Every minister, according to the hazard of the distribution of cerebrums, ordered, prohibited and revoked what another seemed to have ordered, prohibited and revoked the day before. Sometimes, the skulls came back into possession of their legitimate cerebrums; those days were days of rest; but one might have thought that Marforio was arranging things so that they would be rare.

While a kind of delirium stirred the destiny of the principality, Lorenzo was sad, unable to find in his happiness the forgetfulness of his political anxieties. He never ceased imploring Heaven, with a fervent ecstasy with which Marta was associated, for the return—or, rather the advent—of common sense and reason: a superfluous prayer that Heaven would not grant. One might have thought that Providence was taking pleasure in that debauchery of government and was lending ironic encouragement to the imbroglio, which had no logical issue.

Colbertini was the only one who was not duped. He became impatient in his retreat, biting his fists at the thought of seeing the prancing of administrators and the principality's inhabitants accepted as progress. I shall tell you in due course in consequence of what imprudence, believing that he was opening abysses, he closed all the crevasses of the revolutionary volcano, and how, by making himself necessary, he made himself redundant. That will, in fact, be the hypothetical resolution—I might even say apotheosis—of this instructive and moral tale.

I say the hypothetical resolution because it is always the case that nothing is resolved in life, and that the history of a State, no matter how minimal it might be on the map of the world, changes and is modified, but is never fixed in an invariable fate. The principality that Bonifacio XXIII inherited from Bonifacio XXII no longer exists, and has been subjected to many contrasting destinies, but the soil there is as rich as it ever was, the women as are lovely as they used to be. There is still a party of the young there, and a party of the old, but the party of the young has aged and is no longer content with appearances; it has no need of a French cook to make demands and achieve them, and the struggle is much more serious than in times past. There would, therefore, be further dramas to recount if this story were a series of annals instead of an episode; it is, in consequence, in obedience to a pure hypothesis that I shall conclude it by exposing the ministry's final catastrophe.

X. In which the ministers make the people happy by no longer trying to do so

Everything in the principality, therefore, was proceeding at a violent rhythm, but the illusion, far from decreasing, was augmented thereby, and Bonifacio's popularity had attained limits that defied ingratitude. As for Marforio, he was beginning to want to play the part of benevolent God in his experiments, always promising not to trespass too much on His privileges, for fear of eventually exciting His resentment. That sentiment on the god doctor's part was so naïve that it cannot be reckoned blasphemous.

Alas. Marforio had no suspicion that the impotence and vanity of science were about to be demonstrated to him in a terrible fashion, by an ignoramus.

One morning, the doctor had just entered the Treasury Room, with the radiant expression that no longer abandoned him, in order to carry out his important functions when he suddenly ran out again, uttering a loud cry, and came to fall down at the door of Lorenzo's apartment.

The heir presumptive, whose marriage had not augmented his occupations and who still had plenty of leisure time, was getting ready to set out with Marta on a botanical exploration; he was continuing to educate himself in the study of herbs—as if that were the best way of learning to govern human beings!

The doctor was lying on the ground, motionless. Marta saw him first, and, falling upon him, tried to lift him up, making him breathe smelling salts while weeping and stammering questions at Lorenzo, who knew no more than she did.

"Father, Father," she said, sobbing. "What's wrong? What's happened to you?"

Marforio came round gradually, and as Lorenzo had summoned servants to carry him, he indicated to his son-in-law that he wanted to be alone with him. When everyone else had gone, he said, with a sigh: "Oh, my dear Lorenzo, my last day has arrived."

"What's happened, then? Is it a disgrace?"

"You've hit the nail on the head: a disgrace, but the cruelest and the most unexpected: the disgrace of science. I'm dishonored; there's nothing more for me to do than die."

"You're scaring me!" said Lorenzo, who was thinking about the famous system. "Tell me, quickly!"

"Well, my child—oh, I shan't survive it!—a horrible conspiracy has been woven against the prince, the ministry and me. They're jealous of my glory."

"Speak, Doctor, speak!"

"I've just been, in accordance with the obligation imposed upon me, and in which, as you know, I never fail, to place the cerebrums in the skulls. I had such fine plans for today!"

"And?" said Lorenzo, breathless with impatience.

"Well, I find, as usual, the door locked—nothing to advertise the horrible discovery externally. I go in..."

"And? Come on, hurry up!"

"I go straight to the table where the bowls are, and..."

"What? Good God!"

"And I don't find anything there: the bowls are empty."

"Even the one..."

116

"Yes, even the one that had the honor of containing His Highness' cerebrum."

"Perhaps you're mistaken?" stammered Lorenzo, gripped by terror and sensing that he was on the edge of a precipice.

"Oh, I searched! Then I understood that it was all over for my glory, and thought I was about to die." Marforio fell into his son-in-law's arms. "Oh, my friend, people will think that I was a charlatan. My experiment has been spoiled, my system will be ridiculed by the ignorant!"

Lorenzo dared not measure the full depth of the gulf that this emblematic theft had hollowed out beneath his feet. He dragged the scientist to the Treasury Room. They searched all the cupboards. The empty bowls, gleaming in the sunlight, seemed to be laughing at their visitors' anguish.

Lorenzo felt his knees trembling; the good hereditary prince was sincerely mourning Bonifacio, and giving scarcely any thought to inaugurating his reign. "My father! My poor father!" he said, covering his face.

"Alas," said Marforio, piteously, "he has no suspicion of the misfortune that has overtaken him."

The remark had such a frightfully grotesque character that Lorenzo looked at his father-in-law in shock and surprise.

"Yes," the scientist went on, "He's asleep, perfectly tranquil, not knowing that he won't find his cerebrum again on awakening."

"He's asleep," Lorenzo stammered. "That's true."

"Of course! Did you think he was dead?" Marforio retorted, who found a small quantum of comfort in that contradiction.

"But if he's alive, all is well!" cried the good prince, thinking only of his filial dreads.

"He's alive, and all the ministers are alive, but don't expect any thought or reflection on their part, or even a parody of intelligence. They're alive in the fashion of automata, devoid of distinct speech. They'll live thus for a few months or a few years; I don't know exactly how long, for I've never carried out that ultimate experiment."

"Come on, Marforio," the young prince said, animatedly. "Perhaps all is not lost."

They went to the room in which the ministers and the sovereign habitually enjoyed their unconscious sleep. On opening the door they heard a dull and rhythmic rumbling that attested to the ardor with which the august individuals carried out their task and honored the scientist who put them to sleep. Lorenzo sighed; that candid snoring was the very image of confidence and innocence. Bonifacio was smiling; he had presumably gone to sleep with the smile that no longer quit his face.

Marforio and Lorenzo stood there, grave and composed, thinking hard.

"I've got an idea," said the doctor.

"So have I," said Lorenzo, with a sigh. "Let's hear yours."

"Well, everything can still be repaired, but a few sacrifices will be necessary. You know, thanks to the phenomena produced lately, that cerebrums removed in the appropriate manner can serve any body that comes along. I'll go find a few poor devils importuned by thought, ambitious for power, philosophers dreaming of government. I'll offer them, in return for a fee, the possession of power and honors. I'll open their skulls and bring the new cerebrums here—which might seem a little out of place at first, but will at least introduce some variety into the Council..."

"Oh, enough experiments!" said Lorenzo. "Enough sacrilegious attempts and temptations."

"Oh, my son-in-law," said Marforio, animatedly, excited by the prospect of a new scientific struggle, "so you doubt your father-in law! You're insulting his system!"

Lorenzo could have retorted that there was a good reason for that, but he was too intent on following a plan that he had formulated, and was still developing, to attach much importance to Marforio's recriminations and demands.

"Think, Prince, about the immense advantages of that new combination," said the scientist. "The ministers would become master-keys. We'll give them the ideas—I mean the intelligence—necessary to happiness of the principality. The government will become truly representative of popular opinion, since, according to the circumstances, we can transplant into the skull of the ministers the cerebrums of the leaders of opinion---if they consent, of course. As soon as a cerebrum has produced what was expected of it, we can return it to its original possessor. The State, as long as this system prospers, will be founded on the participation everyone in government—but as the people need to get used to the faces of those who govern them, so as to avoid a confusion of physiognomies as well as to maintain an invariable decorum, cerebrums will succeed one another, but the ministers will always be the same..."

Already consoled, Marforio, rubbing his hands together at this prospect, could already see himself as the dispenser of social life in the principality. His scalpel would become a scepter.

Lorenzo, as we have said, was following his own train of thought and not listening to the doctor. He was thinking about Marta, and, remembering the advice that her dear soul and valiant bounty had often given him, had conceived a bold project that was ripening in his mind and rendering him increasingly grave as its realization gradually became more plausible.

As Marforio did not receive any reply and did not find the enthusiasm in his son-in-law on which he had thought he could count, he touched his elbow. "Well, what do you think?" he asked

"I think," said Lorenzo, with a gentle firmness and a visible effort, "that God doesn't want us to trespass any further in his domain. In permitting an enemy to attack your work, he's warning us to stop these operations, this butchery..."

"Butchery!" cried Marforio, indignantly. "Oh, my son-in-law, you don't deserve my daughter!"

"Excuse me," said Lorenzo, "I'm ignorant—but I have duties to fulfill as a prince and I want to fulfill them. So long as my father appeared to be acting of his own free will, I was obliged to bow down before his whims, while perhaps regretting them. Today, I believe that my honor and the interests of the principality require me to substitute for the dead thought."

"Say the absent, or lost thought—for after all, the cerebrums might perhaps be found. What if we were to put up posters?"

"Oh, Colbertini—for he's undoubtedly the one who has carried out the coup—will have taken his precautions. The traitor is taking his revenge. Why did I forget to demand the key from him?"

"Admit too, my prince, that one does not leave a key to the house with an enemy that one has expelled. You want to reign, and you begin like that!"

"I was wrong, it's true, but the time has come to put things right, and I feel that I'm up to the job. Marforio, will you promise to support me in everything and to keep the most rigorous secrecy?"

"Will I have to renounce my experiments?" the scientist asked, sadly.

"Are you not constrained to renounce them? From whom will you obtain the authorization to continue your proofs? If you don't help me, I'll allow public curiosity and indignation to discover the truth and follow its course, and you'll lose your honor along with your system."

"Oh, above all, let's save the honor of science!" exclaimed Marforio. "What do I have to do?"

"I've told you: keep the secret and help me maintain the principality in an illusion that, I hope, will not be prejudicial to its interests."

"Oho! Are you getting an appetite for power, my son-in-law?"

"Call it an appetite for devotion. You can assure me that the bodies lying here can go on living?"

"Of course. Since they're asleep, they can wake up.

"And when they wake up?"

"They'll have the same face and the same gait as usual, only they'll be empty heads, without cerebrums. For some, the change will be insignificant."

"And you think that unless someone looks inside the head, no one will notice...what's missing?"

"Provided that no one questions them, the void will be unobserved."

"In that case, Marforio, wake them up; I'll think and act on their behalf. But make sure that no one ever suspects the truth. Our honor is at stake, and perhaps also our lives."

"In truth, my son-in-law, this new fashion of utilizing the vicissitude that that devil Colbertini has contrived for us is quite pleasing. You'll see that I'm adequate to the role. I swear by Albertus Magnus to keep the secret."

Marforio approached the ministers and Bonifacio and interrupted their sleep. Then something frightful happened, of which Lorenzo had always had a profound terror. The bodies got to their feet, got dressed, walked, yawned, smiled, stretched their limbs, and opened their mouths as if to talk, but without pronouncing a single word. The prince tried to take his father's hand; Bonifacio allowed him to do it, and smiled. By virtue of a mechanical instinct, the ministry followed in its sovereign's footsteps and the silent procession marching in step, striking the marble paving-stones of the gallery, went to the dining-room. That was the first ordinary task of the day. As it was a matter of animal instinct, it was carried out punctiliously.

The breakfast was grave. The watchful servants did not understand that unaccustomed silence; for some time now, such gatherings had been noisy. Lorenzo, sitting to his father's right, began his princely comedy and lied in the good cause; he leaned toward Bonifacio respectfully, and put on a show of receiving orders, which he immediately transmitted.

Toward the end of the meal, a rumor rose up from the street. The people, secretly roused by Colbertini and his agents, were demanding to see their sovereign. The rumor had gone around that he was ill, perhaps dead, and that Marforio's maneuvers had compromised the days of a prince and a ministry that were in the process of winning popularity.

Lorenzo took his father by the arm, made a sign to Marforio and stood up. The entire ministry, moved as if by a spring, immediately rose to its feet. The two princes, followed by the ministers, went on to the balcony. Frantic cheers greeted them. As soon as a measure of silence could be established, Lorenzo asked to speak.

"Dear friends," he said to the populace, "my father is too deeply moved by the evidence of your sympathy to speak; he had asked me to thank you on his behalf and to tell you that all your wishes will be granted."

A quiver of joy ran through the crowd. Marforio, placed behind Bonifacio, pushed him lightly on his upper body, and His Highness bowed and saluted. Motionless, and rolling their wide eyes, the ministers stood to the right and left of their sovereign.

"Yes," said Lorenzo, "the reforms, so long postponed, will be executed this very day. The streets will henceforth be supplied with lighting that will substitute daylight for moonlight at night." (*Applause.*) "No more filth on the sidewalks! Taxes on consumer goods will be the object of examination, and everything leads us to hope that they will be progressively abolished."

Cries of "Long live Bonifacio!" were heard; even Marforio was violently acclaimed. As for Lorenzo, a constraint and chagrin had been observed in his tone that was interpreted as resentment, and people refrained from associating him with the testimonies of gratitude of which the government was the object. The young prince accepted this first mistake as a favorable augury.

So much the better, he thought. *It will be easier to deceive them.*

The cortege quit the balcony and headed for the Council Chamber. Everyone took his habitual place. Lorenzo made sure that the ministers had everything they needed and went out with Marforio, carefully locking the door and making sure to take away the key.

He even took the further precaution of sending to the barracks for a few soldiers who had not forgotten how to handle weapons and had not sold the equipment supplied by the State to buy ribbons for their mistresses. He summoned them and said: "His Highness is working and will be working for some time. He must not be disturbed; in consequence, I order you to stand guard outside the door of the Council Chamber. You are to prevent anyone from going into the room by any and all means, including the use of weapons."

Colbertini will have to be very clever, he thought, privately, *to thwart those precautions*.

Colbertini did not even try. The police were on his track, but he hid so carefully that they were forced to concede the futility of the quest. He had taken part in the quasi-seditious demonstration of which he was the instigator. The appearance of Bonifacio and his ministers on the balcony of the palace had astounded him.

"Decidedly," he said to himself, "there's sorcery behind it."

He dared not admit to the criminal spoliation that he had committed. It was a serious offense, and he might have paid for Bonifacio's cerebrum with his own head. He judged it more prudent to stay one step ahead of popular justice and left immediately for the frontier, where a number of his friends were waiting, to whom he had promised a part in the administration of government if the plot he had hatched had come to fruition. He had taken care to send a small parcel to Marforio when he had departed, containing a letter and a key.

You are victorious, traitor! said the letter, *but not for long. I'll rouse all the thunder of Heaven against you. Pray to the devil who inspires you to help you escape the Holy Inquisition.*

Marforio laughed long and hard at the note.

"The simpleton!" he said. "He claims to be a Statesman, and he's sulking! He confesses defeat."

Lorenzo, worn out by emotion, had hastened to tell Marta everything.

"I've lied in the face of God and men," he told her, as soon as he saw her. "My vocation is commencing. Oh, you have to help me with your wisdom and your advice."

"I'll help you with my prayers and my love," Marta replied.

The struggle so heroically undertaken by the hereditary prince continued the next day, and the days thereafter, God knows with what terrors and what infinite precautions, not only without anything betraying Lorenzo's generous, but with a success that surpassed his hopes. He put his father and the ministers to bed at night and got them up in the morning, made them eat and drink, and then, when they were suitably locked away, he worked with Marta and governed according to the inspiration of their two hearts.

That they made a few blunders, and that the generous illusions of his soul caused him continually to fall into traps and enormous errors, I will admit; but he had such an active good will and such a righteous intention that the faults brought their own remedies and everything always worked out for the best. Lorenzo, of course, left all the glory to his father, and the people continued to think that he was not responsible for anything.

An era of prosperity began for Bonifacio XXIII's Estates. It was the most glorious period of his reign. It was in that era that he and his ministers acquired the glorious titles of which history has never wanted to deprive them. Those men without cerebrums were credited with all the genius and all the maturity they had been denied a few weeks earlier. The perfect dignity with which those automata of flesh and bone took part in ceremonies, what they gained in eloquence once they no longer said a word, and in wisdom once they were no longer thinking, fulfilled all the desires of the party of youth. It had rejoiced in the noisy and active period, but it rejoiced even more in that taciturnity.

Bonifacio became a politician superior to Machiavelli. Aphorisms, to which Lorenzo was no stranger, began to circulate. Some affirmed that the empire of the world belonged to the phlegmatic; others rejoiced in the fact that the reign of the loquacious had ended. As Bonifacio was unapproachable, and as he always went abroad in the midst of an escort of devoted servants, it became impossible to talk to him. Sometimes, profound and sublime words were attributed to him. Lorenzo racked his brains in order to invent them.

Without infringing upon any of the liberties that the people thought they had enjoyed thus far, because they had squandered them, order was gradually established. A singular emulation was manifest between the prince and his subjects. Everyone wanted to work hard, because the Head of State was working hard. After six months, Bonifacio was able to pass in review a nice little army, balance budgets without making use of beautiful phrases as counterweights, encourage business without harming intellectual labor, and realize everything of which he had never dreamed.

That prosperity filled Lorenzo's heart with joy and a secret pride.

"You're a great man, my son-in-law," said Marforio, who was a little less presumptuous since his disappointment

"How glad I am to love you!" said Marta.

"And when I think that the public attributes all this to the fat body that's digesting his food over there!" added the scientist.

"So much the better," said Lorenzo, smiling. "I have all the advantages of power with none of the inconveniences. I do good, and I have no flatterers to compensate."

Marforio was spared ingratitude to a greater extent than Lorenzo. People even went so far as to attribute to him, if not all the good that he accomplished, at least the fecund initiative whose results were now being reaped. Gradually, however, as public satisfaction increased, Bonifacio became the sole object of love and esteem. That good king, so paternal and so quiet, that mysterious intelligence, who was manifest in his good deeds, was the object of a worship that varied its forms without ever being exhausted. Monuments in honor of the sovereign, and statues, with or without drinking fountains, decorated the capital.

As for Lorenzo, hardly anyone recalled his existence. He was only talked about as a naïve young prince who had made a silly marriage—for the people most democratic on their own account adore princely unions in the aristocracy and are humiliated by their leaders' misalliances, often fatal to their glory. That fine young man, so pure and so poetic, was reckoned to be blockhead.

He laughed at that, and found a veritable and piquant satisfaction in the injustice that he had sought. His filial piety, which had not been compensated by anything received from his father, was further excited and alimented, and, having no flatterers to corrupt his inspirations or rivals to challenge his zeal and divert it into dangerous exploits, he continued to do good, in a tranquil, honest and saintly fashion, solely for the joy of making his father beloved and being loved by Marta— who, for her part, did not remain a stranger to the increase of the population and the consolidation of the dynasty.

Good kings deserve to be immortal, but a question arises as to whether perpetuity might corrupt the most precious virtues, and whether the people who became weary of Aristides[18] would not have revolted in the end against a sovereign as immutable in his justice as in his duration. Nations have a weakness and a tenderness for princes who are old devils, but no one has ever heard mention of any who were coddled under the pretext that they were good gods.

Bonifacio XXIII seemed assured of long life, especially since he was no longer living—by which I mean, since the worries of his intelligence no longer cast a shadow over his

---

[18] The Athenian statesman known as "Aristides the Just," well known by virtue of being featured in Plutarch's *Lives*, ostracized as a result of his conflict with Themistocles after a ballot whose result that Plutarch attributes to ignorant stupidity.

body. However—and it is here that the fragility of science becomes strikingly manifest—Marforio's conjectures proved unjustified, and it was observed with surprise, in the intimacy of the castle, that the health of His Highness and Their Excellencies the ministers was declining rapidly, even though nothing had changed in the regularity of the automatic functioning of those illustrious individuals. They took their four or five meals a day with the same abundance and exactitude; their slumber and their strolls were untroubled; they vegetated in that somnambulistic locomotion without chagrin and without dolor. In spite of the excellent hygiene to which they were subjected, however, dark circles were seen to surround their eyes, their cheeks became hollow, their stature curbed, their stride slowed.

At first, Marforio thought it might be a temporary malaise, but he soon realized that death was going to vanquish them, and that his scientific presumption was on the point of receiving a counsel of modesty.

Lorenzo anticipated that denouement without dolor. It was not that the ambition to succeed his father had altered his sentiments of filial tenderness, but he had been wearing secret mourning-dress for Bonifacio for a long time, and that automaton devoid of speech and amity who ate and drank beside him appeared to him to be an effigy of his father, but no longer his father.

All ingenious resources that could be deployed for the prolongation of life, Marforio attempted on behalf of the prince and his ministers.

"It's monstrous," he said. "These rogues have made a pact with Colbertini. Since they aren't thinking any longer, what the devil can they die of?"

They were dying precisely of not thinking any longer, and that was what Marforio did not want to recognize. He had difficulty admitting that matter, in order to flourish and to endure, needs intelligence; he did not understand that there is in ideas, in mental life, a nucleus of life itself, and that, in the same way that one sees sickly bodies maintain themselves and persist for a long time on the threshold of the tomb because the energy of the will or the imagination gives them a kind of fear of matter and death, one also sees more robust bodies weaken and perish when the interior flame no longer sustains and illuminates them.

Bonifacio was nothing but an animated cadaver, one of those whited and renovated sepulchers of which scripture speaks. His ministers were no better.

Marforio was desolate, and struggled with all his might; on the rare occasions when the public exhibition of the government was a necessity, His Highness and Their Excellencies were heavily made-up, but that small lie, that mask, was one irony more, and did not prevent active decomposition from attacking those noble and powerful individuals.

The people, whenever they saw their sovereign, cried at the top of their voices "Long live Bonifacio!" but if the voice of the people is the voice of God it was not, at any rate, the response of Heaven to the questions addressed thereto by the doctor.

After a few months, all the powder and cosmetics were powerless to conceal the ravages of decrepitude. Lorenzo, who feared that in the first impulse of its grief the nation might direct some excess against Marforio, had the rumor put about, first of the prince's indisposition, and then of his illness. The churches were besieged. Candles were burned to all the saints in the calendar, who were not too many. Pilgrimages were made to various places of pleasure where industrialists had established pious drinking-dens. Charlatans offered themselves with heroic remedies. People begged "the father of the nation," in eloquent speeches, not to work so hard. The party of the future, which had partly disbanded, was reorganized, and peppered Lorenzo with brochures and manifestoes, accusing that egotistical young man of leaving all the cares of government to his father.

"Oh, the fools!" said Marforio, whose humor was becoming visibly embittered, and who swore that he would not survive the failure of his system. "They don't know what they're talking about. If they only knew, my son-in-law, that you have done everything, governed everything!"

"They'll never know," Lorenzo replied. "Can I admit—can we admit—that we've deceived them?"

One morning, the bells rang a funeral knell. They were beautiful new bells that had recently been installed, and represented as a gift from Bonifacio. All the inhabitants burst into sobs and only remarked on the sweet tone of the bells to say, with desolation, that their sovereign would not hear them.

A few hours before, High Highness had passed away, painlessly. The cadaver was hideous to behold, so hasty was the matter to dissolve, but Bonifacio was buried with his smile, which never left his lips.

The ministers fared no better. They died at soon after the prince, following him within the week, like faithful servants. In the intervals of that decease, the end of the model government was announced.

I shall not describe the relative magnificence of Bonifacio's funeral celebrations. It was a memorable day, and as great dolors are never unaccompanied by great hunger pangs, there were splendid feasts, which might have led one to think, at first glance, that the principality was celebrating a wedding.

Lorenzo, pale and sad, as every hereditary prince must be in the procession of his predecessor—the last had been his father—led the tragic cortege.

Marforio, as the prime minister, was constrained to be there, but to tell the truth, that was the day when his responsibility weighed upon him most heavily—or, to put it more accurately, weighed upon him more veritably—for it was something more than a prince, whether it be Alexander, Caesar or Bonifacio XXIII, that he saw buried; it was all the effort of science, all the discovery, all the work of his genius.

By way of consolation, the poor scholar said to himself: "Perhaps, if the infamous Colbertini had not stolen the cerebrums, they would have lived." But there was in that regret the very condemnation of his system, for, from the moment that the cerebrum was sustaining the body, it was no longer a destructive and pernicious agent.

Lorenzo did not point out to his father-in-law the formal contradiction that existed between his theory and his sighs; he was at odds himself with serious difficulties that were about to put his courage to the proof once again.

The day after the funeral, seditious placards were found posted at street-corners, between the images of the blessed Virgin that were above them and the heaps of ordure that were beneath them. In these posters protests were made against the elevation of Lorenzo to the throne occupied by his forefathers. They did not propose that the principality should do without a sovereign; that would have been too radical a means, which could not come from the party of the future, deeply imbued with the past, but, in accordance with the ancient fashion of the petty states of Italy, it was patriotically proposed that the money, crops, soldiers and all the other wealth of the principality should be offered to an old foreign sovereign, who, having absolutely no right to Bonifacio's heritage, would doubtless show his gratitude for what was granted to him.

Colbertini had something to do with the drafting of this program. Since he had fallen from power, the Statesman in question had come to regard himself as infallible—a rather common error. Add to that the fact that he had emigrated, and that peoples, although pitiless toward exiles, have a sufficiently great consideration for flight. The traitor was avenging himself on his successors and the prince. He dared not claim payment of the debt contracted toward him by the late Bonifacio, but he thought he might well have it paid by the prince designated in the proclamations.

Lorenzo would have been quite happy to leave the palace and abdicate the honors, but he had duties to fulfill, and a heritage to claim and defend. He tried to resist peacefully, to make promises—but what promises could he have made that were not beneath the reality that his father had so liberally heaped upon his people? When he spoke about doing his best, people laughed in his face, saying that he was incapable of doing better or as well as Bonifacio XXIII, whose example had been sterile for him, as he had proved abundantly.

We know full well how that model of sons and modest princes, as well as heirs, could have responded, but it was precisely his silence that constituted his glory and his merit in his own eyes. He did not want to reign by stigmatizing his father. How, in any case, could Lorenzo tell the people that they had been tricked, and inform them of the horrible and sinister comedy that he had played? How, moreover, could he prove to them that all those dead or dying ministers were marionettes?

Lorenzo attempted to struggle as a prince; he ordered that the walls be cleared of the seditious placards that covered them. The armed revolt was only waiting for that signal. The cry of tyranny went up. The instincts of the young sensualist—he was called that because of his haste to marry legitimately rather than content himself with the wild amours permissible at his age—were finally showing themselves in all their perversity. Then, the lamp-posts that Lorenzo had installed in every street were ripped up and hurled as projectiles at his palace; the beautiful new rifles that he had distributed to the civil guard were used for the first time against him.

Blood would have flowed if Lorenzo, sufficiently edified as to the principality's sentiments of gratitude toward his father, had not renounced convincing himself any further advantage of the services he had rendered himself in the name of Bonifacio XXIII. He understood the difficulty of monarchical power and admitted humbly that he was not sufficiently ambitious to begin slaughtering his subjects in order to force upon them the happiness that he felt capable of procuring for them.

"The scoundrels!" said Marforio—who was not, however, enveloped in the disgrace. "I'd like to hang the lot of them."

"Or at least remove their cerebrums," added Lorenzo, and continued: "No, Doctor, they're being logical. Peoples can't be paid off with conjectures and hypotheses; they have an ingratitude that is the condition of their independence, and if they subjected themselves to an entire dynasty of imbeciles in memory of a benefit rendered, they'd always be under the yoke. One can tame them by force, seduce them with pomp, and please them by trickery, but good will without ostentation annoys them. I'm no conqueror; I have simple tastes, and I have no wish to deceive them. It's therefore just that they image that they've lost everything with my father's death, whose works are recent, and that they're suspicious of me, who don't resemble my father."

"But my son-in-law, since it's you who reigned so well...!"

"Ah! That's what it's necessary not to tell them—and would they believe me, anyway? Come on, Marforio, let's make a decision. One act of violence, a crime of State, odious to my conscience, could maintain me, but I'm not certain enough of being infallible to commit that crime."

The worthy Marforio did not understand such subtleties. "You're not talking like a prince," he said, veritably indignant.

"I'm talking as a citizen."

"You're talking as an honest man," said Marta, throwing her arms around her husband.

Prince Lorenzo was indeed a very honest man. Should that development of instincts of candor and good faith be attributed to the education received from his French governess, reading *Télémaque*, or his poetic vocation? That is what I cannot affirm, in the dread of suggesting an ineffective means to princes tempted to be honest. What I can say is that he preferred to renounce power than claim it by force, and that he left the principality without leaving a single drop of blood behind.

As soon as the departure of the incapable prince became known, cheers saluted the deliverance. Even Lorenzo's generosity was reckoned a crime. Peoples in revolt usually expel princes who resist them and despise those who do not. A prince who cannot defend his crown does not deserve to wear it. Lorenzo's horror of civil war passed for cowardice.

A delegation went to offer the power to the foreign sovereign whose name had been mentioned. The latter hastened to gratify his new subjects with a portion of his debts, and made his entrance to the capital a few days later.

He was received and complimented by Colbertini, whom he named as his first chamberlain, ministers having been abolished by a radical measure that ought to have made Bonifacio shudder in his tomb—with the result that the infamous Colbertini had the right to wear, suspended from a sash, the famous key to the Treasury Room that had finally permitted him to accomplish his vengeance.

As for the party of the future, the new sovereign who owed his crown to it hastened to disperse it and threaten it with *carcere duro* if it ever reformed. As it had acted badly out of pure patriotism, it doubtless ought to have declared itself satisfied with that recompense.

Lorenzo was exiled, but he had his love and liberty, and that was sufficient to provide him with an ideal fatherland. He brought the worthy Marforio with him to France, where the soil is particularly hospitable to exotic princes. In any case, Lorenzo left the title of prince to slumber; he was poor and needed to work; hereditary pretensions were no longer of any consequence. He studied, and became in a matter of months a distinguished naturalist, published several articles, took part in scientific debates and won several crowns that did not alter European equilibrium at all.

It should not be thought, however, that in quitting the principality, Lorenzo had renounced his affection for it. On the contrary, it seemed that he loved it more since he had lost it. He thought about it night and day, and if he strove to educate and applied himself with all his heart to forming the hearts of his children, it was because he thought that if they ever returned to it, it was necessary to render to his homeland devoted citizens who had forgotten everything and learned everything.

Marforio continued to pursue his chimeras, but he noticed that the soil of France rendered them more fugitive; he renounced experimenting on cerebrums, the French much preferring natural cracks in the skull to those the doctor could contrive; he resigned himself to lesser problems and limited his ambition to the squaring of the circle and discovering the philosopher's stone.

Lorenzo lived happily, the absent fatherland gave his domestic happiness the melancholy and sadness that freshens, so to speak, the perfumes of the soul and prevents them from evaporating. He had children as lovely as Marta and as good as himself. He strove to give them an honest and inflexible conscience, the sentiment of honor and the passion of duty; he taught them that they were princes, and told them his story, in order to preserve them from vain ambitions.

Perhaps there was one sin that I ought to confess on his behalf, and of which he did not repent when he died: he raised his sons in utopias and persuaded them, for instance, that peoples are the masters of their own destiny, that princes are not indispensable to the prosperity of States, and that justice and liberty are more necessary than bread and circuses.

These paradoxes, which caused Lorenzo to be mildly slandered by his entourage and attracted accusations of republicanism, unfortunately bore their fruit, and seemed to condemn his children to a very long exile, for they swore not to return to their homeland until Italy was free, from the Alps to the Adriatic.

THE WHITE LADY OF BADEN

Toward the end of the month of January in the year 1852, the Grand Duke of Baden, Leopold I, took to his bed with an attack of gout. The physicians declared that the malady was not dangerous, and that His Highness, only sixty-one years old and of robust constitution, was strong enough to fight off that indisposition. After having prescribed the necessary remedies, they withdrew, perfectly tranquil, forbidding the circulation of any bulletin regarding the prince's health, judging it inappropriate to alarm the court and population of Karlsruhe.

Strangely enough, however, scarcely had the rumor spread that Duke Leopold had taken to his bed than funereal presentiments immediately seemed to agitate the castle and the city; visages betrayed anxiety, and, in spite of the oracle of Epidurus, people began alarmed and began to tremble for His Highness' life. The physicians affirmed a cure, but people listened to them while shaking their heads; they specified almost to the day when the Duke would be fit and well again, but people sighed and gazed at the heavens. By the middle of March, more than one lady of the court was secretly preparing mourning-dress, as if the prince's death were inevitable.

A young Frenchman, witness to these presentiments, which insulted the prognosis of the Faculty so forcefully, expressed his astonishment one day to the Baroness von B***, a respectable dowager in whom age had not extinguished intelligence, and who had just enough devotion not to be an atheist.

At the first word, however, the Baroness became pensive, and let the knitting that she was undertaking with an entirely national ardor fall on her knees. She stopped her interlocutor with a gaze dispirited by sadness and fright.

"Alas, Monsieur," she finally replied, "our fears are all too justified. It's now three times that the White Lady has appeared in the castle."

"The White Lady?"

"Yes, don't you know the legend?"

"I know of no other White Lady than Boieldieu's," the young Frenchman replied, smiling.[19]

"Well then, listen," said the dowager von B***, staring her needles in motion again. "There was once…"

Before beginning, however, the Baroness glanced slyly at her interlocutor; she noticed a mocking smile on his lips.

"You're nothing but a Frenchman," she said, growling and hitting his fingers with the knitting needles. "You laugh at everything. Go away! I shan't tell you the legend."

As he went down the stairs, the young Frenchman said to himself: "I've had a narrow escape. It's singular how national prejudice harms the free flight of the mind. That old baroness has one of the youngest, most charming imaginations, and yet she was about to murder me with some tenebrous local legend. The woman was brought up in the eighteenth century; she scarcely believes in God, but she believes in the Devil. She'd have put out my eyes with her knitting-needles if I'd expressed any doubt after she'd told her tale. Why, in any case, should I take instruction regarding a superstition from an old dowager, who's too German not to be superstitious?"

---

[19] The reference is to Adrien Boieldieu's opera *La Dame blanche* (1825), based on episodes from novels by Water Scott. It is, however, a trifle odd that the narrator is claiming unfamiliarity with all the numerous legends of supernatural "white ladies" current in France, especially in Normandy and Brittany. Germany also has its fairy share, including a white lady of Baden, but the latter is the ghost of Princess Jakobea (1558-1597), who was sometimes compared by historians with Mary Stuart. Ulbach's story is entirely improvised.

And he young Frenchman went on his way, humming the famous operatic refrain: *Look out! The White Lady is looking at you.*

At the corner of the street he bumped into one of his friends, a young native of Baden, and a student of diplomacy. *Of course!* he thought. *Just the man! He must be above prejudice.* And after the handshakes customary in such an encounter, he asked the newcomer: "Have you ever seen the White Lady?"

The young German replied, perfectly seriously: "I haven't seen her myself, but one of my uncles, the Duke's chamberlain, once encountered her in a gallery in the castle."

The Frenchman was nonplussed. *What!* he thought. *He believes in the legend too! It's hardly worth the trouble of being an apprentice diplomat.* Smiling, he said: "What does this redoubtable apparition look like?"

"You haven't seen her portrait?"

"What! The mysterious lady has gone to the trouble of having herself painted?"

"Of course—and the Duke, who is going to die, has taken care to have the portrait removed from the castle of Baden-Baden last summer, when he was in residence there, he was so frightened of encountering that sinister visage. He had it brought here, into the crown wardrobe. The White Lady will avenge herself, alas!"

"*Au revoir*, my dear chap," the Frenchman interrupted, shaking his interlocutor's friend vigorously.

The Badois was deceived by that demonstration, which he took to mean: "Poor Duke; poor Duchy; poor White Lady," when in reality, the pressure was ironic, and signified: "Poor fellow!"

"Decidedly," muttered the young skeptic, "the Grand Duke will be failing in the respect that he owes to the legends of his homeland if he recovers from his illness."

The idea of visiting one of the castle physicians with whom he was slightly acquainted seemed piquant to the French traveler.

He found the doctor somber and preoccupied. "How is the Duke?" he asked him.

"Well enough," replied the physician, "And yet..."

"Do you, by any chance, Doctor, also believe in the legend of the White Lady?"

"I don't believe it, but that doesn't prevent others from believing in it, and the prince will end up divining the secret of the alarming sympathies that surround him. In his state of mind, it doesn't require any more to disturb the brain. Oh, I wish I could send to the devil all these inventors of devilries and spells, and the first time I find myself facing the portrait of the White Lady, I'd pass my cane through her eyes. It would be a pity, though, for the woman is beautiful."

"Really?" said the Frenchman, who found the doctor's spite more attractive than the naïve faith he had encountered thus far.

"What! You haven't yet seen the portrait of the White Lady, when no one's been taking about anything else for nearly two months?"

"I believe, Doctor, that I can scarcely dispense with paying a visit to the portrait, while waiting for someone to tell me the legend."

"Oh, the legend is absurd," said the physician, with the gesture and the smile of a strong mind, "but the portrait is superb! What eyes! What a complexion! I'm going to the castle now; if you like, I'll take you with me, and we can go to present our compliments to the White Lady of the House of Baden."

"I accept," said the Frenchman.

On the way, the physician waxed lyrical about Duke Leopold's illness. He demonstrated in a peremptory fashion the pusillanimity of the Badois. With furious arguments he tore away the lugubrious veils with which they enveloped the horizon. He mocked the legend and those who believed in it so fervently that the young Frenchman ended up concluding that, in spite of his rationality and the testimony of science, the scholar became a little bit afraid of the popular vision.

At the castle, they were separated for a hour. The doctor went to visit the illustrious invalid, whom he found in the care of several of his colleagues. A thoroughly reassuring statement was drawn up and signed. Within a week, the Duke would be able to go out and travel.

When he rejoined the young Frenchman, the doctor affected a great cheerfulness. "All's well!" he exclaimed. "We shall triumph in spite of the phantoms. I can now look at the diabolical portrait without fear."

"Don't take your cane, though—that will be more prudent."

"Have no fear: I defy all the White Ladies in the world!"

They arrived at the wardrobe. It was not easy for the two curiosity-seekers to get to see the portrait in question. The Grand Duke had manifested such a repugnance for the image, the last time he had seen it, that it had immediately been made to disappear, enclosed behind a triple lock. In Baden as in Paris, however, there is no lock without a key, no key without a turnkey, and no turnkey without a stomach, and the curiosity of the young Frenchman was able to produce shining arguments that triumphed over all reluctance. The mysterious cupboard was opened, and a portrait brought out that was about four feet in height.

The young Frenchman uttered an exclamation and lost himself in admiration. Against a dark background, which time had darkened further, a figure of sinister beauty stood out; she was pale, and her lips, bewitchingly graceful, were slightly parted, like a crimson flower in the midst of a bouquet of lilies. Her jet-back hair was taken up and knotted in a sixteenth-century hairstyle.

Her hands, on which blue veins could be seen, were folded on the back of an armchair. Her dress was black, bordered with fur. An escutcheon, on top of which two bears were supporting a comtal crown, shone in one corner of the picture. Nothing was simpler or more severe than that portrait, but all its charm—I ought to say all its horror—was contained in the fixed and penetrating eyes with which the unknown lady was gazing. One might have thought that the painter had punctured the canvas and set a veritable flame in the place where the irises should be.

Beneath thick eyebrows describing an irreproachable arc, a singular and inflexible light-source seemed to be emitting horizontal rays that could not be avoided. A magnetic force always drew the attention toward the marble forehead sheltering those two funereal lamps. There is a somber portrait by Raphael in the Louvre that exercises the same fascination. The eyes attract, and no matter from one direction one looks, one is troubled and tormented by those two immobile and penetrating sparks.

The portrait of the White Lady of Baden, due to some unknown of genius, or perhaps one of those mediocre painters who have a single moment of sublime inspiration in their life, was a masterpiece of pride, sadness and beauty, but as one studied that fatal physiognomy the enigma was spontaneously deciphered. That lip, so admirable in its design, seemed to tremble with the breath of terrestrial passion; those eyes devoid of tears, if they shone like steel, were just as hard; that pallor was a shroud and not a veil.

The young Frenchman was plunged into an ecstasy mingled with fear. He felt his heart beating faster at the sight of that sad and regal beauty. He found her as ideal as Ophelia, as sad as Lady Macbeth; he floated between love and terror.

The physician, who, for his part, had gazed with an attention no less profound, although slightly mocking, at the portrait of the While Lady, clapped the Frenchman on the shoulder and said to him: "Well, what do you think?"

The young man shuddered, and tried to conceal his emotion.

"I think," he replied, "that she's an admirable woman, a trifle pale, but whose eyes and mouth announce that she has a proud mind and an ardent heart. What passion there is in those lips! What an infinity in that gaze!"

The doctor shook his head. "Fine phrases in relation to an execrable woman! Not so much enthusiasm, my young friend! What you're reading in those eyes is murder; what you're admiring on those scarlet lips is spilled blood. Your heroine is a monster. I know that you Frenchmen, when you don't guillotine such creatures, set them on a pedestal and award them the aureole of genius, but it would be difficult for you to poeticize the White Lady."

Is there any need to say that the young Frenchman was listening to the doctor with impatience? Now, he desired with as much ardor as he had previously manifested suspicion to hear the story of the famous legend that stirred up so many presentiments regarding the castle of the Duke of Baden.

He sensed a vague interest palpitating in the depths of that lugubrious history, and it must be admitted that even the crime of which the White Lady might have been culpable was a forceful stimulant for his curiosity, so true is it that we all have, to some extent, a passion for the horrible, and that certain terrors are the source of the keenest enjoyments of the mind.

The doctor saw his companion's desire, and linked arms with him. "Don't overheat your imagination, my young friend," he said. "There's nothing very interesting about it. In a few words, this is the story..."

"In a few words!" exclaimed the Frenchman. "Thank you, Doctor, but you're too brief; besides which, you're not sufficiently disinterested in the question to speak about the White Lady as an impartial storyteller; I don't trust you."

And, disengaging his arm from the physician's, he ran back to the Baroness von B***'s house.

He found her in the same armchair, beneath the same ray of sunlight, working on the same knitting.

As soon as she saw him, she said: "What brings you back, Monsieur Incredulous?"

"Repentance and faith," the young Frenchman replied, sending a salutation full of humility and supplication from the threshold of the room.

The old Baroness smiled, looked at the penitent sideways, was sufficiently satisfied by his compunction, and pushed out a small tapestry footstool buried beneath the folds of her skirts.

"Come and kneel there," she said, "and make your confession; if you offer proof of contrition, I'll absolve you."

"And you'll tell me the legend?"

"Of course."

The young man came to fall at the dowager's knees, with a vivacity that amused her.

"That's how it was, once," she murmured, with a sigh. "People knelt there, but to tell stories, not to hear them. Bah! The past is also a legend, and you're not here to listen to my sighs."

The young Frenchman told her about visiting the portrait, his impressions and his ardent curiosity.

The Baroness gravely wound up her knitting, took a few morsels of licorice from a little ivory box ornamented with a magnificent portrait, slid them between her lips, sat back in her armchair, coughed slightly, pulled her mittens over her fingers, and began.

Once there was a young Margrave of Baden, very handsome, very knowledgeable and very good. That young prince, as is scarcely ever seen, had but one fault; he was irredeemably sad, possessed by a melancholy that nothing could dissipate. His father and mother, who contemplated that unique scion of their family with pride, wondered what desires had hollowed out abysms in their child's heart.

The Margrave, however, was not yearning for anything and was not in love with anyone. I mean that he was had no other love than that stemming from his filial piety, for no son was ever more submissive to the wishes of his parents, from whom he received advice with a perfect humility. You can see that the prince was definitely a very extraordinary prince.

One day, the Margrave was taken by the two venerable authors of his days into a hornbeam grove in the park, and there, in the sight of the good God, far from importunate courtiers and curious servants, they tried to fathom the mysterious wound that was bleeding in the young man's heart.

He lent himself meekly to that examination, but it was impossible for him to confess any secret. To every question the Margrave responded that nothing was wrong, that there was nothing he desired, that the burdensome ennui from which he was suffering would doubtless dissipate, and that he had nothing else to ask of Heaven than the continuation of his parents' calm and serene days. A respectful kiss completed that reply, and the two august old folk, after having blessed their son, went back to the castle, very frustrated, but very moved by such exemplary tenderness and such perfect innocence.

The night inspired the old folk to think of a cure, however, and as soon as the next day dawned, they summoned the melancholy Margrave again.

"My son," his father said to him, "We've decided that you ought to travel. I don't know what plans God has for us, but it might be the case that we shall soon join our ancestors on the marble pillow of the family vault. You might be suddenly called upon to reign; it's therefore essential that you be prepared for that great event. Now, the sadness to which you are prey is a bad disposition for government. What will happen, my son, when you see the underside of human nature and the interior of consciences? I don't want you to be a misanthrope, and I love me subjects too much to bequeath them a tyrant or an unbeliever; it's necessary to seek a cure for you. I think that traveling will give you an opportunity to distract yourself, by completing your education. One does not know oneself well until one has seen oneself in multiple mirrors; in the same way, one does not understand humankind until one has been brought out of oneself. Go forth, then, my son and study people in their various lands. You're prudent; I have no advice to give you; you have my blessing…"

The old prince did not reason too badly, for a simple German prince. The remedy was good; the Margrave consented to try it. He packed his bags in a docile fashion, not forgetting to take a Plutarch and a Seneca, which he sometimes read to maintain in his mind an appetite for the good; polished his sword, which he suspended by his side; tenderly embraced his father and his mother, bowed down beneath their benediction, and set forth.

On the threshold of the castle, his mother, who had followed her son, took him in her arms one last time, and held him momentarily against her heart, murmuring in his ear those supreme exhortations that always spring from the maternal bosom, multiplied by anguish and separation.

"My son," she said to him, in a low voice, "bring your heart back from your travels; whatever the occasion might be that tempts you, remember that a respectful son must have his marriage blessed by his mother and father, and that a prince of the house of Baden must not offer his blazon in a bouquet."

The margrave smiled, blushed, kissed his emotional mother three more times, mounted his horse and departed sat a gallop for his tour of Europe.

He went to France, to Italy and to Spain, and all the sunlit lands of poetry and love, but the gaiety of those privileged regions, far from dissipating the young traveler's melancholy, had the contrary effect of thickening the lugubrious veil that enveloped him. His heart recrossed the frontiers as free and insensitive as it had crossed them to begin with; as for his intelligence, he enriched it during every new excursion with one disenchantment more.

The North suited the margrave's pensive character more. He headed toward those melancholy lands, and the pale sun seemed to vivify him and cause him to blossom more than the warm radiance of Naples, Venice, Madrid or Paris.

One day, in Denmark, the young prince lost his way while riding in the countryside by himself. After making fruitless efforts to recover his route, as night was falling, he took the opportunity to ask for hospitality in a manor house whose marvelous situation on the edge of a lake he had admired a little while before.

An old majordomo came to take the bridle of the Margrave's horse and informed him that he was in the house of

Countess Olamünde, a young widow, who had lived in absolute retreat since the death of her husband, and no longer went to court. The Margrave solicited the honor of being introduced to the Countess, and the old domestic led him on to a terrace where the latter was breathing in the fresh air of the evening, seated between her two children.

The Margrave had never seen a woman as beautiful as Countess Olamünde; never in his dreams had he imagined a face as pure, eyes as penetrating, hair as black. He saw combined in a single individual two very different beauties: the milky whiteness of the women of the North, and the flashing gaze and ebon hair of the women of the South, all of it harmonized by a languor and a charming sadness that removed the excessive keenness from her irises and gave her pallor an energy full of mysterious thoughts.

I don't want to hold back surprises, nor launch myself into analyses of sentiment irrelevant to what you want to know. You can deduce, without having the penetration of Oedipus, that the Margrave fell in love with Countess Olamünde. How could it be otherwise?

Can you, who have seen her marvelous portrait, not understand with what violence the heart of that contemplative young German must suddenly have expanded under the gaze of that strange woman, spreading severely enclosed perfumes?

If ever a passion was as rapid as lightning, it was that one. On setting foot on the terrace and perceiving the Countess, by the last rays of the setting sun, sitting there and searching infinite space with her gaze, the young man felt a spring well up within him. A secret voice said to him: "It is her for whom you have been searching!" By virtue of an instantaneous revelation, he understood that these secret of his sadness was there, and that all his melancholy was the idleness of his heart; henceforth, it would live.

He approached slowly and respectfully, not daring to interrupt the profound meditation that absorbed the Countess' thoughts.

Alas, thought the young Margrave, *she's probably thinking about her husband.* And the prince was jealous of that memory given to a dead man.

My privileges as a story-teller permit me to admit to you that the Countess was much more preoccupied with the unknown husband that the future had in store for her; and this is the time to tell you, without reticence, what kind of soul it was that was consuming itself within that transparent alabaster, and what kind of gleam was seen to rise in the most beautiful eyes in the world.

Countess Olamünde was ambitious, A descendant of a royal family, which revolutions had transplanted far from the throne, she lived with the incessant idea of raising her family up again, of reclimbing the steps descended, of one day mingling the gold of a princely crown with the ebony of her hair.

Count Olamünde, her first husband, had been a very modest gentleman, incapable of understanding his wife's immense ambition, and having the simplicity to believe that a sufficient fortune, with two beautiful children and a tranquil conscience, was a very adequate portion, in Denmark as elsewhere, with which one could be content.

Having suffered ten years of discontentment stimulated by a spouse so ill-made to aid her in her endeavors, Countess Olamünde had become a widow. I cannot affirm that the deceased had been mourned; he died so conveniently that suspicious minds might have thought that something other than chance was involved in that coincidence, but the Countess' reputation for virtue and the long-unsteady health of the Count appeared, in Denmark, to be plausible reasons to deflect all suspicion, if one can admit that suspicions were ever excited with the regard to the event. At any rate, mourned or not, Count Olamünde had a grandiose funeral and a gigantic marble cenotaph with a Latin inscription, and if it is true that death is nothing but human life seen in reverse, the deceased would have had to agree, in enjoying such as magnificent monument, that there was something rather agreeable in the ambitious aims of his spouse.

Countess Olamünde considered widowhood as a transition between the disappointments of her first marriage and the hopes of a second. So, on the evening when the Margrave came to request hospitality, the beautiful widow was plunged in ardent contemplation, seeking her star through the clouds. Brought back down to earth by the stranger's arrival, it was without disappointment—or, rather, it was with a shudder of joy and pride—that she saw the handsome young man bow respectfully and heard him pronounce his name and his qualities. The Countess enveloped the Margrave with a rapid glance, and, satisfied with that examination, brought to her lips the most dazzling smile that has ever caused a poet to dream.

This would be an opportunity to play you one of those beautiful tunes that youth plays so well, but my old fingers have been stiffened by knitting, and would pluck that enchanting string poorly. Let your imagination, then, come to the aid of my sterilized heart. Picture that beautiful evening, that terrace, Countess Olamünde, with the two eyes that you know and the ambitions that are agitating her, and the young margrave with his candor and his naivety; think of the sublunar conversations of Romeo and Juliet; invoke and evoke all the gracious phantoms that the breath of night promenades over the terraces of castles on the edges of lakes, and you will have no difficulty substituting for the elegy which I shall spare myself.

Let it suffice for you to know that the margrave was so well received in the house of Countess Olamünde that he came back the next day, and the following days, and that a fortnight after their first meeting, the Margrave and the beautiful widow launched forth in thought, into the same ideal regions in the same winged chariot. But as that intimacy developed in the heart of the young prince one of those eternal sentiments that are only extinguished by death, gaiety lit up his gaze and enthusiasm cleared his brow; he smiled at nature and at life, and he went with a marvelous candor at the forefront of all illusions. The love of Countess Olamünde, on the other hand, was

147

a flame that hollowed out her face and paraded sinister reverberations beneath the brows of her large eyes.

One evening, when they were both on the terrace, the Margrave let his emotion overflow and, informing the Countess of his imminent departure for Karlsruhe, painted his regrets and hopes in touching terms.

"I have had a beautiful dream, Madame," he said, in conclusion. "If I were able to change reality, God is my witness that the most beautiful day of my life would be the one on which I could bring you back to the castle of my forefathers as the Margrave of Baden."

The eyes of Countess Olamünde flashed, and her lip trembled. "And what could prevent you from the realization of that beautiful dream?" she replied, with a somber energy.

"Alas," replied the Margrave, "there are four eyes opposed to that happiness. So long as those four eyes reflect the azure of the heavens, our union is impossible."

"And if those importunate eyes were extinguished?" asked the countess, with a terrible tremor and a strangled voice.

"If those four eyes were closed," the Margrave replied, sadly, "you would be my wife."

"I will be the Duchess of Baden!" cried Countess Olamünde, in a savage outburst.

The prince gazed at her in astonishment, seeking to understand what was happening in that tenebrous heart, and doubtless finding an explanation in accordance with his desires.

"Yes, Countess," he said to her, in an emotional voice, while kissing her hand. "Yes, you shall be a Margravine! Adieu! I shall return; I shall bring back faith and courage."

The Margrave left, and the Countess, leaning over her terrace, followed him from afar with her somber gaze. When he had disappeared entirely into the mists of the road, Madame Olamünde got up, as white as a ghost.

"I will be the Duchess of Baden," she repeated, proudly, folding her arms over her breast, "but before that joy..."

Her two children were brought to her then for their evening kiss, but the countess pushed those two innocent children away, in alarm.

"Why are they not already asleep?" she said, violently. "Why are those four eyes so shiny, so awake at this hour? Let them be veiled! Let them be extinguished! I do not want to see them any longer!"

And, waving her arms as if she wanted to be rid of serpents that were biting her, the Countess expelled them from the terrace; she did not go to bed that night, but wandered through the schloss. It is probable that she did not go to visit, in al her wanderings, the marble bed of Count Olamünde.

Two months went by. The Margrave of Baden came back to Denmark; he was in haste. He was bringing good news, and his horse could not keep up with his impatience. A complete transformation had taken place in him; the sickly dreamer had blossomed into a charming and robust cavalier; happiness had smoothed his forehead and brightened his visage, and his gaze as overflowing with hope.

In the last town that preceded the Countess' manor, the young voyager paused and collected himself. He was bringing so much joy that at the moment of his arrival, the burden seemed heavy; he had so many things to tell the Countess that he needed to put his ideas in order. He took off his dusty traveling clothes, decked himself out as if for a betrothal, and set off again with such a rapid heartbeat that he as obliged to stop frequently, fearing that he might suffocate.

A league from the manor, the Margrave encountered the old majordomo who had taken his bridle on the occasion of his first visit; he was dressed in mourning, walking with his head bowed, carrying a package under his arm.

"Where are you going in this fashion, my good man?" asked the traveler, alarmed by the costume and lugubrious expression of the old servant.

The majordomo raised his head, recognized the Margrave and went pale, but made no reply. When the young man persisted, and demanded news of the Countess, he murmured: "The Countess is waiting for you, my lord." And, without adding another word, uttering a profound sigh, he continued on his way.

That's strange, the Margrave said to himself, seized by a lugubrious presentiment. *Has some misfortune struck the manor?*

When he perceived an inn, he stopped at the door, had a measure of oats given to his horse, and attempted to interrogate the innkeeper.

At the first word, the landlord shivered, looked fixedly at the traveler and replied: "You're the man who is awaited at the manor; you have no need to stop so close to your goal!" And with an alacrity imprinted with a kind of superstitious dread, the innkeeper went to pull the horse away from the manger, handled him the bridle and closed his door, making no response to the Margrave when he called him back in order to pay him.

This time, the young prince was gripped by fear; he departed at a gallop. Soon, he perceived the countess' manor house. The gate was open; two village children were sitting on the edge of the moat; when they heard the horse they got up and ran away, crying out, as if at the approach of a sinister vision.

The Margrave crossed the threshold with one bound; his mount's iron horseshoes struck sparks from the pavement. He called out but no one came. Then he tethered his horse to a ring at the gate. The courtyard and the vestibules were deserted. The Margrave went up the stairway leading to the Countess' apartments. He was afraid of running into a coffin. Death was floating so visibly over the house, transformed into a sepulcher, that the young prince expected to find the woman he loved in the folds of a shroud.

At the top of the stairs he stopped, put his hands on his heart to compress its beating, addressed a brief prayer to the God who blesses pure sentiments, and then went into the widow's apartments.

Having passed through several rooms as abandoned as the rest of the house, he reached a remote chamber, and a groan that made him shudder informed him that he was no longer alone. Countess Olamünde, crouching rather than sitting in a large armchair, her hands in her hair, staring straight ahead, seemed to be concentrated in one of those grim and insensate dolors that only superhuman sentiment or remorse bring out. An almost complete obscurity reigned in the room; the curtains were drawn, the shutters half-closed.

Hearing footsteps on the floor, the Countess raised her head.

"Who's there?" she asked, in a voice so troubled that the Margrave scarcely recognized it.

The prince advanced toward the Countess then, and, taking her hands, which were inundated with cold sweat, he bent his knees with a controlled piety and said, softly: "Greet the Margrave of Baden!"

The countess uttered a cry, threw herself upon the curtains, which she tore away from the rail, abruptly thrust back the shutters, and recognized in a flood of light the man for whom she had been waiting for so long, hurled herself upon him like a raptor on a prey and hugged him as if to stifle him, murmuring: "It's you! You're very late!"

The prince was struck by the change that had taken place in the Countess' face. The orbits of her eyes were hollow; she was as pale as a ghost; and a sinister flame was vacillating in her gaze.

"What's wrong, Madame?" he exclaimed. "Are you ill?"

"It's nothing," she said, with a burst of laughter that resounded in the deserted rooms. "I was waiting for you, and had lost hope of seeing you, but here you are! Oh, I can forget!"

"You're really alone, Madame?"

"You think so? Oh, but I've been afraid of hearing someone *come back*."

"What has happened, then? Why this abandonment?"

"What has happened? Don't you know? Oh, I'll tell you on the way...but let's flee, let's flee! You've come to find me, haven't you? I'm your fiancée; nothing any longer opposes my being your wife; the jealous eyes that frightened you are extinct!"

"God be praised, Countess," the Margrave interjected, swiftly, "those four eyes still reflect the heavens, but they have smiled upon me and have acceded to my dearest wish."

"What are you saying? That those eyes, those torches, those four pupils still live? You've seen them?"

"Why this disturbance, this alarm?"

"Oh, but I'm certain that I saw them close forever!"

"What are you saying? My God!"

"Nothing—let's go. You can see, Margrave, that everyone knows that I'm about to leave, and has abandoned me. Come, come; your horse is down below, pawing the ground with impatience. You can carry me on its rump."

And the Countess, with a violence that betrayed crazed terrors, dragged the Margrave away. The latter, dazzled and fascinated, but yielding with a kind of fright that had replaced confidence, allowed himself to be led. He found his horse outside the door, took the Countess in his arms, and climbed into the saddle.

As he was about to shake the bridle, an idea occurred to him. "We're forgetting your children, Madame. Where are they?"

The Countess twisted in the Margrave's arms like a serpent thrown on to a fire; she looked at him with frightened eyes, placing her trembling hand on his shoulder. He repeated his question. She replied, her teeth clenched, with a hiss: "You're asking for my sons! But did you not tell me that their eyes could not contemplate our happiness?"

"It was the eyes of my father and mother that I feared on your behalf, not those of your children, Madame—but my father and my mother having consented to our marriage..."

The Countess cut him off with a frightful scream. "You're lying!" she said, deliriously. "You're lying! It's impossible! I could not have become an unnatural and sacrilegious mother in vain!"

The Margrave understood everything. He parted his arms in horror; the Countess slid to the ground, but, immediately coming to her feet, she clutched at the saddle, the stirrups, and the prince's hands, uttering faltering moans.

As for him, glacial and terrible, unable to find any cry to express the frightful ripping of his soul, as inflexible as God's curse, he thrust the child-murderer away with his foot, who ran into the castle, roaring. Then, causing the horse's blood to spurt with his spurs, he rode through the gate flat out...

The road circled around the manor; as he galloped along the lakeside, the Margrave perceived the Countess leaning over the terrace; the breeze brought him these words, uttered with all the force of despair: "Margrave of Baden, whether you like it or not, there is a pact of blood between your family and mine! I am yours for all eternity!"

Then the countess was seen to extend her arms and jump; the waters of the lake were agitated; the price uttered a violent cry and wanted to run to the rescue—but he thought that he ought not dispute that criminal's fate with the judgment of Heaven.

The Margrave returned to the Duchy of Baden, to die there after a few months of languor. Remorse for the crime of which he was innocent crushed him and led him to the tomb. By virtue of a singular whim, he wanted to have in his room, beside the bed, a portrait of Countess Olamünde. He sent agents to Denmark to seek out the magnificent painting that you have seen.

A few days before his death, the young margrave affirmed that he had seen the Countess. His tearful parents tried to persuade him that it was a hallucination of his fever, but he persisted, and said to his aged father who sought to reassure him: "You will see her too, Father!"

Indeed, when the old duke died, a few years after his son, he similarly affirmed that he had encountered the phantom of Countess Olamünde in the corridors of the castle. Since then, it has been a tradition of the House of Baden that when a prince of the family is about to die, the White Lady appears to him.

"And now," the dowager added, "you will no longer doubt the reality of our presentiments, when you hear that Countess Olamünde has been seen three times since His Highness Leopold fell ill..."

As she concluded her story, the Baroness von B*** unrolled her knitting, set the needles in motion again, and awaited the young Frenchman's impressions. When the latter did not say anything, the dowager asked him what he thought.

"I'm searching for the moral of the story," he replied.

"Behold the skeptic!" she said, laughing. "You take our national history for an imitation of Bluebeard."

"No, Madame; I know that all royal castles have owls in their cornices, and that on certain nights those lugubrious birds flap their wings in the great halls. In France it's the little red man of the Tuileries; in Prussia it's the woman with the broom; in Norway..."

"Enough! Enough!" said the dowager, whose patriotism was offended, and who was too insistent on the originality of Badois legends to content to seeing them confounded with all superstitions of the same stripe.

The young Frenchman fell silent, and, after offering his thanks, changed the subject. However, as he was taking his leave of the Baroness, he moved closer to her and said to her, as he kissed her hand: "I've discovered the moral of your legend."

The dowager von B*** shrugged her shoulders. "Let's hear this discovery!"

"Your story demonstrates clearly that young men expose themselves to great dangers when they want to marry widows who have children."

The Baroness turned her back on him and nursed her resentment for three days. At the end of that interval, she consented to forgive him, on his solemn attestation that he firmly believed in the apparition of Countess Olamünde. That response was no more than a polite concession to hospitality, and we ought to declare that the Frenchman went back to France with as little superstition as he had left,

As for Grand Duke Leopold, he was too perfect a German to give the lie to the national legend, so he died punctually at the end of April 1852, in spite of the assurances of his physicians, and for the greater glory of the White Lady.

Paris, 1854.

THE LITTLE RED MAN

One morning in the month of October in the year 1773, when the entire court was at Versailles, three young women, who had doubtless made plans to breathe the final perfumes of autumn, went into the park before anyone else was awake, holding hands and talking about a thousand things. They sometimes paused to hurl bursts of laughter and lines of songs into the marble face of some old astonished faun, and then went on their way at random, without appearing to have any other objective than to breathe as much of their air of liberty as possible, and to trample with their little dew-dampened feet the leaves that were beginning to fall.

All three of them were beautiful, with the primal beauty of youth that derives as much from the purity of the soul as the purity of the lines of the face, and those three limpid foreheads, which were brightened by a serene inner light, animated the deserted pathways like a poetic vision. Had it not been for the mantlets that each of them pulled around their shoulders from time to time when the breeze rose slightly, and the clouds of powder that remained from the previous day's toilette in their curly hair, one might have been able, in that time of gallantry, in the midst of that mythological garden, to compare them to three nymphs emerged from tree-trunks searching the avenues for some sylvan to torment, or some sleeping shepherd to drive to despair. But that day, the three matinal divinities—to continue the gallant metaphor—seemed to have forgotten to steep their beautiful eyes with victorious darts, and appeared to have come into the park in a vulgar and human fashion to twitter away there at their ease, while listening to the bird twittering.

It was with the most sincere enthusiasm that the three deities of the court of Louis XV forgot the Olympus, then best by mortal ennui, of which they were the ornament. To judge by the clamor of their voices and their free movements, one might have thought that they had taken flight from one of those sad aviaries known as convents, and were of a mind to make up for all the time of lost gaiety.

One of them, especially, whose simple peignoir of gray taffeta tied with black velvet ribbons contrasted with the lavish embroidered and florally-enameled dresses of her two companions, seemed to be avidly enjoying a few hours of stolen independence from etiquette. From time to time, she glanced in the direction of the doors of the palace with a little resentful moue that required no commentary.

Suddenly, she stopped, and, raising her pretty shoulders as if to shake off heavy memories that were pressing on them, she said: "Mesdames, does it not seem to you that this life is torture? Personally, I'd gladly exchange the destiny that awaits me, and which you probably envy me, to become a simple little girl again, running and playing in the green by-ways of my homeland."

"Alas, my dear," another replied, "what is the homeland you speak of by comparison with the Savoy?"

"Oh, yes, the Savoy," added the third, with a deep sigh.

"Will you please be quiet, with your silly expressions," the young woman with the black ribbons replied, smiling. "It seems to me that you have lips full of snow, and you're making me shiver merely by talking about it."

"Have you not seen our mountains, my sister?"

"Have the two of you seen Vienna, my sisters? You see, the most beautiful place in the world is one's homeland, and the homeland is where one loves and is beloved."

"In that case, you're French, you stubborn Austrian!"

"French! No, not at all—not as much as I'd like to be." And she paused to wipe away a tear that as shining among her long lashes. A word emitted at hazard had just awakened painful thoughts.

They walked on for a few moments among the hornbeams, without speaking and without even looking at one another, each one relaxing into her reverie. Finally, the one who had interrupted herself continued: "If Louis had wanted it, however…!"

"Hope, my friend, hope."

"Alas, I no longer hope—I regret."

"Well, you bad girl, at least try to regret patiently."

"That's it! Wait, always wait! But who can tell whether the coldness of a husband that I love might not last forever? So you think that in becoming less young, one becomes more smitten? You don't understand it; you're happy, you're beloved. But since I've been in France, I've reflected a great deal, and I have more experience than you, Mesdames; when one is suffering, one might as well be old at seventeen!"

As she said that, she passed the prettiest hand in the world over her dewy and transparent temples, as if searching for wrinkles and to detect her suffering there. A smile of incredulity was the mute commentary of her two friends; as for the young victim of neglect, she seemed to have fallen back into her meditation momentarily.

Meanwhile, the excursion that no one had yet had any idea of cutting short, so pleasant did it seem to wander thus at their ease, even chatting—or, rather, especially chatting—about their petty chagrins, had extended a long way, and they were already far advanced into the park when, at the corner of an avenue, the three young women heard a noise. They stopped immediately, raising their pretty heads in surprise, and they stood still, listening with palpitating hearts, breathing the air in the charming fashion of startled hinds.

"If someone were to see us!" said one of them, in a low voice.

"If someone were to recognize us!" said a second.

"If the king knew!" added the third

And they all turned aside, in order to go forward, raising themselves up on tiptoe, to scout out the enemy and identify him.

"Shh!" said the boldest of the three, eventually, who had just gone to explore a suspect arbor. "It's coming from in there!"

They conferred in whispers, and then moved forward with the utmost precaution, waiting to take each step until the rustling caused by the previous footfall on the leaves had died down, and parting the hornbeams as they went, until they reached the place from which the mysterious rumor was emerging. Then, climbing on to a bench that happened to be there and moving a few branches with the reticent curiosity that the three young women were experiencing, torn between the desire to know and the dread of learning too much, they urged one another to take a look.

One put an end to her resolution and extended her neck ; a second, emboldened, leaned on her companion's shoulder in order to do likewise; then the third, not wanting to have more scruples than her two friends, slid her anxious head between the two that he preceded it. All three linked arms in order to support one another, leaning forward with the same movement, and were then able to see at their ease.

Four your women, sitting in the middle of the arbor, each with an open notebook in her hand, were lending a somewhat mutinous attention to a handsome young man standing in front of them. He was complaining and they were arguing. He was trying to give his voice the exaggerated tones of a false anger, and they were interrupting him and giggling. Then the disconcerted speaker plunged his right hand into the gap in his waistcoat, while his right hand crumpled a manuscript stitched together with pink ribbons, at which he gazed despairingly, as if calling upon it urgently as a witness.

Modestly dressed in a brown buckram jacket, wearing his unpowdered dark hair long and loose, contrary to the fashions of the period, pale, with large blue eyes, a high forehead and protruding veins, the orator of the arbor displayed in his face and attitude the feverish animation that makes one dream so many beautiful things and say so many silly ones between the ages of sixteen and twenty. One divined, by the seemingly-luminous kind of sweat that bathes inspired faces, that his soul was tormenting his body. He had to be an embryonic man of ambition, or a madman, or a poet. As we shall discover, by keeping company with the three young ladies behind the horn-beams, he was a poet—which also means, of course, a man of ambition and a madman.

Adrien, for that was what one of his companions had just called him, had just left school; at present, he was confiding—to ears too frivolous to understand them, according to him, the precious fruit of a year of divagation and enthusiasm. At all times, the schoolboys of all lands have been labored, at the age when the passions awake and love is glimpsed, by that ardor of expansion that is most commonly expressed in verse. Poetry is the dew of early years; the midday sun subsequently causes it to rise and drinks it all.

In the epoch in which our story is set, youth had not yet thought of turning its enthusiasms toward abstractions and despair. One did not make one's debut with a plaint against the century. Maladies of the lungs generally respected poets. It was the heyday of the idyll, but the idyll in furbelows. The first muse was young, curly-haired, powdered and wore a floral hat; sometimes she chased snow-white sheep before her with an elegant crook; despairs were modulated on a bagpipe; there were no vile pistols or heavy gas to aid the suffocations of a misunderstood love, but emblematic birds in little reed cages, knotted ribbons around bouquets of roses: all the frivolous and coquettish apparel that rendered Olympus uninhabitable without a dresser and a coiffeur. The eighteenth century dolled up the scraps of the seventeenth; the pretty and the dainty replaced the beautiful and the severe; Marivaux and Florian became the leaders of schools, like Watteau and Boucher.

Adrien would necessarily have satisfied the dominant taste of the era. In his long reveries, along the obscure corridors of the Oratorian college where he had studied, which had made is young head seethe, there was a vision that remained with him of a fête at Versailles in which he had glimpsed little feet shod in white satin, the beautiful heads of duchesses in aureoles of powder, handsome aristocrats in velvet garments. His father, who had a modest employment at court, had told him marvelous stories about what could be seen in antechambers; and all those memories, all those images had taken on a luminous form in fixing themselves in an eighteen-year-old imagination. You will not be astonished, therefore, to learn that Adrien, at the moment when we make his acquaintance, was in the process of conducting a rehearsal of a three-act pastoral in verse, into which he had poured all the ardors of his soul and all the riches of his fantasy.

In this regard, I doubt that Corneille, that author of *Le Cid*, who despised with modesty because genius was sufficient for him, and who was frankly great, had a breast swollen with more pride, on hearing his Rodrigue speak, than our young poet had in reading aloud his innocent declamations. He would gladly have put on his hat: *I am Adrien, the author of Agénor et Chloé*! But, forced to renounce that unusual form of publicity, Adrien had had recourse to four young women of his own age, and it had been agreed that, for the birthday of one of his parents, our poet would have the satisfaction of seeing his work performed, as best it could be—but performed, at any rate—by his childhood companions.

Given the disposition of the play, which was very clever, although very natural in appearance, there was only one male role, which alleviated many difficulties. First of all, no other adolescent would have found himself admitted to the intimacy of these demoiselles, and Adrien was pleased with his isolation, which was not without charm; secondly, the admission of other male characters would have produced rivalries regarding the distribution of parts. So, in order to avoid having to defend or yield the leading roles, Adrien had said to himself: *There will only be one male role and I shall play it*. That way, there would be no arguments! He would not offend anyone, would remain in charge of the company and could act as its master. That last privilege, however, was hotly contested, and, as we shall see, Adrien experienced in his autocracy all the inconveniences of constitutional government; he reigned, but did not govern.

Let us return now to take our place beside the three young women behind the hornbeams. That rather long digression was necessary. In order for his conduct is to be understood, Adrien's character had to be explained. Having done that, let us get back to his sheep, for there were—or rather there were supposed to be—sheep in the play; the embarrassment of disciplining that unintelligent part of the company had caused them to be omitted in reality, although they still had to subsist in the imagination of the audience.

Our poet had been unable to make the sacrifices to female vanity on which he had courageously resolved for reasons of masculine self-respect. Unless he composed a dialogue, in the strict acceptance of the term, he was obliged, in the interests of plausibility, and perhaps also for the sake of the magnificence of his play, to admit more than one female role. We dare not say that that was a mistake, but it was certainly a misfortune. Until this final rehearsal, which was decisive—the play was to be solemnly performed the next day—the roles had been studied separately, without worrying about their relative importance; but when they came together, and the position of each one was designated, there were exclamations of surprise, resentment and disappointment; thus was produced the tumult that had distracted the three young ladies during their stroll in the park.

According to the poet, Agénor, the prince or marquis of a country forgotten by map—but not by the Carte de Tendre[20]—

---

[20] The *Carte de Tendre* [Chart of Affection] was an actual document produced as an amusement by several hands, working in collaboration, which was reproduced as an engraving in the first volume of Madeleine de Scudéry's novel *Clélie* (1654). It offers a symbolic representation of the path to love, in which the river of Inclination flows through such villages as Billet Doux, three alternative routes taking it to worthy destinations, while a few side-branches lead to dead ends. Passion, by contrast, sails the uncharted and reef-strewn *Mer Dangereuse*.

guided by desire, very innocent for a marquis, to pick a bouquet of wild flowers, was wandering sadly through a meadow when at the foot of a willow tree, he suddenly discovered a shepherdess, peacefully asleep. At the sight of her, transports of delight caused Agénor to forget the glamour of courts and the sumptuous elegance of great ladies. The charming simplicity of the shepherdess—in a white satin dress and a straw hat ornamented with ribbons a flowers, holding a similarly beribboned crook—bowled him over. He knelt on the grass and threw himself into the most hyperbolic exclamation that ever made tender green foliage tremble in an eclogue.

Meanwhile, the shepherdess woke up and, understandably confused by having been taken by surprise in the joys of sleep, apologized with a naïve grace that completed the turmoil in the head of the sentimental marquis. Delicate insinuations were then made with the aim of ascertaining where there might perchance be a vacancy in the heart of the delightful shepherdess.

On Chloé's confession that only the countryside in spring and a few lambs in her flock had, for the time being, found the flowery path of her soul, Agénor, authorizing himself by the example of a great lord of antiquity named Hercules, who had spun at the knees of a great lady name Omphale, had no scruple about falling at Chloé's feet, offering her his heart, his hand and his name, calculating with sufficient justice that the distance between a marquis and a shepherdess is the equivalent of that between a demigod and a princess.

These heroic sentiments certainly did great honor to a marquis of that era, when prejudice had greater empire, but the young woman who was charged with playing the role of Chloé did not want things to happen thus. Under the pretext—frivolous, to say the least—that she did not want to sleep in public, she demanded that Adrien change the scene. Then again, as the heroine, she claimed the right not to commence the act, and only to appear after having waited for a while; that, in her opinion, was the means of producing the greatest effect.

Adrien was not at all convinced, for numerous excellent reasons, but it was impossible for him to explain them, as he was being tormented by the rest of the troupe, who were also soliciting numerous changes.

In the second act, Agénor and Chloé, arm in arm, went to offer a cage, in which two doves were sighing, to a locally-celebrated prophetess, who was to pronounce a verdict on the union insistently claimed by Agénor and gently refused by Chloé. The prophetess in question, in Adrien's conception, ought to be enveloped in a loose black robe whose dark color and amplitude seemed an insult offered to the elegant and gracious contours of the figure of the actress, as well as to the freshness of her youth. The latter was, therefore, complaining about not being clad in a satin dress, as Chloé was.

A third actress, for analogous reasons, did not want to appear too old, while appearing as the grandmother of the shepherdess, She consented to understand and bless the amours of her grandchildren, but only on condition that it was made manifest that it was not solely the effect of memory and regret on her part. In addition, she was superstitious and dreaded that the temporary disguise might bring hr bad luck; she was afraid of not reverting thereafter to the young and pretty girl she had been before, and of really aging.

Finally, there remained a fourth, even more difficult to satisfy. Her entire role displeased her—and yet, the ingrate, she was playing a priestess living in, or ostensibly living in a temple of jasper ornamented with flowers. She it was, according to the rites of the little-known country, who had to sanctify the union of Agénor and Chloé, and marry them by virtue of love and her magic wand. As she did not appear until the denouement, however, she judged that there was no point in creating a role for four lines and wanted the role either to be extended or abolished completely.

Adrien found himself, in consequence, greatly embarrassed. He did not know how to respond. He exhorted them all, begged them with joined hands, lamented the destiny of poets, and sought to make the grace and simplicity of his pastoral work understood.

Wasted effort! They all seemed to be conspiring to drive him to despair.

There was a moment when, no longer able to contain himself, he threw is manuscript away, folded his arms and raised his eyes to the heavens, as if requesting that they bear witness and to implore the intervention of some Providence.

Suddenly, it seemed to him that his wish had been granted, and that the Providence in question had come—an angel, a fairy or an enchantress—to help him and extract him from difficulty. The foliage in front of him parted gently, and a radiant face showed itself in the midst of the branches, gazing at him with an expression of compassion and sympathy.

At that sweet apparition, the poet, his eyes staring and his hands extended, was on the brink of proclaiming a prodigy, when the sight of two more beautiful faces framing the first, and a few trivial details of attire doubtless unfamiliar to celestial providences, caused him to tumble from the heights of ecstasy and caused him to think that they might simply be three curious young women, listening to what he said and witnessing his humiliation.

For their part, the three ladies, seeing that they had been discovered, bravely advanced through the foliage that could no longer serve to hide them, and leapt into the middle of the arbor. After a profound bow to the stupefied assembly, the one who was wearing a peignoir and seemed to be the most determined of the three, took the floor.

"Monsieur et Mesdemoiselles," she said, "forgive us for having disturbed you. My friends and I were walking in the park; the noise of your dispute drew us in this direction, and we've been listening for half an hour. Now that we're up to date with the affair, would you like us to arbitrate? Have no fear, Mesdemoiselles; we appreciate your forceful reasons—and you, Monsieur poet, please believe that we understand the full value of your beautiful lines."

At this proposition, made in a slightly mocking tone, the insurgents bowed their heads without making any reply; they were ashamed of having been caught in *flagrante delicto* in their vanity and teasing. In general, if women fear the judgment of other women, it is because they know full well that their judges will pronounce in accordance with the denunciations of their own conscience, and that there is no reply possible to conclusions that commence with a confession.

Adrien was therefore very glad of such a gracious intervention, while his four companions, humiliated and nonplussed, were beginning to regret their disputes to direct more conciliatory gazes toward him. It therefore required little argument on the part of the three unknown women to determine the mutinous debutantes to recognize their sins and rein in their pretentions.

Chloé asked for nothing better than to be asleep in the first scene; the prophetess consented to the costume in question; the girl playing the role of the grandmother subscribed, in all their rigor, to the requirements of her role; and the priestess, this time exaggerating her zeal, proposed that if her friends thought she had too much to say that it should be cut in half, reduced from four lines to two.

Adrien refused that sacrifice, but was not entirely convinced of the good will of his troupe. He advanced, trembling with a delightful emotion, toward the young lady in the gray peignoir, expressed his gratitude in a stammering fashion, and concluded, with the aid of respectful circumlocutions, by asking her to come and witness herself, with her two friends, the solemn representation of his pastoral.

That invitation, addressed with joined hands and an imploring gaze, made the three young ladies smile and glance at once another. Before replying, they appeared to confer together. It was deducible from their whispering that it was not an easy thing for them to accept.

Finally, after a very animated deliberation, in which the majority seemed to be in favor of refusal, the young lady in the peignoir, whom we have seen exercising a certain ascendancy over her two friends, and who constituted a very influential minority, took the responsibility of acceptance upon herself. Turning her head from right to left and from left to right with vivacity, like someone refusing to hear any more, who wants to dispel poor reasons, she replied to the delighted Adrien that, on the following evening, they would all three be glad to come and applaud *Agénor et Chloé*.

The time and place were settled; then, after deep curtsies, mingled with some embarrassment on the part of the young actresses and full of affability on the part of the three unknowns, they went their separate ways, the latter to return to the château, the former to replace with distractions of a less noisy kind the stormy debates of the rehearsal.

Now, when the young woman what was to play the part of Chloé's grandmother the following day closed her lovely eyes in order that they might be covered with the innocent blindfold of blind man's bluff, and Adrien, having put all the cares of a director in his pocket, along with his handkerchief, set about tightening his muslin cravat with the most rigorous severity over the charming eyelids of the pretty duenna, the latter pinched his ear and said to him: "Adrien, do you know who those three young ladies were?"

"No, Amélie, do you?"

"Oh! I thought I recognized them."

"Well?"

"Either I'm much mistaken, or the two sisters in embroidered dresses are the two princesses of Savoy, the Comtesse de Provence and the Comtesse d'Artois."

"Are you sure, Amélie? What about the lady in the peignoir?"

"The lady in the peignoir must then be our gracious dauphine, Marie-Antoinette."

"Is that possible? My God! The princesses alone in the park!"

"I can assure you, Adrien, that it was them."

"And I invited them to our fête! How they must be laughing at me now!"

"You mean at us, Adrien."

"Oh, no, at me alone—I was the one who issued the invitation."

"Do you think so? It seemed to me that they accepted in good faith."

"What folly! The princesses! The dauphine!"

"We shall see, won't we?"

"Alas!"

"Don't worry about it!"

"Above all, Amélie, don't tell the others—they'd make fun of me."

"Have you quite finished?" cried the lovely demoiselle who was to lend her pretty face the next day to the shepherdess Chloé, and who was a trifle jealous of the prince's tête-à-tête with her pretty grandmother.

"It's done," was the reply—and the young woman with the bandaged eyes launched herself into the avenue, extending her arms, running to the right and the left, everywhere she could hear laughter and chatter.

There was a long interval of gaiety then, and vocal outbursts worthy of bringing smiles to the faces of the marble gods, the insensible inhabitants of the park.

Meanwhile, Adrien, bowled over by the confidence he had just received, had retired to a corner and set about dreaming profoundly; and while his friends frolicked and let the hours pass insouciantly, he put his hands to his heart, which was beating violently in his chest, and murmured in a low voice: "As long as they come tomorrow!"

What did the ambitious poet hope to come, then, from the august presence of the three grand-daughters of Louis XV at the performance of his pastoral? We cannot say. That evening, however, when he went into his bedroom, he went to kneel down at the foot of the bed, then joined his hands with fervor, and, gazing at the starry heavens through his window, he said in a soft voice:

"Dear God, who have taken my mother and refused me a sister, you know that I'm alone, and that those innocent young girls will never understand all the love and faith that there is in my soul; you, who have caused me to be born proud in order to conserve me as a poet, I beg you, O my God, to permit that the angel who will one day love me, who will come to claim her part in my burden and whom I shall name me wife, shall be as gentle, good and beautiful as Her Highness Madame la Dauphine Marie-Antoinette."

Having said that prayer, he lay down, and did not sleep a wink all night.

All the annoyances that Adrien had experienced in bringing his pastoral to completion, all the anxieties that the coquetry and caprices of his troupe had caused him, were forgotten. His work, so long caressed in the shadow of his soul, was finally about to appear in the broad daylight of publicity, and the gracious children of his imagination, whose innocent chatter had filled all the echoes of his head and his heart for such a long time, were about to receive the baptism of his family's applause.

Certainly, in default of a numerous audience, there was already a great joy for our poet in bringing tears to the eyes of a hundred people, even in the land of acquaintance. We can therefore affirm that Adrien experienced the overflow of joy mingled with disturbance that a first performance always causes. The chances of success were good, the sympathy of the audience was acquired, and we could not explain the provenance of the slight cloud that occasionally veiled the radiance of his brow if we were not in the confidence of his ambitious hope.

He attached a superstitious notion to the coming, which was rather improbable, of the three princesses. It seemed to him that to triumph in the eyes of the grand-daughters of the king was to triumph in the eyes of the entire court, and it seemed to the presumptuous poet that an approving smile from those three divinities would transport his Parnassus to Olympus. Perhaps the ideal of glory was not alone in agitating his heart, and more temeritous hopes were germinating there, without his daring to admit them to himself in the utmost depths of his thoughts. At any rate, he had been in a fever since the morning, and in moments when his delirium could be exhaled without witnesses, he surprised himself by appealing to the three noble visitors to the arbor aloud, by darting to one side and the other the intoxicated and ecstatic glances of a conqueror who wants to please, and passing his hand violently through his hair, making it stand up on his head, like a madman trying to lift himself up by that means and place himself on a pedestal.

Thus, the hours that went by until the time came for the performance appeared to him to be very long; he thought he had lived a week in a day, and when the sun, to whom he had addressed the wish of Joshua twenty times over since its rise, slowly set behind the yellowing trees of the park, he ran, quivering with joy, to preside over the installation of his theater.

The material part of his task did not offer any less difficulty than the speculative part, and the embarrassments of the stage-manager were equal to the worries of the director. The problem that the poet had to solve in order to surround his pastoral with as much magnificence as possible was, given a chamber, to construct with the aid of two armchairs, a curtain, a screen and a carpet, a landscape in which beautiful green trees provide melancholy shade for a sleeping shepherdess, in which the blue sky, filtering the rays of a sun such as is only seen in eclogues, is mirrored in crystal waves; in which meadows enameled with flowers serve as tender pasture for little white sheep.

We already know how the flock was only to appear in the dialogue, but it was impossible, in the absence of any form of illusion, for the scenery and other accessories also to be relegated to conversation. It was therefore necessary to utilize the resources of the store-room. The carpet employed as a backcloth was already a fortunate find. Apart from the fact that magnificent birds—peacocks with large tails, pheasants and swans—were needlessly spread all over it, the neatly-woven trees were satisfactory to obliging eyes. It is certain that no one would quibble about the border of flowers and fruits that framed the forest. The screen could serve both to hide the actors and complete the horizon. A broad sky, turquoise in color, pretty, well-painted trees, finely designed pathways, silvery waterfalls and, on boldly-projected bridges, fishermen clad in lampas and dangling huge golden fish on the end of their lines—all that was a luxury of ornamentation that Adrien could use to his profit. It is true that the landscape, with its kiosks fitted with bell-turrets, its fishermen with long moustaches, had a certain Chinese air about it that might be misinterpreted, but in the evening, thanks to a complaisance of the imagination that did not prohibit transporting the action to the vicinity of Peking, everything might settle into place—and everything did.

The shepherdess Chloé installed herself as best she could in an armchair that had to pass for a grassy bank, and, the three strokes having been solemnly sounded, Adrien pulled back the large curtain that hid the splendors of the theater from the public. Then, the last duty of the stage-manager fulfilled, he went behind the screen and made his entrance, in the midst of the applause of all the spectators.

Fortunately for the poet, it was almost impossible for him not to remember his lines, because he was momentarily stunned, dazzled and overwhelmed, not knowing where he was, speaking the first verses of his pastoral mechanically and unconsciously. One sole idea was whirling in his head and confusing everything: his eyes wandered from side to side, only seeking to recognize a single person, and his straining ear only aspired sound with the chimerical aim of assuring himself as to whether, amid the applause, he could distinguish the sound of two small hands that he had glimpsed the day before.

When the first act finished, the spectators stamped their feet. Grandparents wept. It was a concert of praise that would have overwhelmed the most modest poet, but Adrien did not hear it. He had retired behind the screen, pale, his eyes swollen with tears. What good was all the testimony of listeners indulgent by reason of vanity and ignorance? The embraces and blessings with which he was threatened seemed to him to be an odious disappointment by comparison with the ineffable smile from royal lips for which he had hoped.

The unfortunate poet was deeply disenchanted. The glory that he had personified in one of the three princesses had already played him false. Thus, it was with a profound discouragement and an inexpressibly heavy heart that he reappeared in the second act.

Gradually, however, the verses that he recited carelessly warmed his lips as they flowed over them; gradually, the poetry that he could not touch without something vibrating within him raised his head again and reilluminated his eyes. Then, in a desperate effort, he contrived to look out into the hall, and—good God!—what became of him when he perceived, ten paces away from him, three mantlets and three commonplace bonnets, beneath which he recognized the gracious trinity of the arbor and his dreams!

He stopped in the middle of his line; the joy that flooded his heart prevented him from speaking; then, with a gesture that must have seemed strange to the actress in the scene, he put his hands together as one does in ecstasy, and let himself lapse into a contemplation from which Chloé had a good deal of difficulty extracting him.

Until the last line of the play, there were henceforth two men within him: the one who was giving the replies and declaiming, the other indifferent to everything, concentrating his entire soul in his eyes and his eyes on a single point.

In spite of those distractions, everything went well, and the denouement, touching in its simplicity, produced an irresistible effect.

Adrien was, therefore, subjected to congratulations that were for him pure torture. Finally, when the tumult of conversations and commentaries was well enough established for him to be able to escape, he ran to the place where the three princesses were. He was afraid that, in the fear of being recognized, they might already have withdrawn, but he saw, on the contrary, that they were waiting for him.

172

Confused and trembling, he advanced, tried to speak, but could only bow profoundly, murmuring: "Highnesses!"

At that word, a blush of resentment and disappointment passed over the three august faces, and Marie-Antoinette, who seemed to take the responsibility for initiative upon herself in all circumstances, put a finger over her lips to demand silence from Adrien.

Smiling, she said to him: "I see, Monsieur, that it is necessary to renounce our role as unknown Providence. That's a pity, but I hope that the princesses have not been undeserving of the confidence you accorded yesterday to the three indiscreet individuals in the arbor."

"Oh, if only I'd known!"

"You would have declined our intervention, wouldn't you? That would have been wrong of you. But when we lost the prestige of anonymity that rendered us so powerful, Monsieur, as we were decidedly very curious, we wanted to know who the young unknown poet was whose anguish we had soothed. Your father, whom we chanced to address for that purpose, informed us fully. It was him who took responsibility for bringing us here, and it's him that we have asked to escort us back to the château. Now listen to me, Monsieur Adrien; you are frank and honest, and it will not be in vain that one appeals to your devotion and discretion."

"Highness, my life would be torn out of me before a secret!"

"Oh, it's not a matter of putting your life in danger. My God, how dramatic these poets are! The conspiracy that we would like you to initiate—for it is a conspiracy—is entirely peaceful. What we would like to overthrow is the ennui that reigns at court, and we are only conspiring to amuse ourselves. Don't think, therefore, of perilous sacrifices; merely present yourself at the château tomorrow morning; have the manuscript of *Agénor et Chloé* under your arm, and you'll know them what we require of you. *Au revoir*, then, Monsieur—until tomorrow. Be punctual. Above all, don't forget the pastoral."

And before the poet, confused and disturbed, was able to find a response, the three princesses had disappeared. There is no need to add that Adrien did not sleep any more that night than the previous one.

The next day, dressed up, made up and resplendent, carrying his head high, trying to impart the solemnity of a conqueror to his stride and surprising himself by jumping for joy, tormenting a ruff of freshly-starched lace with a feverish hand, his hat under his arm and a radiance in his eyes, as pale as an ambitious man within reach of a reward and as starved as a lover who lives entirely in heaven, the poet presented himself at the château. The password having been given, he was introduced into a small drawing-room in the entresol, where the three princesses were assembled, and behind their armchairs, the three princes, their spouses.

Adrien would have preferred not to encounter those august protectors. Having not stopped in his bold suppositions, and being internally flattered to have a secret in common with the king's grand-daughters, he was momentarily disappointed by the presence of the husbands, but he was soon consoled.

Marie-Antoinette explained to her stupefied and dazzled friend that she had conceived a plan to organize a theater in the petty apartments, and that it was his work that had been judged worthy of opening the series of performances. She even went so far as to let it be understood, as she had the day before, that the court was suffering a great ennui, and that it was to counter that ennui that the young dauphine had had the idea of staging a comedy.

Adrien was slightly surprised to learn that people could become bored at court, but he told himself silently that perhaps the complaint was a pretext invented to cover the urgency that was being put into applauding his work. Poets always have such fashions of explaining things away, but in fact nothing was more true. The court, toward the end of 1773, seemed to have been struck by the paralysis that sometimes precedes death by a short interval. People were no longer talking, but whispering; the corruption of the courtiers was the same, but it had lost the kind of cynicism that had been able to excuse it during the regency and the early years of the reign. The debauchery had become hypocritical, which left it hideous.

In his intervals of rationality, the king, old and suffering, having lost his taste for pleasures and only running hither and yon out of vestigial habit, sensing that the throne was creaking beneath him and that his successor's task would be a heavy one, sighed and bowed his head before the thought of the future. "Poor France!" he had said, a few years before. "A king fifty years old and a dauphin of eleven!" The Dauphin had grown up, but the embarrassment of the crown had increased, and Louis XV, who, when he made that exclamation, already understood the inevitable slope down which the monarchy was rolling, now closed his eyes to hide his tears and in order not to see the abyss.

The depression and disgust that seizes a man whose entire life has been given to dissipation in his declining years is a surprising, and almost providential thing to behold. When a sensualist senses that the terrestrial world is escaping him, he becomes frightened of the unknown and celestial world in which he begins to believe. Souls devastated by the passions are afraid of the night of the tomb, as children are of the obscurity of the dusk. The imagination that has nourished itself in caprices and whims finds reality monstrous, and those who have abused the emotions end up developing a strange impressionability. They were crazed in their joy, they are exaggerated in their sadness. Louis XIV, by the austere fireside of Madame de Maintenon, prayed piteously for the redemption of his sins, and Louis XV, in the milieu of Versailles, depopulated of amours, took pleasure in funereal ideas.[21]

---

[21] The author inserts a supportive citation from the memoirs of the Nicole du Hausset, one of Madame de Pompadour's chambermaids, here: "King Louis XV was extremely melancholy, and liked anything that recalled the idea of death, while dreading it greatly."

One can imagine, therefore, how the dauphine and the two young princesses of Savoy, all three young and pretty, all three cheerful and insouciant, must have suffered in that dismal and dispirited court. In an era when Louis XV spent entire hours watching the clouds pass over the park and the leaves turning yellow, it would have been a crime of lèse-majesté to manifest the intention of amusing oneself, so the three young rebels had taken the greatest precautions to maintain silence regarding their plans.

Marie-Antoinette had shown herself the most impatient to liberate herself from the ennui; she was the soul of the conspiracy, for she was the one who was suffering the most. Lively and bright, devoid of false coquetry, habituated by her mother Marie-Thérèse to a simple and modest life, understanding that dignity resides less in vague precautions than in self-respect, she had felled chilled on entering Versailles, by the ceremony that preceded her slightest movement. Then, she had experienced regrets and presentiments, and had thrown herself into the arms of the Duchess de Noailles, her maid of honor, begging her to love and guide her.[22]

Madame de Noailles, however, whose rigidity in observing traditions and customs had earned her the nickname of Madame Etiquette, was exactly the person who was to be least sympathetic to the young and independent dauphine. The latter was thus obliged to turn her gaze in another direction. The dauphin, from whom she had a right to expect affection, showed an inexplicable indifference toward his young spouse, a coldness that often degenerated into harshness. That disdain for so much youth and beauty, whether it sprang from intrigues on the part of courtiers or whether it resulted from the prince's natural apathy, had offended the proud and loving heart of the dauphine.

---

[22] This detail is historically inaccurate; Sophie de Noailles, Comtesse de Toulouse, who married one of Louis XIV's legitimized sons and became one of Louis XV's confidantes, died before Marie-Antoinette arrived in Versailles.

There remained, in consequence, for confidantes and friends, the two Comtesses de Provence and d'Artois. They welcomed their desolate sister-in-law with open arms. The three young foreigners became united by a keen amity, and found a great charm, as we have seen at the beginning of this story, in isolating themselves from the crowd of courtiers in order to talk, at their ease, about their absent homelands and their chagrins.

The encounter with Adrien in the park, however, and the performance that a disguise had permitted them to attend, had suddenly revealed to them a means of cheering up the winter, which seemed bound to be lugubrious at Versailles. The three spouses had immediately been taken into their confidence. Apart from the fact that it was scarcely possible to conceal the plans from them, they needed actors and an audience. The Comte de Provence and the Comte d'Artois gallantly subscribed to everything that was demanded of them. The former pledged himself for severe roles, the latter for amorous ones. The dauphin declined his services, and said that he would represent the audience. His two sisters-in-law wanted to insist that he lend a more active co-operation, but Marie-Antoinette, who doubtless had a secret reason for him to witness her success, decided that the troupe was sufficiently numerous and that her husband had all the desirable impartiality—she dared not say indifference—to be an excellent public. As she was ordinarily the arbiter of last resort, the question appeared to be settled, and it was agreed that it would be for the greater amusement of Monseigneur le Dauphin that Their Highnesses would make up a repertory.

The goal of the comedies not being purely literary, and the fantasy of costumes playing a major part in the pleasure that they anticipated, the future *fermière* of the Trianon wondered, while looking at herself in a mirror, whether an elegant shepherdess' costume, a hat ornamented with broad ribbons and a crook might not suit her. It was on the affirmative response of the mirror that Adrien was invited to come to the château with is pastoral—and, a few days later, everything was disposed in a room on the entresol for the debut of the new troupe and a second performance of *Agénor and Chloé.*

As we have said, every possible measure had been taken to ensure that not a word about the important project was breathed outside. They had to make certain that neither the king, who might be annoyed by it, nor Mesdames the princes' aunts, who would have been scandalized, nor the public, who would have mocked, ever learned about these scenic distractions, in which the role of Agénor was given to the young poet.

Since external etiquette must not suffer and no curious gaze could be allowed to penetrate as far as the illustrious actors, they thought that it would be unwise to deprive themselves of the benevolence of an intelligent actor whom they had seen at work and who would be a useful resource. Then again, they regarded it as a delightful prank to admit a young man of the people to participate in the amusements of princes. At the end of a reign in which the entire nobility had made it glorious sometimes to seek pleasure in the crowd, descending as low as necessary in order to encounter it, they had no qualms about indulging, within honest limits, in a little rakish fantasy, and "slumming" with a charming and loyal fellow: it was an innocent caprice that they were satisfying, without admitting it—but one that might cost a fanatic like Adrien dear.

Who could list all the intoxicating hopes that went through his young head? Him, the plebeian, the poor poet, living in intimacy with the greatest personages in the realm, acting on stage with Highnesses, and, in the quality of shepherd, putting himself at the knees of a future queen of France, taking her divinely beautiful hand, talking to her for entire hours, and seeing her smile: understanding her, in sum, exchanging with her the soft words of love that, although he had drawn them in advances from his own funds, would nonetheless appear to him, at certain moments, one either side, to be improvised.

That was enough to drive anyone mad; but Adrien soon lent himself to that magnificent dream. At his age one easily attains the height of exaggerations of fate. Gradually, it seemed to him that the distances were reduced. His timidity disappeared. He took on the allure of a marquis, and when he gave his performances, he entered proudly, his fist on is hip, feigning forgetfulness of the fact that his father introduced him clandestinely, and went up the hidden stairway that led to the meeting-place with the triumphant lightness of a elegant lord, content with himself and his ancestors, climbing the great stairway of the château on the day of a celebration.

The famous pastoral was performed with great success. The audience—which is to say, Monsieur le Dauphin, assisted by His Highness the Comte d'Artois, who had found no means of employment this time—covered the author, the actresses and the actors with applause.

We say "the actors" intentionally, for, although the poet had originally thought it prudent only to put one male role in his play, the impossibility of casting four ladies at the château had caused him subsequently to change the sparkling priestess of the denouement, who married the lovers with a crown of roses, into a majestic priest decorated with a venerable beard and hair "whitened by the snow of years." Monsieur le Comte de Provence was charged with the metamorphosis, and acquitted it in a fashion worthy of great eulogies. Monsieur struck poses that the foremost models of the Académie of Painting might have envied, and his gesture of benediction was utterly sublime.

The stage-setting bore a strong resemblance to the one deployed by Adrien for his first performance, except that, to one side, a huge cupboard, always open, seemed ready to swallow at the slightest sound the screens that formed the theater's entire scenic equipment. That was a precautionary measure, in case—although it was unlikely—someone in the château had occasion to come in. Rackets and shuttlecocks were diplomatically strewn on an armchair, similarly to serve, in the event of interruption, to deflect attention from Their

Highnesses' veritable recreations. A broad line traced in chalk indicated the limits of the stage, and took the place of the barrier to the indiscreet incursions of the public.

We have observed the legitimate success obtained by the pastoral, but what we have not mentioned in the very particular impression that it made on Monsieur le Dauphin. That day, he noticed for the first time that Madame la Dauphine had beautiful blue eyes and a nice figure, that all her movements were full of grace, that she spoke her lines with talent, that she had profited considerably from the lessons of Aufresnes and Sainville, two French actors who had been her speech tutors in Vienna, and that, in sum, the young Austrian, about whom he had been told so many bad things, might very well be a superior woman in terms of intelligence as well as beauty.

He observed that at a certain point in the play, when Agénor was excitedly proclaiming his love, tears appeared in her eyes, and that she seemed to be looking at him. That mute reproach went straight to his heart, and if a residue of shame prevented him, at the end of the performance, from coming to beg her pardon, frankly and humbly, it is still the case that he began from then on to applaud frantically; his enthusiasm even became so loud that the actors were obliged to interrupt themselves to recommend moderation; furthermore, they took advantage of the interruption to prohibit the applause of the public; perhaps it was a means of forbidding whistles. At any rate, the dauphin had to content himself with rapping lightly on the fabric of his hat—but that tolerance soon became a grave infraction, when His Highness, who was giving a remarkable imitation of the march of the French guards, let himself get carried away and played it entirely on the most sonorous part of his hat. There was a protest, and a reminder of the terms of the decree against marks of approval, but the prince, for his parts, claimed that he was furnishing agreeable accompaniments, and taking the place of the orchestra. Marie-Antoinette, who sensed that she had something to do with the expression of that tumultuous contentment, forgave him. Nevertheless, when they went, she made a comment about the incorrigibility of the public.

The success of that first attempt persuaded the actors to continue their experiments. Other plays were put on, in which Adrien naturally played his role. The poor child only rarely came down to earth; his days were spent in ineffable ecstasies and his nights in mad invocations. The image of the three princesses, and Marie-Antoinette in particular, floated incessantly before his eyes. He dared not look into the abyss that separated him from the dauphine, and sometimes surprised himself—the insensate!—wanting to reveal his agitation to her. He told himself that she would understand all the ardor and poetry that he had in his soul, and he dreamed of a sublime and chaste communion of ideas between the woman who would one day be queen of France and Navarre and him, the poet, who would also have his royalty and his crown.

The winter had passed in the midst of these amusements. Adrien's exaltation had only increased, and we cannot say what would have become of the impetuous flood of love that caused our young friend's heart to beat so violently, and threatened to burst forth at any moment, if an unexpected event had not cast a disturbance into those charming but dangerous pleasures.

It was in the month of April. His Majesty Louis XV, fatigued by a walk in the park, returning to the château, turned round to contemplate the last rays of the sun on the tender greenery of the trees. The birds, which were untroubled by the king's moods, were fluttering back and forth in the air, uttering their joyful and insolent notes like childish laughter. A gentle perfumed breeze as circulating in the foliage; the marble gods, over which the breeze agitated the silhouettes of branches, seemed to be trembling with ease and smiling at the spring. The arbors took on mysterious hues and invited conversation on the benches.

Everything, in sum, was resplendent with a calm and mild joy. One might have thought that Nature was in ecstasy, and the sky was so transparent that the eye sought God beyond it. But all that joy of the awakening earth sickened the soul of the king; that day, his funereal presentiments were agitating him, and, by virtue of a rather ordinary contrast, he saw hovering, in the midst of his lugubrious ideas, the phantom of his beautiful lost loves and his vanished felicities. The pathways along which he had just strolled, the bushy arbors that he no longer dared enter, which he venerated as the sanctuaries of his first illusions, had evoked numerous memories in him, and he climbed the stairway to the great apartments shaking his head sadly, like a man who has just said sad and painful good-byes.

When night fell, he was afraid. The obscurity, as it increased around him, seemed a funereal drape, and his room a tomb. He rang loudly to have the lamps lit. The glare of the candlelight brought a slight smile to his lips, but he soon fell back into melancholy, and then large tears swelled his eyelids and slid down his cheeks. The poor king sensed his decline, and reviewed his life. In the perfumes of spring he had rediscovered the perfumes of his youth, and the comparison with the present day with days gone by had depressed him.

For more than an hour he went back and forth from his armchair to the window, gazing at the stars that were shining like silver tears on mourning drapery, shivering at the thought that he might perhaps have seen the sun for the last time. That mental disposition is not astonishing in a prince who had always lived a sensual and frivolous life, and who was unable to receive serious impressions. A weighty idea, on taking possession of him, depressed him instead of fortifying him; he did not understand the tenderness of tears; he was only familiar with their bitterness.

That evening, more depressed than usual and not being interrupted by anyone in his dolorous reveries, he had experienced strange hallucinations. He had remembered the bizarre tradition of his family according to which a little red man, a fantastic and infernal genius, appeared every time that a catastrophe menaced a Bourbon, and at the slightest sound, the slightest creak of the parquet, he raised his head fearfully, expecting to encounter the piercing and fatal gaze of the terrible phantom.[23]

However, the hour at which it was customary for him to go every evening to see Mesdames having chimed, he made an effort to pull himself together, got up resolutely, seemed to drive away his lugubrious preoccupations, and opened the door of a secret corridor by means of which he communicated with his daughters without going through the great apartments.

The burden that he had resolved to shrug off fell back heavily upon his heart, however, to such an extent that instead of turning right, in the direction in which Mesdames resided, he made a mistake, absorbed as he was in his meditations, and turned left, heading in the direction in which Madame la Dauphine was lodged.

He had only taken a few steps when he heard the sound of a door closing abruptly ahead of him. He raised his eyes and perceived, by the rapid light of a candle that was blown out, a strange and fantastic figure.

It was a man of short stature, whose face was brightly lit. He was wearing a mantle with red stripes, a toque of the same color, and he had a long épée under his arm.

---

[23] According to popular legend, the first person to encounter the apparition in question was Catherine de Medicis in 1564; the inventor of the tale probably intended the scarlet costume to symbolize the blood later to be shed during the St. Bartholomew's Day massacre. The figure was eventually introduced to an anecdote relating to Henri IV and (inevitably) anecdotal accounts of preludes to the deaths Louis XVI and Marie-Antoinette. It had gained sufficient currency by then for Napoléon Bonaparte to think it politic to make up a series of encounters with the phantom in his *Memoirs*, as if to secure the "legitimacy" of his doomed empery. It was his publicity that made the figure famous, and has sustained that celebrity since—an observation not without irony in the context of the present story and the moment of its composition.

That apparition, in the darkness, and at a moment when his mind had surrendered to superstitious dread, gave him vertigo. He tried to speak, but the words died on his lips, and, even by summoning up all his effort, he could scarcely contrive to murmur: "Who goes there?"

The mysterious individual paused momentarily; then, the regular sound of his footfalls on the parquet became audible again. The king glimpsed him vaguely in the shadows, still advancing, ready to touch him.

Then, an indescribable fear took possession of him. He wanted to flee, but remained glued to the parquet; he extended his arm in an instinctive moment to repel the frightful vision, and his hand encountered the épée. Then he could no longer contain himself and, uttering a terrible scream, he fell to his knees, convinced that he had seen the little red man, and that a great misfortune was about to occur.

After a few moments of anguish, he heard the footstep of his infernal messenger decreasing in the distance, then a door closing, and then nothing. And the pale and superstitious monarch, who had tried to pray, got up again, and, leaning on the wall, went back to his room, where the threw himself into an armchair, half-dead.

As you might already have guessed, Madame la Dauphine's theater had something to do with that inopportune phantasmagoria, and the supernatural vision that had acted so violently on the king's tormented soul could be explained perfectly naturally. This is what had happened

The young troupe had intended to give itself the pleasure, that evening of performing *Les Folies amoureuses.*[24] During the scene of the military travesty, Agathe's épée could not be found. Profuse apologies were made to the audience, aug-

---

[24] By Jean-François Regnard, first performed in 1701 and loosely modelled on the Italian tradition of the *commedia dell'arte*. The heroine, Agathe, adopts various disguises and feigns madness in order to avoid her guardian's vigilance and meet her lover, Crispin

mented by Madame la Comtesse de Provence, who had no role in the play. Monseigneur le Dauphin was asked to perform on his hat one of those accompaniments that he played so well, and Monsieur Adrien was asked to be good enough to go and fetch the épée in question from a cabinet that was indicated to him.

In spite of the seraphic tendency of his thoughts, Adrien had been constrained, for that performance, to deck himself out in the costume of Crispin.

Let us mention, in passing, that the costume of Crispin, strictly speaking, ought to be entirely black, but that the young troop, by no means severe in the matter of tradition, had judged it appropriate, for the sake of increased gaiety, to adopt the red-striped costume of Sganarelle.[25] That change might have been the cause of all the misfortune that followed.

Our young friend had, therefore, without disturbing his costume, gone to the designated place in order to obtain the complement indispensible to Agathe's warrior dress. As he came out of the room, he heard a noise and, in order not to be seen in an accoutrement that might have compromised the secret that had so far been scrupulously kept, he blew out his candle and tried to grope his way back to the room where his august comrades were assembled.

He distinctly felt that he had bumped into someone, but how could he possibly have imagined that it was the king? Thus, he did not worry overmuch about the exclamation he had heard, and went back to the stage laughing at the fright he had doubtless just given some poor domestic. He thought, however, that he ought to recount what had happened. They laughed with him; Monseigneur le Dauphin's accompaniment was suspended, and the play was completed without any further hitch.

---

[25] Molière's works feature several characters of that name; the costume in question is presumably the one worn by the valet in *Dom Juan, ou the Festin de Pierre* (1665), who provided the inspiration for Leporello in Mozart's *Don Giovanni.*

The next day, however, the rumor spread through Versailles that the king was very ill, and that the little red man had appeared in the apartments. When Adrien arrived at the château he was introduced into the presence of Madame la Dauphine, who, her eyes filled with tears, said to him:

"You should not be unaware, Monsieur, that the incident that we regarded yesterday as a frivolous matter, has become very serious today. The king, whom he have sought in vain to reassure, is convinced that his family's fatal spirit has appeared to him. He is delirious. That accident has hastened a malady whose symptoms have already been evident for a long time. His majesty probably only has a few days to live, and we are the innocent cause of that frightful tragedy. You will understand that it puts an end forever to our performances, but I didn't want you, in leaving us, to take away the idea that I might be ungrateful. No, I wanted to see you to tell you how much I have learned in knowing you, how good and devoted you have appeared to me. People like us have few friends—especially me, whom they call 'the foreigner' and 'the Austrian woman.'"

"Oh, Madame! Is it possible not to love you?"

"I can assure you, Monsieur that in this court they slander me. To you, I can confess everything, because you are not an ungrateful and perfidious man like the rest, and you would not betray me. Well, these courtiers, to whom I have never done any harm, had set to work to rob me of the dauphin's affection, but thanks to you and our plays, I am very happy now."

"How can it be thanks to me, Highness?"

"Oh, you wouldn't understand that—it's a mystery of coquetry."

On the contrary, Adrien understood very well that the performances of which he had been the cause, in which the Dauphine had reserved the attractive roles for herself, had caused the Dauphin to devise his unjust prejudices regarding the intelligence and beauty of his spouse; but he could not congratulate himself internally for having contributed to that result.

Marie-Antoinette continued: "It is your adieux that I must receive now, Monsieur Adrien, but permit me before then to ask you how I might acquit my debt to you. If an employment at court..."

"At court? No, I too have enemies to my happiness; I would suffer too much, Highness; but I thank you. A single one of your words is worth more to me than all the favors in the world. I was ambitious a few months ago, but I no longer have any ambition now; I have something else in my heart to fill my life. Be happy and beloved, Madame. If Heaven permits that you soon become the queen of France, be avenged by the love of your subjects for the shameful calumnies of the courtiers."

Adrien was suffocating. Sobs were pressuring his breast and all his limbs were agitated by a convulsive tremor. There were a few moments of silence; then, making a great effort to control himself, the poet went on: "I've refused your offer, but before reentering my darkness, permit me, Madame, to take away a memory of you, that would be like a gentle light for me, and an ineffable consolation."

"What do you mean?"

Instead of replying, Adrien flexed his knee, and looked up at Marie-Antoinette with a gaze so imploring that she, understanding all the contained ardor and religious respect that there was in the young man, smiled and held out her hand. Adrien placed his lips upon it and left there, along with a kiss, a burning tear that made the Dauphine shudder. Then he got up and went out, unsteadily. Marie-Antoinette watched him go compassionately, and murmured, in a very low voice: "Poor child!"

As for him, he went to take refuge in a remote area of the park, where he could weep at his leisure, and when his soul was somewhat relieved, he went home, saying as he went: "Dear God, I've had a beautiful dream; why have you woken me up?"

Some time afterwards, on the tenth of May 1774, a light placed in the window of the great apartments informed France that Louis XV had ceased to live, and that His Highness Monseigneur le Dauphin had become His Majesty Louis XVI.

Nothing more was heard of Adrien; but when Marie-Antoinette organized a theater at the Trianon, much later, it was noticed that she was preoccupied and distracted on the first night. Perhaps she was thinking about *Agenor et Chloé*, and also about the little red man.

Troyes, 1849

THE ORIGINAL CONCLUSION TO
"THE LITTLE RED MAN"

(The version of the story just reproduced is the one re-printed in Prince Bonifacio, *and presumably represents the author's final judgment as to how the story ought to conclude. In the version that had previously appeared in* Les Secrets du diable, *however, the word "peut-être" [perhaps] is omitted from the final sentence, and the text continues as follows.)*

One would like to stop there, but alas, one cannot touch upon the history of Marie-Antoinette without arriving at its terrible denouement.

One day, a miserable cart carried the daughter of Marie-Thérèse to the scaffold, and in the crowd, behind the hideous cortege, marched a pale man, emaciated by suffering, his eyes fixed upon the discolored forehead of the poor queen. When the vehicle stopped, the widow of Louis XVI paraded her merciful gaze over the executioners, and got ready to climb up courageously to the guillotine, in order to rise up to Heaven. It was then that the half-dead man parted the crowd around him in order to cry, with a supreme effort: "Vive la Reine!"

At that voice, Marie-Antoinette shivered, searched for the man who was risking death for her, and, having seen him, said with a heart-rending expression: "Poor Adrien." Then, she murmured, as she closed her eyes: "The red man! The red man!"

They seized the poet, who, proud of being recognized, died smiling on the scaffold on to which André Chenier was later to climb.[26]

---

[26] The poet André Chenier (1762-1893) initially penned idylls and elegies, but developed philosophical ambitions and planned to write a long poem summarizing the world-view of

And all the pastorals commenced under Louis XV died then, in that fashion.

---

the *Encyclopédie* as an Enlightenment replacement for Lucretius' *De rerum natura*, of which he only completed a few fragments. A believer in constitutional monarchy, he was a trifle too loud in expressing that view and took to writing satirical verses attacking Robespierre, in a manner of which Ulbach/Ferragus could only have approved wholeheartedly; his efforts got him guillotined shortly before the suspension of the Terror. He was posthumously hailed as a significant precursor of Romanticism.

THE DEMON OF THE LOCH

I. The Tomb and the Cradle

Toward the middle of the month of December 1542, Falkland Castle in Scotland was filled with tumult. A portion of the nobility had gathered there in the expectation of a great misfortune and good news. The misfortune was about to be completed in the very castle where King James V had retreated after his army's defeat by the English at Solway Moss; the good news would be brought from Linlithgow Castle, where the queen of Scotland, Marie of Lorraine, the daughter of Claude of Lorraine, was in residence.

Scotland was going into mourning and hopeful expectation at the same time. One reign was ending; another was announced. While poor James V was battling against the phantoms surrounding his death-bed, the queen, very sorry not to be able to mop the sweat-soaked forehead of her beloved spouse, was waiting far away for the first wail of the child that was to replace her two sons, dead in infancy.

Finally, on the eighth of December, a squire left at the gallop for Falkland, and spread along his route the glad news of the birth of a little girl, who would be called Mary, after her mother. That same day, King James fell prey to an ardent delirium. His companions waited for glimmer of reason in order to notify him of the event, but reason seemed to have fled forever.

Scotland was a rude land in those days, full of ignorance and brutality. The noblemen there took up the profession of murderers and brigands when the need arose. Murder was the ultimate resort of politics. James V, a delicate and poetic spirit, was not made for that savage land and that savage epoch; he had soon been forced to renounce his illusions, his adven-

191

turous excursions and his life of gallantry. A fervent Catholic and an implacable administrator of justice, sacrificing the interests of his dynasty to the principles of his faith, he had fought unsparingly against the Presbyterianism of his uncle, Henry VIII. He had stifled his generous instinct in vain, however; in vain he had had recourse to the sword, the ax and the pyre; abandoned by the cupidity of his nobles and the indifference of his people, twice defeated by Henry VIII, weeping for the shame of his arms and the futility of his rigors, devoured by remorse, pain and fever, he was in no condition to receive the consolation that Providence had sent him.

His eyes ardent and sunk in their orbits, his hair spare, his lips contracted, his nostrils flared and his fists clenched on his bed-sheets, James struggled desperately against the frightful visions that where swirling around his chamber.

Sometimes, it seemed to him that all the victims of his intolerance,[27] escaped from the pyre, had come to place the faggots and flames of their torture under his bed, and the unfortunate king, believing that he could feel himself being consumed, cried "Fire!" and tried to flee, moaning that the blaze would char his bones. If the servants and gentlemen dared to approach and restrain him with their arms, the dying man would faint in terror, taking those officious hands for bloody pincers, Specters, to which he gave names, came in turn to salute and summon him. One of them, he said, had cut off his arms and legs and had promised to come back to cut off his

---

[27] Author's note: "For the historical details, and often for the legend itself, see the moving history by Monsieur Dargaud." The reference is to Jean-Marie Dargaud's *Histoire de Marie Stuart* (1850), and is slightly misleading. In fact, Mary only spent a few weeks at the Priory of Inchmahome, and there is no particular link between the folklore of kelpies and the Loch of Menteith. The latter is nowadays known as the Lake of Menteith, or sometimes Monteith, but I have used the translation that would have been current when Ulback wrote the story.

head. Another drew him on to a lake whose waters were bloody and tried to drown him in it.

The death-throes of the young king were horrible to behold, and the most insensitive eyes melted in tears by his bedside.

On the fourteenth of December, in the morning, James' passion appeared to be reaching its terminus. After a torpor lasting several hours, the king woke up calm and weak but having recovered all his reason. He raised himself up on his elbow, scanned the room with the astonished gaze of a man emerging from a dream, unable as yet to get a grip on reality, made a sign to demand the opening of a window, breathed deeply of the winter wind that was stirring the leafless trees, and then fell back on his pillow, murmuring: "What a hard sleep you have made for me, my God, and what a sad awakening you have prepared for me."

People crowded around the royal bed. Recognizing clearly, by the sad smile with which he saluted the courtiers of death, that his mind was no longer calm, a Scottish laird knelt down, took the moist hand that the king held out to him, bore it to his lips and announced to James V the birth of Mary, his daughter.

A divine dew extinguished momentarily the blaze that was consuming James. He closed his eyes beneath an ineffable caress. His poor heart, so swollen and so bruised, overflowed in a sigh of joy and triumph. The inferno vanished; the heavens opened; the king gave way to the father, and that word—daughter—drove back into darkness all the tearful specters that had mounted a vigilant guard around the royal bed.

"A daughter!" murmured the invalid, and a tear rolled between his lashes; then he fell into a gentle reverie, and it was evident, by the creasing of his lips, that his soul was flying through space to Linlithgow, and floating, glad and reconciled, above his child's cradle.

Poor king! Poor father! He smiled at that frail offspring born at the foot of scaffolds; the still-open tomb of his two sons was closed; the horizon, so bleak, disenchanted and darkened, brightened, and from afar, through the mists, he saw the face of a blonde child, who was smiling at him. The entire indescribable poem of the joys, caresses, impertinences and affections of infancy appeared to him as if in a flash. A gust of life and hope blew into his heart, while the keen air came in through the window that was still open.

Alas, the respite was brief; the mirage disappeared very quickly; the consciousness of his imminent death returned to the king with the sweat he felt forming on his brow. He shivered convulsively; the window was closed again, the fire reanimated, but the wind of the tomb never ceased to agitate that royal specter.

"A daughter!" James murmured. "Poor child, who will wear mourning for her father, and for Scotland!"

And as that thought recalled all his phantoms, the king raised his hands to his eyes as if to close them against frightful images. "Those," he said, "who have not respected the royal thistle and have caused the crown of Scotland to wither, those who have profaned that crown on my head will tear it away from hers. From a daughter it came, and from a daughter it will go."

After having pronounced these prophetic words, the exhausted moribund turned over in his bed, uttered a loud cry, and expired.

The gentlemen then approached the funeral bed, one after another, to say a last farewell to the dead majesty, and then went sadly down to the courtyard of the castle, mounted their horses, and departed for Linlithgow Castle. They went to salute their six-day-old queen, Mary Stuart.

The king's prophecy seemed to precede that somber cortege, and, in spite of their roughness, those lairds understood that the open tomb was too large for a single victim, and that Scotland was about to enter a long and bloody widowhood.

II. The Kelpy, or the Demon of the Loch

Six years have gone by. Young Mary has blossomed like a wild flower on the banks of the Loch of Menteith. Raised in the Priory of Inchmahome, the child queen knows no other life as yet than the sheer rocks, the wild heather and the verdant banks that witness her excursions and her games.

Cheerful and madcap, she gets up before daybreak, she knows no other pastime than wandering the stony paths that rip and shred her black satin plaid, with a golden clasp bearing the arms of Lorraine and Scotland. The soul that is waking in that joyful heart wants no other emotions than legends, ballads, music and dancing.

She is the sylph of the strand, and the fishermen smile blissfully when they see her running, or rather fleeing, through the long grass. She is the joyful sprite of the region. Everything about her—her pale and pink face; her gaze, so shiny and limpid, which exercises a fascination that she will later abuse; her hair, whose curls float freely around her lithe neck; her charming voice, which alternates between command and coaxing—is charming, seductive, generative of affection.

The highlanders leave the doors of their huts open when the weather is fine, for they know that the daughter of James V often appears on the threshold in a ray of sunlight, coming to request a piece of black bread and songs. Sometimes a boat is heard on the loch full of laughter and rapid speech; it is the young queen going out with her companions. Mary has an entire petty court of children of her own age and name. The queen mother, having a profound veneration for the Virgin, has wanted all those close to her daughter to have the same reasons to intercede with the Mother of God. In consequence, they are all named Mary, and that miniature court is vowed to the same worship.

Often, therefore, all those little Marys leap into a boat with their child queen and have themselves rowed over Loch of Menteith, and the green and profound waters serve as a mirror for all those coquettish faces, search beneath the oars for the naiads and sirens or ballads.

One day, the young queen learned that she was about to leave for France. On her sweet, pure head God was to set a double crown, and she was promised, at Saint-Germain-en-Laye, a little husband of her own age, the dauphin François. Although the idea of traveling, of a change of climate, and of leaving the monastery that had been her somber cradle caused Mary's heart to beat faster, she nevertheless regretted her beautiful loch, its green heather and its sad landscapes, which she had animated with her gaiety.

She was going to see her mother's homeland, her uncles de Guise, who sent her such beautiful presents and affectionate messages; she was going, clad in rich finery, to take her place at the court of Saint-Germain; but it was necessary for her to renounce her liberty. The little peasant-girl was about to become a true queen, which is to say that she would no longer be able to go out, to run where she pleased; and the playmate she was promised, the dauphin François, frightened her by virtue of the thought that he would one day be her husband, which is to say, her master. So Mary wanted to make one last farewell excursion on her beautiful loch, and the four usual companions of her life, Mary Fleming, Mary Seton, Mary Livingston and Mary Beaton, escorted her to the boat that was waiting for her.

That day, the sky was heavy and full of tears, like the heart of the little queen. Scotland seemed to be sad; that lock was agitated, as if to speak and murmur a complaint. The fishermen, who had run to the bank to watch their fairy's last excursion, watched silently as the five Marys installed themselves in the boat, giving no thought to uttering their customary cries of delight. The little queen, over whose sadness all that exterior sadness had come to weigh, tried to laugh, to excite her companions, and not being able to distract them, began singing a ballad—but her voice was not as pure, not as clear, as usual; she dared not continue, and stopped at the first chorus. Then as Mary Fleming was closest to her and seemed saddest, she put her arms around her, kissed her and said;

"Come on, darling, try not to make me cry. Let's think about the beautiful country we're going to see."

"Alas," replied Mary Fleming, "is there any beautiful country without lochs?"

"Poor loch!" said the little queen. "I wish I could take you with me! And, leaning over the edge of the boat, she dipped her little pink hand into the water, filled it, and raised it swiftly to her lips, from which the droplets trickled.

"Be careful, my queen," said one of the little Marys. "Don't lean so far—the Kelpy will catch you."

"The Kelpy," Mary Stuart replied, "is a good demon, who has always smiled at me and who loves me; he wouldn't want to harm me."

"If he loves you, it's all the more reason to be careful."

"My friends," said the young queen, getting to her dainty feet, "let's say farewell to the demon of the lock, that old companion who can't follow us, and to whom no one will any longer come to sing our songs."

Then Mary Stuart stand up straight in the boat, which the tumultuous waves were beginning to rock, and the young enchantress spoke thus:

"Old Kelpy, you who are as black as night, and have long arms filled with weeds, demon of Loch of Menteith, whose horse's hooves gallop over the waves and whose human head shows itself to the drowned, and whose cold hands cling on to doomed boats; demon who has always caressed me, I bid you farewell, and I give you, as a souvenir of your beloved Mary, this clasp with the arms of Scotland and Lorraine, which has touched my heart and will touch yours."

And, swiftly snatching the retaining clasp from her plaid, Mary threw it into the waves; then she knelt down, tried to plunge her gaze into the depths of the water, as if to see the Kelpy there. All her companions did likewise, and the five Marys bent down and leaned over so far that the waves, lifted by the wind, rose all the way to their faces and seemed to kiss them.

Suddenly, whether because the oarsmen, frightened by that imprudent game and despairing of being able to put a stop to it by remonstrations, wanted to force the reckless girls to give it up, or because the tempest blew up then, or, finally, because, as the ballads assure us, the Kelpy, the demon of the loch, wanted to render Mary a prophecy in exchange for her farewell, there was a great tumult along the sides of the boat, and a water spout sprang forth, inundating the excursionists. Mary Stuart uttered a loud scream and threw herself backwards, pale and half dead, on to her bench, murmuring that she had seen the demon of the loch, that the watery Centaur had gripped her in his arms and tried to draw her toward him.

The queen's young companions tried to reassure her, without themselves feeling well-armed against the terrible vision. They dared not look at the loch, for fear of encountering the large glaucous eyes of the monster: the eyes that infallibly brought misfortune and announced the death of the person who met them.

As for Mary Stuart, she trembled, and passed a quivering hand around her waist, as if to efface the grip that she said she had felt. She had distinctly seen the demon cling on to the boat and shake it, and she affirmed that at the moment she had screamed, commending herself to the Virgin, her patroness, the monster, who was mortally afraid of the Mother of God, had plunged into the loch, darting one last terrible glance at her.

The boat soon landed at the threshold of the monastery. The young girls dared not tell the story of their excursion. As for little Mary, her heart was squeezed more tightly still. The presentiment completed the darkening of that voyage to France, with which people tried in vain to dazzle her. She was put to bed with a fever, and all through that night, which was filled by a terrible storm, she thought she could distinguish in the whistling of the wind and the roaring of the loch the plaints of the Kelpy, who was calling to her, claiming his young and royal bride.

Her nurse, rendered anxious by that agitation, remained by her bedside, and heard her murmur, several times: "My good God, who has destined the genteel dauphin François to be my husband, don't permit me to remain here as the wife of the demon of Menteith!"

Toward morning, sleep calmed her terrors, but the departure from France was due to take place that very day, and when the hour chimed, Mary allowed herself to be led away trembling, and kept her eyes closed while the loch was in view.

III. The Two Crossings

They embarked at Dumbarton, but scarcely had the fleet serving as the queen of Scotland's escort drawn away from the coast than the wind blew violently and the ships, shaken by the waves, creaked and threatened to break up.

The little queen thought more than ever, then, about her vision. Evidently, the demon of the loch was pursuing her, and the waves were becoming deadly to her. Putting her hands together, the daughter of James V begged the evil genius of Menteith to spare her companions and only to strike her. That prayer, which departed for a pure heart, rose up to Heaven through the heaped-up clouds. A rapid wind pushed the fleet toward the shores of France, and on Sunday the twentieth of August 1548, the vessel bearing Mary Stuart landed—or, rather, ran aground—on the headland of the Baie de Morlaix, in a lair of smugglers and pirates, at the port of Roscoff.

That was not enough of presages. The Kelpy's influence seemed to pursue Mary all the way to the lands where she would reign. As she emerged in great pomp from the church of Notre-Dame de Morlaix, where the *Te Deum* had been sung, and as she went through the gate of the city known as the Prison Gate, the drawbridge split and fell into the river. The Scots cried treason, but, as the chronicler says, "The Seigneur de Rohan, who was marching on foot beside He Majesty's litter, cried 'No Breton has ever committed treason!' and for the two days that the queen stayed to recover from seasickness, he had all the gates in the city unhinged and broke the chains of the bridges."

At Saint-Germain-en-Laye Mary Stuart soon forgot the adieux of the demon of Menteith and the auguries of her voyage. She spent happy years there, in a continual whirl of hunts, fêtes, dances and concerts. Ardent as she already was at the Priory of Inchmahome, the little queen surrendered herself to pleasure with an extraordinary enthusiasm. The entirety of that sparkling court of the Valois, of which Catherine de Medicis was the shadow, intoxicated Mary and shone upon her youth, her precocious beauty and her intelligence.

Ronsard, Joachim du Bellay, Amadis Jamyn and all the poets ravaged Parnassus for her and made her a litter of roses and lilies, which she trampled, laughing. Scotland, cold and misty, was sometimes completely forgotten, and when, from the height of the terrace of Saint-Germain, she watched the Seine unrolling its sash, or when she traveled, in a gilded and flag-laden boat, over the pond of Fontainebleau, the daughter of James V scarcely gave a thought to the lugubrious Kelpy. The Naiads of France made so many pearls sparkle in their joyful frolics, that one could not recall, in the presence of those charming waves, the deep waters of Menteith. It was always a young and beautiful divinity, sitting on a nacreous shell, that one sought on the silvery surfaces of rivers, no longer the hideous Kelpy that had received Mary's golden clasp.

Alas, one may forget the Centaur, but the Centaur does not forget. The daughter of James V had been blessed by her father in a bloody agony; pyres had been lit beneath her cradle; happiness could not be anything for her but an ironic interval between two dramas. Scarcely had she turned nineteen, scarcely had she been intoxicated by all the perfumes that expanded in her wake, than death took her beloved husband, François II, and an illustrious and brilliant cortege, full of mourning and sadness, headed for the sea, to take the desolate Mary Stuart back to her ships, exhaling her plaint in tender prayers and harmonious verses.

On the fifteenth of August 1561 two galleys and two sailing ships left Calais. On one of those ships, Mary Stuart, leaning sadly on the stern, watched the coasts of France diminish and whiten on the horizon. History has conserved the queen's costume on that occasion; she was wearing the white velvet dress that served for the grand mourning of the queens of France; a wimple trimmed with lace enveloped her neck; her heavy veil fell in folds upon each shoulder; the silver fabric of her sleeves was narrow at the bottom, bouffant at the top; her hair, smooth on the head, was curled over her temples and attached behind with knotted ribbons; a light bonnet descended over her forehead in a heart-shape and covered, without hiding them, three rows of pearls of the most beautiful clarity; a necklace of other pearls, which she preferred to all her gems, streamed over her neck.[28]

Poor Mary! As she saw that she was drawing further away from the shore, inexpressible anguish awoke in her soul; she was leaving behind in France a tomb in which all her dreams and all her illusions had been laid to rest with her husband, and she was going to find in Scotland pyres that were hardly extinct, and gibbets that were still bloody. She was leaving a charming court, hearts warmed by her memory, and she was going to encounter somber and mistrustful subjects, an arrogant and jealous nobility. In France, she was loved; in Scotland, alas, no one knew her any longer; perhaps they would even hate her there!

Crossings were catastrophic for Mary. Since the day when the demon of Loch of Menteith had appeared to her, she had not been able to set foot on a ship without some misfortune following. The Kelpy did not miss that opportunity. When they were some distance from land, two boats bringing the people of Mary's escort to the ships capsized; six men

---

[28] Author's note: "*Histoire de Marie Stuart*, par M. Dargaud."

disappeared into the waves; the foam leapt all the way to the queen's face; she called for help but it was in vain; the sea did not surrender the holocaust and, after futile efforts, someone came to inform Mary Stuart that the crew had lost six men.

The royal widow let two large tears fall from her beautiful eyes, and as the ladies in waiting surrounding her tried to console her, she said to Mary Fleming, her favorite: "My faith forbids me to believe in spells, my heat reproaches me for foolish terrors, but in spite of my heart and my faith, I've seen the demon of the loch put his arms around those boats and drag them under."

"Dispel these illusions, my queen," said Mary. "It wasn't the demon of Menteith; it was only the wrath of the Ocean and the mercy of God that permitted the deaths."

"Oh, I believe in God," Mary replied, excitedly, "but I can't chase away that other belief of my youth."

And, quitting her faithful companion, the young queen went into a quiet part of the ship to meditate and weep in private. She was sometimes heard bidding melancholy adieux to France; she sent her, on the wings of the wind, her most ardent caresses; then she lamented the deaths that her vessel left in its wake, and when the idea of the demon of the loch came back to mind, she evoked all the memories of her childhood and compared the sad queen who was returning to Scotland a widow with the little girl who had gone to seek fugitive joys and eternal regrets in France.

At least, the queen believed in the eternity of her dolor; although Mary Stuart had one of those thirsty natures that absorb tears as the burning sands of the desert absorb dew, and are never finished with the temptations of the earth and the intoxications of the heart, she was sincere in her despair. During that crossing, in the presence of the beloved shore that she was quitting forever, after that scene of mourning that had moved her profoundly, she believed in good faith in the impossibility of recovering her regal smile and her youthful gaiety—but she was to pass alternately between the violent alternatives of insensate joy and terrible despair many more times.

The crossing was, therefore, sad; Mary wept a great deal. She asked the helmsman to wake her at daybreak if the coast of France was still visible. The old man did not forget the order, and Mary saluted the shores of her adoptive homeland one last time by the light of dawn; then everything disappeared, the horizon became infinite, and the queen found herself alone with her regrets, between the sky and the sea.

They arrived on a Sunday morning, but a thick fog prevented the disembarkation, and it was not until the following day, the nineteenth of August 1611, that Mary Stuart set foot on Scottish soil.

IV. Loch Leven

Years have passed. The insouciant young girl of the monastery of Inchmahome has become an energetic and violent woman. Passion has replaced the limpid flames of her first innocence on her forehead and in her eyes. The sprite of Loch of Menteith has lost her aureole.

She is still loved, and will always be loved, but with a fatal love, full of frenzy and remorse, a love that withers and kills. She is loved because she is beautiful, because her gaze is irresistible, because her mouth knows magic words; but no one any longer has the supreme veneration for her, the religious worship that made highlanders and fishermen adore her.

That is because Mary Stuart is no longer only the widow of François II; it is because she is also the widow of Darnley, immolated for her and by her; it is because the blood of Riccio, the Italian singer, stabbed in her bedroom, has spurted over her dress; it is because Chastelard has died on a scaffold for having loved her and having believed that she loved him;[29]

---

[29] The French poet Pierre de Bocosel de Chastelard would probably have remained almost unknown to history but for the fanciful account of his doomed passion for Mary Stuart given in the *Memoirs* of Pierre de Bourdeille, Seigneur de Brantôme (1665-66), a work of highly dubious accuracy. He was, how-

it is because, after so much bloodshed, she has given herself freely to Bothwell the pirate, Bothwell her third husband, the murderer of her second husband Darnley; it is because the daughter of James V has not only been as pitiless as her father with regard to heresy, but because she has merited being cursed by John Knox, the invincible apostle of Presbyterianism, the only man that she tried in vain to seduce and fascinate;[30] it is because James Murray, her brother, whom she has heaped with honors and wealth, finds his glory and his virtue in ingratitude; it is because misfortune and shame follow that unfortunate queen, full of genius and resplendent in beauty, everywhere; it is by dint of strange caprices, disorders and crimes that she would have become odious to history had God not wished that she commence her expiation on earth.

A forgetful spouse, she will be a forgetful mother; an impudent queen, she will be abandoned and betrayed; then, finally, she will redeem by her immolation all the precious blood that she has caused to be spilled.

At the moment when we find her again, Mary Stuart, vanquished but indefatigable, has escaped from Loch Leven castle, where her rebellious nobility imprisoned her, to recommence her life of conflict, war, violence and passion.

It was the second of May 1568. The queen had been waiting impatiently, for several days, for the signal of deliverance that had been announced to her by George Douglas and

---

ever, beheaded after being found in Mary's apartments, and one can only conjecture as to the exact circumstances of his presence there.

[30] The evidence that Mary tried to "fascinate" John Knox, the leader of the Scottish Reformation is slight, and hi famous pamphlet *The First Blast of the Trumpet Against the Monstruous Regiment of Women* (1558) is sufficiently vague in its misogynistic targeting for it to be uncertain as to whether he was including her along with the regent who reigned on her behalf, Marie de Guise, and the English queen Mary Tudor.

John Beaton, two of her most faithful and last remaining friends.

George, a relative of the Laird of Loch Leven had not been able to see Mary without submitting, like everyone else, to her fascination. Charged with guarding her, he had wanted to favor her escape, but, discovered and forced to flee, he had assembled a few of the queen's partisans outside, and left to one of his youngest relatives, a child of sixteen known as "Wee Douglas" the care of opening the doors of that seductive and fatal beauty's prison.

Wee Douglas had carried out the mission he had been given with all the more ardor because he too had felt moved by a tender pity for the enchantress.

On the second of May, after supper, as Mary withdrew to her chamber, someone knocked on the door. Wee Douglas appeared and, placing a knee on the ground, announced to the queen that she was about to be free, and that he had stolen the keys to the castle.

"Free!" murmured the queen. "Be blessed, you who have taken pity upon the woman whose people have abandoned her!"

"Time is pressing, Madame," Douglas interjected, embarrassed by that testimony of gratitude.

"I'm ready," Mary Stuart replied, getting to her feet—and a few moments later, placing her arm on the tremulous arm of her young liberator, wearing a disguise, she passed through the castle gates. A boat was moored on the shore. Loch Leven, somber and silent, rocked the skiff. The moon, accomplice to the flight, was veiled. It was an admirable night for an escape.

Before setting foot in the boat, the sprite of Inchmahome remembered the Loch of Menteith, her childhood excursions, perhaps also the Kelpy. Holding Wee Douglas back as he got ready to depart, she said: "Every time I have embarked, alas, it was for misfortune, and the waters I have crossed have always received my tears."

"The waters of Loch Leven will receive my blood rather than your tears," Wee Douglas replied, forcefully. "If I don't succeed in setting you free, I shall kill myself."

"Be quiet, child, and pray to God!"

Then, turned to the somber walls that had been the confidantes of her dolors, the queen of Scotland addressed an ardent prayer to Heaven. Strangely enough, the more her heart was calcined by the fire of human passions, the more it also opened to divine effusions. The daughter of the Catholic James V experienced, beneath all her sensuality, an inexhaustible thirst that could only be really satisfied by prayer.

When she had finished, Mary leapt into the boat, and the boat, borne away by the oars, flew over the loch like a kingfisher.

A little way from the shore, the queen looked at the beacon that she had left in her window to inform her friends hidden in the vicinity of the exact moment of her flight. Wee Douglas made out a sigh.

"What are you regretting, Madame?" the child asked, timidly.

"I'm not regretting anything; I'm afraid," said Mary Stuart. "That red light is a dark star; one might think it a bloody gleam."

"It's liberty that's shining, my queen!"

"Yes, the liberty of combat, the liberty of punishing rebels. Blood! Always blood! Douglas, Douglas, I wasn't made for this terrible life."

Douglas put down the oars and, seeing Mary Stuart pensive, contemplated her sadly.

It seemed that the moment was all meditation. Loch Leven was forgotten, the dangers had fled; one might have thought it a placid and pleasant excursion. Mary gazed at the waves, Douglas gazed at Mary, and the silence was only interrupted by the lapping of the water at the sides of the boat.

In that peaceful night, the fugitive queen deflated her heart and breathed in the perfumes of her past life in the perfumes of spring. She thought about her beautiful sojourn in

France, her sad return, her sins and her crimes; purged of her remorse in that vast serenity, she felt her soul gradually shedding its anguish.

"Douglas," she said, finally, as if she were summing up her meditation, "never love. Keep your heart as pure as the flash of your gaze. It's the only advice I can give you in return for liberty."

"It's too late, Madame," Douglas replied, in a trembling voice, setting himself to his knees. "I've seen you weep, and when I swore to save you, I swore to love you until death."

"You too, poor child!"

There was a long silence, which neither dared break. The moon, veiled until then by cloud, suddenly showed herself, and her pale radiance enveloped the boat. Wee Douglas perceived a water-lily then, on the surface of the loch, whose flower was slightly closed: a touching emblem for a queen of France. He leaned out of the boat, reached the flower with the aid of an oar, and offered it to Mary Stuart. There was a shiny pearl on the edge of the calyx: a drop of water or a teardrop.

"Madame," said Douglas, "You have made the loch flower, and the demon of Loch Leven has ornamented himself to watch you pass by."

"What! This loch has its demons too?"

"Undoubtedly, and the ballads relate..."

"Oh, don't talk to me about ballads, Douglas—I loved them too much and sang them too often. The demon of Loch Leven is no better than the demon of Menteith, and it won't render the sad queen any better auguries than those the Kelpy rendered the child."

And Mary Stuart, smiling bitterly and gently mocking the superstition that she dared not admit frankly, told the story of her excursion on the Loch of Menteith, her betrothal to the demon, and the sad voyages she had made over water since then.

When she had finished, Douglas exclaimed: "I know an offering agreeable to the Kelpy of Loch Leven"—and, taking from his bosom the keys of the castle, which he had brought with him in his flight, he threw them into the loch.

Scarcely had the water closed over them than a gunshot rang out. The queen's escape had been discovered, and they were firing at the boat.

Douglas went pale. Mary Stuart uttered a cry, and the boat resumed its course—or, rather, its flight—toward the opposite shore. The journey was made in silence, but when they touched the bank, the queen said to her guide: "You see, Douglas—the lochs of Scotland don't want me; death pursues me here."

Some distance from the bank, Wee Douglas picked a thistle, and offered it to the queen, who was already carrying a lily.

"Queen of France and Scotland," he said to her, making allusion to the two emblems, "your subjects await you."

Then he blew into a horn suspended from his belt. George Douglas, John Beaton and Claude Hamilton, who were waiting, hidden in the grass, ran to greet the fugitive.

Mary was soon surrounded by a faithful and devoted nobility. Hope reentered her heart; she believed herself finally to be mistress of her destiny, and cried as she embraced her friends: "I'm saved!"

Alas, she was lost. Her excursion on Lock Leven was only a brief precedent to a long and cruel captivity. On the eighth of February 1587, after eighteen years of torture and prison, the daughter of James V, the window of François II, the queen of France and Scotland, realizing the paternal prophecy, laid her head, still young and beautiful, on Elizabeth's block.

The executioner trembled when it was necessary to strike and had to do it twice. Mary's soul escaped, reconciled with God by repentance and prayer. All our readers know the details of that horrible and sublime agony.

Perhaps, before mounting the scaffold at Fotheringhay, in the dolorous hours she devoted to reviewing her life and offering it to God, Mary Stuart remembered the superstitions of her childhood and the sinister predictions of the demon of the loch.

At any rate, the genius of the waters has taken possession of her memory and wears mourning for her. On the banks of the Nene, which runs at the foot of Fotheringhay, little red flowers are picked, which are born, so the legend says, of drops of the unfortunate Mary's blood.

THE BRELAN

The story we are about to tell is very improbable; some people, among those who only like events ascertained at the court of assizes and do not admit other tragedies than those verified by the victims of the Morgue, will shrug their shoulders and consider this true story as a fairy tale.

A fairy tale! As if anything were impossible in France, where so many people take the moon in their teeth every day; as if it were more marvelous to believe in the atrocious vengeance and terrible power whose effects we are about to relate than the piety of the newspaper *L'Univers* and the miracle of Saint Janvier—meaning no offence to French miracles.[31]

We therefore attest the perfect authenticity of this story; and the proof that it is not impossible is that there will come a day when magetism will be entirely proven and demonstrated—which it to say (it comes to the same thing) when it is definitively denied by scientists.

We got this tale from the mount of an old German of the old rock, and everyone knows that Germans are incapable of lying—in proof of which they used to sing to the tune of *traderi* that they would keep their German Rhine, and they have kept it. Now, this is what the old German told me; I have not changed a word, and that is why my story is not in very good French. I am suppressing the accent, which is why it is not in German.

---

[31] *L'Univers*, edited by the redoubtable Louis Veuillot, was the principal vehicle of French ultramontanism; it was suppressed by the Second Empire's censors some time after the publication of this story, in 1860, but revived in 1867. "Ferragus" would presumably have disapproved on Veuillot's creed but admired his polemical style,

The setting is the reign Louis XV. Because of Mesmer and Cagliostro, I would gladly have set it under Louis XVI, but I promised not to change anything in the story that was old to me, and I can affirm with confidence that it is set under Louis XV.

Would you like a description of the scenery? It has been painted, in England, by a moralist of the palette. Hogarth, in a series of pictures representing the various phases of what he called "Marriage à la Mode," included one canvas, entitled "The Salon," which appears to be very close to the prototype of the décor we have to describe.

Imagine, in a sumptuous apartment, somewhat wrecked by a night of feasting, to either side of the fireplace, a man and a woman exhausted by fatigue, collapsed in armchairs. On the parquet and the rugs, traces of the trampling of the crowd are visible; in the foreground, chairs are tipped over; further away, gaming tables are stained with powder, tobacco and scattered cards; violins and sheet music are piled up in the corners; candles are still burning in the candlesticks and chandeliers; the mirrors are slightly tarnished by the warm vapor of a party: such is Hogarth's painting, and that, very nearly is the sight presented by the Marquis de Thurigny's drawing-room.

We shall eliminate the steward coming to present the bill, who, in the idea of the English painter, constitutes the moral of the work, and we shall modify the physiognomies of the two characters slightly. Hogarth's heroes are not only expressing fatigue; the woman, while yawing, is looking disdainfully at her husband, whose head, heavy with the coarse vapors of vine, is lolling as he slumps in a stupid torpor. They are the image of disorder, completed by ennui and drunkenness.

In the Thurigny household, by contrast, there is no disgust and no corruption mingled with the exhaustion. The Marquise has collapsed carelessly and the Marquis' immobility merely attests to fatigue and preoccupation. Nothing dishonors, as in Hogarth's picture, the frolicsome phantom that the disorder of the apartment seems to evoke.

The Marquis and Marquise de Thurigny, young and rich, having been able to resolve the problem, difficult then, of remaining lovers after a year of marriage, opened their house to pleasure with a crazy fever, a kind of vertigo, but until that night nothing had troubled the couple's insouciant happiness. They were admired and envied, and in consequence, slandered somewhat. Everyone at Versailles was wondering, behind Madame de Pompadour's screen, by what reversal of chronology the heyday of Amadis and Galaor had returned, and that conjugal passion was so perfect, and above all so strange, that people suspected it of being feigned. It seemed impossible that people could love one another as much, naturally, and some wanted to see that rigorous fidelity as a ploy, a role agreed and well played. But what could have been the goal of that dissimulation? It could not be the fear of scandal, since the scandal was, on the contrary, their conjugal love!

Setting all these conjectures aside, Monsieur and Madame de Thurigny were enjoying, in all its plenitude, the beautiful amorous life whose hearth was fueled by their youth and fortune. For a year, nothing had caused the lovers to anticipate that their joy might be sanctified by passing through the heaven of paternal emotions, and they did not complain about it; their intoxication was sufficient for them.

What was astonishing in the attachment of the Marquis and Marquise de Thurigny was not its enthusiasm but merely its object, for, it is necessary to repeat, that was the weakness of that expansive epoch, when one loved ardently, but all the more often by reason of the scant entitlements one had to it, and when duty constituted an impeachment rather than an obligation. Those two perfect lovers had, therefore, in truth, only one fault in the eyes of the world, and that was being married; in other ways, they satisfied the program of the century exactly, balls, feasts and celebrations of every sort being the incessant accompaniment of their melody, their epithalamium. They realized that ideal existence imagined by poets, and their days passed like those of the heroes of Boccaccio and Ariosto. How far could that dream extend? Could human life support to the end, without vertigo and malaise, that intoxication of the senses and the soul? That is what we shall be able to say, before having finished this story.

Monsieur and Madame de Thurigny were, therefore, sitting to either side of the fireplace in their drawing-room, after a night in which all their luxury, all their gaiety and all their youth had welcomed everything that Paris had of the wealthiest, the most joyful and the youngest.

The Marquise, nonchalant and fatigued, like the mistress of a house who has been its queen in terms of beauty and grace, but a queen enslaved to the politeness and regard due to guests, let her charming head fall back on to the back of her chair with impertinent idleness, and, cradling it thus, pleaded for patience with her blue eyes overladen with languor.

But the Marquis was not thinking of retiring; a singular preoccupation was paling his face. His eyes wide open, he was staring in front of him with the fixity of terror. One might have thought that he was following the progress of some hideous reptile over the parquet. He sometimes clenched his hands and clutched the arms of his chair, like a man retaining himself on the edge of an abyss.

That handsome young man, tortured by a great suffering and writhing beneath the talon of a thought, formed a striking contrast with his beautiful and nonchalant companion, who lay back on the gilded wood of her chair, shaking her head, which exhaled a cloud of powder, and from which the pearls of her headdress fell like raindrops, stretching her dainty arms, whose joints she cracked, swinging the hem of her dress with her Chinese feet clad in white satin, completing the savoring, amid giggles and little yawns, of the last voluptuousness of the feast.

The distracted wife had not yet noticed her husband's taciturnity. A profound and heartfelt sigh on the other's part caused her to shiver; she looked at him and went pale, then suddenly stood up and ran to him, took his head in her hands, lifted it up in an affectionate and fearful gesture, and plunged a gaze into his eyes like an ardent blade, in which all the flames of her soul were concentrated, and cried rather than said, in a strangled voice:

"What's wrong, Julien?"

The Marquis tried to smile, kissed his wife's hand convulsively, and murmured: "It's nothing, Louise." An ill-repressed sob gave the lie to those words.

The young Marquise felt stricken in the depths of her being. A rapid frisson ran through her body; the frightful claws of presentiment closed over her heart, squeezing and stifling it. She made an adorable gesture of supplication, and sought once again to read in her husband's eyes the secret that he was hiding, but it was in vain; the sadness of the Marquis was impenetrable.

The poor woman remained motionless for a few moments, contemplating him. She ran through all her memories and impressions of the night, the previous days, and the entire year, but found nothing that might serve to explain Monsieur de Thurigny's strange depression. Waves of a bitter anguish rose within her, filling her bosom. The slightest movement might have caused her to faint fever displayed its first gleams in her eyes; it was a frightful fit, all of whose issues might be mortal.

Julien sensed that; he took pity of that long momentary martyrdom, and, allowing the tears that were burning him inside to show in his eyes, he extended his hand to his wife, saying: "Oh, why do we love one another so much?"

Louise shuddered at that, and understood that he had a secret. With a rapid glance she explored the drawing-room and the surroundings, saw that everyone had retired, that she was alone with her husband. Then, no longer able to contain herself, she covered the Marquis with kisses. Her emotion flowed in infinite caresses; she shook him with the rage of a wife and mother. The sentiment of a suffering to share, a wound to cure, elevated her love to the level of maternal abnegation. Placing Julian's head on her shoulder, like that of a child one is putting to sleep, wiping away her own tears, which were falling on her beloved's cheek, she said to him, in a soft voice calculated to loosen al the cords of his heart: "Julien my love, why are you suffering without me?"

And without giving Julien the time to reply, she stole the words from his lips with kisses. When the initial torrent had passed, when the firm and meditated desire to take her share in the anxieties of the Marquis had left nothing more in Louise's soul but resignation, she sat down on Julien's knees with a child-like melancholy, looked at him with supplicant eyes that she did not turn away again, glued her lips to her husband's trembling hand, and awaited with the ecstatic thirst of a Mary Magdalen the words of her God.

With the hand that remained free, Julien began gently caressing the loosened hair of the angel who was so tenderly claiming her share of his dolor, and, with his brow bathed in sweat, like that of a dying man, he began to speak.

"You want to know why I have reserved such a sad morrow of the fête for you, my love? Heaven is my witness that I would have given my life to spare you this dolorous hour, but it was inevitable. A voice has extracted me from my intoxication, and that jealous voice is as impossible to flee as it is to forget. It's necessary for me to submit to it and bow my head.

"You're astonished to hear me speak like this. Me, your lover, retreating in fear! Listen, Louise, have you never been superstitious? Have you never thought about those hazards that come to trouble the order of things, about that obscure world on the threshold of which human reason takes on the wings of nocturnal birds and takes hectic flight through the strangest reveries? Have you not heard tell of surprising apparitions? Have you not heard mention of powerful men who enchant and excite souls at will?

"Yes? Well, in order to understand me, recall all you children's tales, all your girlish terrors, for that world of phantoms, I have glimpsed; those irresistible effects of the will, I have experienced. Louise, as true as the fact that you are beautiful and I love you, as true as the fact that I can feel your tears on my hand, I swear to you that a demon has taken possession

215

of my life, that tomorrow, I am who talking to you today with a tottering reside of reason, who can still, but only just, act and think spontaneously, if that spirit wishes it, if it pleases that the last spark that I have should vacillate and go out, tomorrow, I shall go mad."

As Monsieur de Thurigny finished that speech, the Marquise, whose gaze was obstinately scrutinizing her husband's eyes, suddenly stood up.

"Julien," she said to him, "pull yourself together! Keep your secret—don't say a word, I implore you. Your head is on fire, don't try to remember; I no longer want that. I have no need to know any more. Forget! Forget!"

"No," said Julien, "you shall know everything. Come on, have no fear; troubled as my poor head is, it will still have strength enough today to resist fever."

"Poor love! I'll help you dissipate these chimeras!"

"You, Louise, will help me to succumb to reality; that will be your sweetest benevolence."

"So be it," replied the Marquise, with a heroic firmness. "Speak, then. I shall listen, I shall be mute until you interrogate me; but I demand in return that after telling your story, you will submit blindly. If they are vain phantoms that are obsessing you, the breath of the woman who loves you will dissipate them; if occult powers of a sinister reality are pursuing you or dragging you away, I who am your wife will follow you, and even if we must fall into an abyss, if you keep me by your side, what does it matter to me? Speak then; I'm waiting."

Louis went to fetch an armchair, leaned on it resolutely, and then, devouring her tears, calm and impassive in appearance, like a marble statue with a furnace inside her, she listened to the bizarre story that Julien resumed in these terms:

"If someone seeking to explain the depression into which I have fallen wanted to recount the events that led to it, he would simply say:

"'That night, at his ball, the Marquis de Thurigny met a German Baron, a short, thin old man named Baron von

Rorenstein. That individual, unknown to everyone, conversed with the Marquis in a low voice for some time; then, he drew him into the gaming room, sat down at a table with him, and everyone then observed that Monsieur de Thurigny was very pale and the little old man very cheerful. The former always lost and the latter sniggered incessantly. At the end of the ball, the Baron left, his pockets full of gold and his lips creased by his most diabolical smile. When he bid farewell to his guests, Monsieur de Thurigny was unsteady on his feet, either because he was worn out by fatigue or because he was more sensitive than was generally believed to his gambling losses.'

"That is what is what you would have been told, Louise, if you had interrogated the crowd, because the crowd only saw my pale face and the ironic visage of the Baron von Rorenstein—but I, who spent that frightful night in any agony of torture, who felt, several times, something like a finger of fire piercing my skull and stirring my cerebrum, who perhaps has no more than this hour to love you freely and be able sable to tell you so, can and ought to add the following commentary to that reply.

"It will be a long story, and I am forced to go back a long way, but none of the details I shall give you are irrelevant to last night's event.

"I have never spoken to you about my father, Gaston de Thurigny, and although the gentle and pious portrait of my mother seems to watch over us and bless us in our bedroom, nothing is alongside that venerated angel to remind us of the man who gave me his name and imposed life upon me, with the heritage of his misfortunes.

"I had sworn an oath never to talk about my father in your presence, in order never to expose myself to judging him, in trying to tell his life story; forgetfulness is the only curse permissible to a son.

"Last night, alas, transported me so abruptly into the past, and I felt the shade of the implacable phantom stir so forcefully, that I am forced to break my oath, and to look that terrible apparition in the face.

"Marquis Gaston de Thurigny was one of those adventurous gentlemen for who martial courage is the principal, and perhaps the only, virtue. He did not bargain with his life, and risked it without scruple; unfortunately, that insouciance followed him everywhere, and he put honor at the same level as life, not in accordance with the idea that it is necessary to quit the latter when one has lost the former, but because he thought one was worth no more than the other, and that one could risk them and lose them indifferently.

"His birth had placed him according to his instincts. He had the arm of a hero and the heart of a pirate. His element was war, but one is not always fighting, and in peace time he regretted the time when gentlemen became brigands. He was melancholy as he gazed at his château, with its broad avenues, modestly situated in the plain, on the bank of a river; he would have liked it to be on a crag, like a citadel, like a vulture's nest.

"It was not, however, that my father was one of those wild moor-slayers who wear formidable moustaches and have the stature of a colossus. Monsieur de Thurigny was slight and slender; his face was mild, his hands delicate and white; he had a sort of feminine beauty; his forehead was nicely shaded by his blond hair; nothing would have caused one to divine the iron beneath the velvet, except that his gaze sometimes had a hawk-like fixity, and only a slight contraction of the eyebrows betrayed his interior storms. His gentlemanly envelope was irreproachable; he had an Asiatic nonchalance that went with his face; women desired him, and his external grace pleaded in his favor for a long time; people refused to believe in the deceptiveness of his fine appearance.

"Such was Monsieur de Thurigny at twenty-five, before his marriage. With his immense fortune, his sensual aptitudes, his frightful passions, and his beauty, he would have played his role marvelously in the Mohammedan lands; he was of the race of Sultans, but his oriental caprices encountered too many obstacles here; he found himself out of place, and that young man, worthy of a seraglio, was merely a dangerous debauchee in France.

"Forgive me, Louise, for dwelling on these sad details; once again, they're necessary, and that reason is the only one powerful enough to make me overcome the repugnance that such a depiction inspires in me. I am speaking to you without anger, but without weakness; this moment is solemn. For the first time in my life, I am formulating an opinion explicitly, a judgment of my father, but I swear to you that that opinion, disengaged from all resentment, could rise, without my blushing, to the throne of God! One does not lie, one does not blaspheme, with one's conscience, and you are my visible conscience, my heart detached from myself.

"You will not be astonished that, given the character I have just described, Monsieur de Thurigny sought excitement, and surrendered himself to the plans best calculated to render his private life tumultuous.

"A ferocious hunter, an ardent drinker and a feverish gambler, he spent his days running after hinds in the forest, his evenings sitting at some joyous banquet and his nights with his elbows on some gaming-table; he quit thickets for boudoirs, boudoirs for gambling-dens, transporting everywhere the need for violent sensuality, the acid thirst that burned him without consuming him. But in all those excesses, in all those intoxications, even the most shameful, the handsome marquis maintained his arrogant and smiling attitude, the luxury of his costume, and his youthful glamour. He descended into all kinds of mire without anything spoiling his external prestige; the vices that escorted him did not touch him, and debauchery could scarcely discolor his cheeks slightly and blanch his feminine lips.

"At twenty-five years of age, Monsieur de Thurigny had not yet given any thought to marriage. His disorderly amours and dissipations did not appear to lead in that direction. One day, however, the rumor went around that Mademoiselle Thérèse de Morvan had consented to part her piously-joined hands, constantly clutching her rosary, in order to place one of them in the equivocal hand of the Marquis.

"There was a great scandal at court, Madame de Maintenon summoned Monsieur de Morvan and demanded to know whether he has lost his child in a game of lansquenet to sacrifice her thus. In fact, it was said at Versailles that after an orgy degrading to both gentlemen, that traffic had indeed taken place, and that the turn of a card had decided the future of poor Thérèse. Some thought that Monsieur de Morvan, whose nobility was doubtful, had sought to graft his heraldic tree on to an illustrious stock, and that his daughter's beauty, as well as his immense fortune, had served that ambitious hope with regard to the Marquis de Thurigny.

"But what do the causes of the mirage matter? For my misfortune and my eternal shame, it is sufficient that Heaven permitted it. Whether it was due to gaming or ambition, my mother became a saintly and resigned victim. Pure and stainless, a lily sprinkled with faith on altars, a heart full of the incense of strong and divine love, she came here to drag her virginal robe in the ill-effaced traces of orgies. She came to offer, in futile fashion, the intercession of her pious life, the baptism of her candid soul, to purify and ransom the heart of her husband.

"During the early months, she was spared disillusion, either because the capricious Marquis really loved her, or because the latter, whose entire existence was a trial of all follies, wanted to give himself the sweet rewards of hypocrisy, or, finally, because his sojourn in France and the maintenance of his rank at court, severely called into question by his bad reputation, demanded that sacrifice to public order. He appeared, during those first months, respectful and gallant with regard to his wife, worthy and conventional in his relationships with society.

"Already astonished by those six months of calm and almost of happiness, people were beginning to believe in a conversion, and one day, the Princess Palatine, who was able to speak freely at court, said to Monsieur Thurigny in front of the king: 'So, Marquis, you not going to be hanged?'

"'Why despair, Highness?' the Marquis replied, smiling.

"A fortnight after that reply, playing cards with the king at Versailles, he came to the aid of chance so impudently, cheated with such effrontery, that the gentlemen who were playing brelan with him threw their cards in his face, and Louis XIV told him to leave the realm as soon as possible if he did not want to remain there in the Bastille.

"Monsieur de Thurigny, laughing at that indignation, which he thought out of place in the mouth of a grandson of Henri IV, returned to his house, where his wife, very happy and very confused, was waiting to tell him that their union had been blessed by Heaven, since Heaven had given her the assurance that she was to be a mother. The Marquis gave her his compliments along with his adieux, regulated his accounts with the gentlemen who had insulted him that evening, and after having laid them out in the meadow, wiped the blade of his sword, threw himself nonchalantly into his carriage, told his coachman to take the road of Germany, and left, insouciant and radiant, for the exile in which he went to seek new pleasures, new amours, new companions and perhaps new dupes.

"My mother wept for a long time. She wanted to flee with the love and honor of her house, fearing for the child stirring in her loins the heritage of a punishment. Oh, your lugubrious presentiments did not deceive you, Mother, and the destiny you feared for your son, after having forgotten me for a long time, has finally arrived!

"Forgive me for interrupting my story, Louise, but I cannot see you looking at me like that without remembering the two beautiful eyes that were extinguished by tears, and I want by virtue of that thought the one who so tenderly opened life to me to descend into that night in juxtaposition with the one who will so gently open death to me.

"After Monsieur de Thurigny's departure, my mother, who had nothing further to do at court, retired to the provinces, to a sad old family château, where she knew, after three months delay, the dolorous joys of maternity.

"My birth, in brightening the desolate obscurity in which the Marquise lived, transported her greatest sadness of the present into the future; she welcomed me as a consolation—but she watched me grow up fearfully, like a victim.

"What shall I tell you about my early years? They went by peacefully and calmly, in the shade of the old manor. I was a silent child. No one taught me to smile; my mother's kisses, instead of causing life to blossom within me, seemed to freeze and extinguish it. Quitting the somber and silent apartments for the lofty, dark pathways of a park two hundred years old, initiated with an austere tenderness into the first elements of thought, having no companion of my own age who might have communicated his gaiety and insouciance to me, I grew up rapidly, but like one of those sad flowers that grow in damp places, devoid of brightness and perfume.

"No one ever spoke to me about the Marquis, and I would have thought that he was dead if my mother, every evening, before I went to sleep, had not recommended me, after our common prayer, to pray for the life and honor of my father, who was making a great and perilous voyage. Except for that, never a word about the man of whom it was only permitted to me to think in confrontation with God.

"Ten years went by like that.

"One evening, I was with my mother on a terrace of the château that overlooked a little lake, and we were breathing, after the heavy heat of an August day, the fresh perfumes that were rising from the shore. Sitting at Madame de Thurigny's feet, with my head on her knees, I was dozing off while my mother, slowly passing her hand through my hair, gazed at the heavens desirously.

"I remember that evening as if the breeze were still bringing me the scents of the valley.

"It was our custom after dinner to go and sit on that terrace. There we waited for nightfall, and when all the stars had come out, when the chill became too penetrating, my mother taught me to pray in that natural and splendid oratory, and then made a space for her kiss between the curls of my hair, and we would go back inside, silent and calm, but full of the melancholy happiness that I already experienced, child as I was, without being aware of it.

"Now, that evening, we had come, as was our habit, to aspire the beneficent breath of the evening. Time went by, and we were about to go back in when, all of a sudden, as the Marquise bent over me to kiss me, three violent blows struck on the main door of the château awoke the echoes of the valley with a start and caused us to utter an exclamation.

"What was that noise? Who was the indiscreet visitor who announced himself at such an hour? I looked at my mother and, by the pale light of the moon, I saw the signs of a great terror in her face. She was standing up, and trembling so forcefully that she was constrained to lean on the balustrade. I was about to question her when I felt two burning tears fall on to my forehead, and hear her murmur: 'Can it be him? My God, thy will be done!'

"At the same instant, footsteps became audible, and the Marquise clutched me to her, violently.

"Then, as we turned round, we saw a man on the terrace, with a sepulchral countenance, thin, bony and arched in the back, whose disorderly vestments betrayed the misery and fatigue of a long journey. He advanced toward us, and I felt my mother's tremors redouble. She made an effort, however, repressed her emotion, and pushed me lightly toward the stranger, saying; "Julien, salute Monsieur le Marquis de Thurigny.'

"That specter was my father.

"I can't describe the sinister impression those words produced in me; even so, cowed by my mother's gaze, I took a step toward the Marquis and kissed his hand.

"'Monsieur,' said the Marquise, trying to smile, 'we've been waiting for you for a long time. What happy thought has brought you back to your wife and child?'

"That soft voice, which offered such a simple welcome, seemed to astonish Monsieur de Thurigny.

"'Ha ha!' he said, with a certain febrile volubility that betrayed a disorder in his thoughts. 'You haven't retained any rancor, Thérèse, and you've kept well; this will be less disagreeable. I've changed a great deal, haven't I? I'm astonished that you recognized me. It's because I've suffered a great deal. I've experienced great…frightful misfortunes. I'm ruined, and I've come to ask you for the hospitality of Baucis for repentant Philemon. Germany is a land of sorcerers; they make contraband there of the mischief of Hell. Don't let your son go there. I've arrived in the devil's claws. Frantz will tell you all about it, won't you, Frantz? But where is he? Has he abandoned me? Frantz! Frantz!'

"'Who is this man you're calling?' asked my mother. 'If he's a servant, he's probably helping in the preparations for your reception; if he's a friend...'

"'Oh no, Frantz isn't a valet, nor is he a friend; he's…why, I don't know what he is. He's Frantz, that's all.'

"A few moments later, we saw a little man of frightful thinness appear, dressed simply, but in mourning. He told the Marquis that everything was ready and that he could go to bed.

"'Thank you,' replied Monsieur de Thurigny. He turned to my mother and added: 'Here's the companion I was talking about. Like me, he has a slight reek of sulfur about him, and I believe he's a first cousin of the architect who built Cologne cathedral, but if he's a demon, it's not by dint of gaiety. Frantz, I'll introduce you to my wife, but tell me what title I should give you: are you my steward or my friend?'

"The singular individual bowed with a hypocritical humility; as he straightened up the reverberation of his sparkling pupils passed over my mother's eyes and mine, and he said to my father, in a tone replete with irony: 'You're asking me for my secret Marquis—what I am to you? Perhaps your Providence.'

"'Say rather my fatality!'

"'Oh, isn't it the same thing?'

"'Let's go inside, Messieurs,' said Madame de Thurigny, unable to master her emotions.

"Such, Louise, was my first meeting with my father; such was the Marquis' return to his wife, after then years of abandonment and forgetfulness.

"A superstitious terror that I saw that my mother shared had dried up all filial aspirations in me, and the phantom who came back that night, that gentleman in rags whose reason had been shaken by the sorceries of Germany, accompanied by that somber an enigmatic individual, bore too much resemblance to an evil genius for my heart to adopt him. Before going to sleep I asked the Marquise, who was in tears, whether I still had to pray for my father, now that he had returned."

"'More than ever, my poor child,' she said, putting her arms around me, and, modifying the formula of my prayers somewhat, she had me invoke God for the Marquis' sanity and the salvation of his soul.

"The next day, Monsieur de Thurigny summoned me to his room. I went in trembling; his mysterious companion Frantz was with him.

"'Julien,' said my father, gravely, 'I sent for you in order to question you. What has been made of you, my son? What do you know? What have you learned?'

"At that question I felt my soul gently stirred. I thought it a symptom of tenderness, a whim of paternal anxiety. I was grateful for it. Convinced that I was about to undergo an examination, I made a rapid mental review of the notions that I had acquired; I had already commenced their enumeration when the Marquis' mocking laughter drove away, with my words, all the pious sentiments that had surged forth within me.

"'That's not what it's about, Julien,' he told me, jovially. 'Do you take me for a pedant? What does it matter to me if you talk like a priggish philosopher, if you don't have the tastes or the instincts of a gentleman? Come on, my son, what's this?'

"And he drew from his pocket a deck of cards, which he laid out on his knees, explaining the numbers and the symbols.

"Raised by my mother, from whom I had never been apart, a sad and studious child, I was completely ignorant as to the value or even the names of the cards. So I thought that I ought to blush at that ignorance, and it was in a tone of veritable regret that I spoke of it to my father. I soon understood my error, however. By virtue of Monsieur de Thurigny's sarcasms, and the confidences that he punctuated with laughter, an unfathomable presentiment made me shudder. I raised my head and, staring at the Marquis, was suddenly struck by the idea that he was mad.

"In fact, at that moment, the radiance of his eyes was astray in imaginary visions. His laughter had a metallic sonority, and while talking to me volubly and incoherently, a mechanical movement made him shuffle the cards. I was afraid, and had turned to flee, when my gaze met that of Frantz, and I felt a commotion, a shock, that made me cry out.

"Like the eyes of those serpents that paralyze their victims, the German's pitiless gaze nailed me to the parquet, and the inflamed dots of his pupils dug into my thoughts. Something akin to intoxication or madness caused my blood to rise to my head and I stayed there, mute and motionless, petrified, as if held in iron shackles. It seemed to me that my forehead swelled up to collide with the opposite walls of the room, and that needles of flame were emerging from my skull.

"I don't know how long that torture lasted; what I can say is that it was frightful; and although I tried to cry out and call for help, I distinctly heard bursts of laughter reverberating within me, as if my bosom had enclosed an echo.

"My mother's voice, which called to me from outside, broke the charm. Frantz turned his eyes away; I felt liberated and I ran, unsteadily, to the door of the room, where I fell, almost fainting, into the Marquise's arms.

"From that day on, vertigo and its terrors floated over the château. My father, always accompanied by Frantz, who served him at table and accompanied him in his walks, following in his footsteps, seemed to be struggling beneath a burden that was crushing his intelligence. Somber and oppressed, he sometimes had fits of feverish and demonic gaiety during which he shouted loudly for a deck of cards.

"I did not speak to Madame de Thurigny about the ordeal to which the German had subjected me. Every time I wanted to confide it to her, an interior voice and a terror surely aroused by that dangerous man froze the words on my lips. The frightful commotion experienced when my eyes first met Frantz's was renewed at every further encounter, so an indescribable terror caused me to remain constantly close o my mother. As for her, calm and devoted, she tried to struggle against the pernicious influence that was killing the Marquis' soul. Armed with her faith and her conscience, she tried to penetrate that darkness.

"One day, she summoned Frantz, who usually avoided her presence, and demanded that he explain himself categorically. Frantz was respectful and calm; he replied that a terrible secret prevented him from revealing anything regarding his liaison with the Marquis; that he had a mission to accomplish; that no power in the world could oppose its fulfillment; but that he would hasten his departure as much as possible.

"Those final words were accompanied by an equivocal smile that chilled my mother. She fell silent, and attempted a completely futile appeal to the Marquis. Monsieur de Thurigny would not hear any talk of dismissing Frantz; he protested like a child, and said that he would not quit his last and only friend until death separated them.

"My mother resignedly abandoned the two accursed individuals to their destiny. She understood that only a superhuman intervention could break the links that bound Frantz to the Marquis, and she waited, calm and collected in her piety, and in her love for me...

"We sensed that the denouement was approaching. Every day, Monsieur de Thurigny's intervals of reason diminished, and at the same time his madness, and his strange sympathy for Frantz, increased. It was more than friendship, it was an invincible and fatal attraction; it was one of those pacts sealed outside this world, in the glimmer of diabolical invocations.

"Everything that I am telling you now, Louise, must seem impossible to you; you doubt it; you're wondering whether it isn't me whose disturbed reason is engendering chimeras; but by the Heaven that hears me, by our love, I beg you to believe me.

"Like you, I've doubted; I've often wondered whether it might not be possible to explain quite naturally and quite simply these bizarre facts of my childhood; but irrefutable proofs and palpitating memories have confirmed me in my terrors; and in any case, even if I had been able to deny it until now, last night was sufficient in itself to prove to me that I was not mistaken, and that Frantz was one of those excessively powerful spirits before whom the barriers of the real and the possible crumble; for whom death has no secrets and life no refuge, and who would make one doubt God if, by good fortune, one did not believe in the Devil.

"Monsieur de Thurigny's humor darkened. His fits of explosive gaiety had entirely disappeared; a kind of somnolence, a torpor, seemed to invade him His perceptions became less distinct; exterior objects no longer awoke any but confused ideas; in his ardent imagination, nothing any longer remained of his thirst for pleasures, his impetuous activity, and no one would have recognized in that languishing and maniac individual the handsome gentleman of the final years of the great century.

"Three months had gone by since his return—three months of apprehension for my mother, three months of agony for the Marquis—when, one day, Frantz, in traveling clothes, hat in hand, came to say his adieux to the Marquise, announcing to her that the time had come and that he was about to leave the château. Then, turning to me, he rested his terrible gaze on mine for a minute, and bowed to me with an ironic gravity.

"'*Au revoir*, Monsieur le Comte,' he said to me, with his German accent, which communicated strange vibrations to his voice. We watched him go, my mother and I, in a silence full of anxiety. That departure was as unintelligible as his arrival and his sojourn.

"We went up to the Marquis de Thurigny's room, and found him lying on the floor, frightfully pale, his hair bristling, breathless, foaming at the lips, exhausted, as if after a struggle, his eyes dilated as if by a frightful vision. It was impossible for us to extract an explanation from him.

"The measure was full; thereafter, and forever, the Marquis was completely mad. On returning to the drawing-room, my mother fund a voluminous envelope on the mantelpiece, addressed to her. She opened it and read, in the numerous pages it contained, the explanation of the mystery. Frantz, as he departed, had left behind, as one last threat and one last vengeance, that commentary on his conduct.

"On her death-bed, the Marquise allowed me to read that strange story; I have not forgotten any of it, and will tell you the principal facts. The night still has two hours of silence to give us; let me, then, my love, prolong this conversation. Alas, it will finish all too soon.

"During the early days of his sojourn in Germany, Monsieur de Thurigny, not knowing what to do and finding himself in a state of uncertainty as to how to employ, in a fashion profitable to his pleasures, the long days of exile had decided to sample a little of those serious amours, those grave and mystical affections of which France is ignorant. Not finding there the opportunity for those noisy and hectic friendships that had assisted him so well in spending his fortune and his life, idle in the midst of that studious population, having only a mediocre sympathy for beer, Monsieur de Thurigny, by virtue of one of those caprices familiar to him, wanted to experience what is doubtless called love in Germany. Rather blasé, in any case, with regard to cheerful tenderness, it seemed to him to be appropriate to refresh himself, if only once, with that languorous and melancholy sentiment.

"He selected his victim with the patience, calm and sagacity of a consummate hunter. He wanted, for the experiment—or, rather, for the whimsical game—one of those meditative hearts ever open to ideal breezes. He seemed to him that it would be charming to squander the pure flowers of one of those celestial gardens, to bring one of those blonde angels always kneeling at the Calvary of the German passion to apostasy.

"It was an impious idea; we support its punishment. Louise, the sacrilege of the father is to be expiated by the son.

"Monsieur de Thurigny, young, handsome and endowed with a prodigious intelligence, able to adapt to his physiognomy all languages and all lies, was an irresistible tempter. He had the suppleness, the glamour and the malice of the Biblical serpent, so, many curious gazes watched him as he passed by when he was walking the streets of Cologne, nonchalant and graceful, affecting the poetic ennui of unoccupied souls, while through the mask of his melancholy he scrutinized his surroundings covetously, and put his desires on the track of the innocent prey he was burning to attain.

"The Marquis' selection was soon made. He had noticed in the temples and the promenades a young woman about sixteen years of age, whose beauty was radiant in her calm face, between the curtains of her long blonde hair. Something harmonious and pure that emanated from her revealed the immaculate candor of her soul. She was an animate lily. Monsieur de Thurigny chose her as the holocaust of his debauchery. Every symptom of virtue that was revealed in her was a further bait offered to his sensuality. The more the cup sparkled, the more he was in haste to drink therefrom.

"The young woman always went abroad escorted by two young men of the same age, grave and austere. The Marquis, slightly surprised at first by those two masculine shadows, for such a transparent vision, soon learned that one of the two was her brother, the other a cousin, and that the most religious peace of feeling and the soul maintained the three individuals at the level of a mild and placid life.

"To capture the amity and the confidence of his stars two vigilant satellites was the first idea that occurred to him and the first step he took. He posed as a dreamer with such a seductive abandon, took such care to find himself in front of the two friends everywhere, with his gaze haunted, that those two simple and honest souls soon imagined that they had found a wound to close, a chagrin to console, and approached the pale unknown effusively. The Marquis remained bleak and taciturn for some time. Irritating the sympathetic curiosity of the two Germans, he appeared to want to bury himself in the silence and bitterness of his memories—but the two friends redoubled their affection, and when he yielded, it was as if he had been vanquished by their persistence.

"Then commenced outpourings, sublime in appearance, although fundamentally imaginary, on the part of the Marquis, handshakes, intimate conversations, future plans, all the exchange of warm and kind words that make up, in youth, hours of amity as well as hours of inspiration and genius.

"Carl and Walter, honest and inflexible, but with the naivety of scientists, were students, the former of astronomy and the latter of medicine.

Carl was Elisabeth's brother, and Walter, as I said, her cousin. All three of them orphaned, they lived together, sheltered by their childhood affection and the memory of the parents who had covered them in caresses. Elizabeth was the good fairy of the household. She it was who prepared the material life of her two companions, with delicate care. Her brother Carl was ambitious; he had taken it for his task to increase the glory of his community, and his dear stars were the focus of his aspirations; he lived more in the heavens than on earth. Walter, whose anatomical labors forced him often to envisage the truth in that which was more material, attached the little colony to the world by more positive links. It was him who regulated the budget and filled the coffers, but he gave without affectations and they accepted without shame, so impossible did it seem to the three friends that anything—ideas, affections, well-being—was not common property.

"Walter thought, quietly, about taking Elisabeth for his wife one day, but while that plan was germinating within him he hid it carefully, not wanting to disturb the security and quietude of Carl and his sister in any fashion, and not wanting his devotion to be attributed to motives of self-interest.

"Monsieur de Thurigny was received by the trio, simply and cordially, as if the family, instead of three members, henceforth counted four of them. He was not even asked to recount his chagrins; he was accepted on the guarantee of his handsome face, veiled by melancholy; his touching attitude dispensed with interrogation. That paradise of German naivety opened without hesitation to the demon's shrewd candor; the periwinkles and symbolic flowers beneath which he crawled hid the serpent's head.

"Carl showed him his observatory, explained his mysterious conversations with the night, and took him for the confidant of his sidereal amours. Walter took him silently by the hand, but that grip signified an immutable devotion. Elisabeth bathed the Marquis' face with the soft and tremulous gleams of her gaze; she welcomed him without suspicion, and began to love him ingenuously; it was, therefore, not difficult for Monsieur de Thurigny to mark his target and to reach it; the victim offered herself to him. Thanks to his marvelous hypocrisy, the languid softness that he gave to his gaze, solitary strolls, conversations in the moonlight—the chaste cortege with which he surrounded his passion—my father had soon attached himself invisibly to Elisabeth's soul.

"Carl and Walter saw that love and rejoiced in it. It did not occur to them to keep watch on the two lovers. Naïve and confident, judging in accordance with their own hearts, they feared to profane, by indiscreet inspection, the pious sentiment whose perfume was revealed to them. Only Walter was sad and anxious or a few days. He regretted his lost dream, but resigned himself in the thought of Elisabeth's happiness, and waited, as Carl did, for the moment when the union would be consecrated. The two worthy and honest Germans did not imagine that such pure oaths could hide a seduction. Having never interrogated Monsieur de Thurigny about his past life, they knew nothing of his marriage, and in the utmost depths of their hearts, they blessed the foreigner who had brought their common sister love and its ecstasies, and them, in the future, the intoxication and sweet cares of a family.

"For the Marquis, immaterial love was the means, so he became impatient with still being in those preliminary delights and wanted to complete his work, but the fire of his senses did not reach the virginal and candid German girl. Elisabeth had transported her love into almost-inaccessible regions, which one reached by descending from Heaven, not by rising from the earth.

"That seraphic countenance and that attitude did not disconcert my father, but it irritated him. He resolved to put an end to it by trickery and, if necessary, violence. Besides which, the comedy was beginning to appear foolish and fatiguing, and his entire past of debauchery and libertinage rebelled against the time wasted in reciting vain words.

"One evening, he made Elisabeth drink a terrible beverage. As soon as the liquor had penetrated the tranquil veins of the poor child, a frightful conflagration lit up in her bosom; her head, overheated by impure miasmas, wandered; a disorderly drunkenness shook all her limbs, numbed until then by a severe virginity. My father, alas, was able to sate his criminal desire in the feverish suffocations of a madwoman.

"The dose, had, in fact, been too strong; Elisabeth had the sad advantage of losing her reason at the same time as her honor. She did not have to blush at her spoliation, and three days after that hour of sacrilegious love, she did, tortured by the most frightful agony, but having no consciousness of herself, burned by the fire in her entrails, howling with pain, and struggling on her profaned bed as if on a bed of coals.

"My father had only intended half of the crime but he accepted the other half with audacity. The debauchee did not reject the murderer. He waited, calmly and disdainfully, only slightly pale, for vengeance to rise up.

"Carl came first. The poor scientist, his teeth clenched and his eyes wide, rushed upon the Marquis, sword in hand. The latter had only to stretch out his arm, and Elisabeth's brother, pierced through the heart in his insensate attack, fell, bequeathing his vengeance to Walter. But Walter, by virtue of an inexplicable resolution, appeared to renounce his friend's heritage. Without shedding tears, without allowing a plaint or an insult to escape him, he buried Elisabeth and Carl, put into their coffin a bunch of those blue flowers of Germany whose name means "Forget-me-Not," went back to his lodgings, packed his bags, put his books under his arm, and left Cologne without paying any heed to the Marquis, without picking up Carl's sword, without leaving the law the responsibility of publishing the rape and murder of Elisabeth.

"Monsieur de Thurigny, astonished by this departure, smiled—but you have guessed, haven't you, Louise, that Walter's vengeance was only suspended, and that that retreat was merely a trap? And as you shall see, his contained anger was implacable in its ferocity.

"Walter was one of those men of bronze who have but one sentiment in their lives, to which they give themselves entirely. Until then, he had loved Carl and Elisabeth. Outside the circle of his labors and studies, he had given no other aliment to his sprit than that pure affection. After the Marquis' crime, when his ravaged soul had lost those objects of tenderness, a terrible despair took possession of him. Before that catastrophe, his existence had been devoted to love, it was devoted henceforth to hatred; but he set about hatred as he had loved, with abnegation, with a cold fury, with a total preoccupation of every instant. He no longer breathed save to attain one objective: that of his vengeance—except that he envisaged the punishment of the Marquis coldly; he did not want to run the risks of a duel that would have equalized the chances. He considered Monsieur de Thurigny as a criminal, not as an enemy; in the depths of his conscience, he judged him, but waited in order to execute the sentence; the hour had not yet come.

"Years went by. The Marquis had gone to Vienna, where a few French gentlemen introduced him to the court. His ostentation, his grand manner and his licentious gaiety soon made him a cortege of all that the imperial city had of debauched youth.

"One night, during the carnival, he perceived that he had been followed since the commencement of the ball by a masked man whose sparkling eyes seemed, by virtue of their obstinate attention, either to be studying him with an exaggerated zeal, or spying on him. Any mystery that did not conceal a woman was not worth the trouble, so far as he was concerned, of being fathomed, so he did not worry about it unduly.

"The next day, however, and the following days, he found that masked man behind him, ten paces away, with the same gaze and the same persistence. It was either a wager or a mania, some imbecile looking for a duel to make himself fashionable, or some German bumpkin who was making himself the Marquis' reflection in order to copy his grace. Monsieur de Thurigny wondered whether he should take the trouble to chastise the importunate shadow, but thought: *What's the point?* and he waited.

"However, he began to perceive that the strange gaze of that domino was not fixed upon him with impunity. At first, there was a kind of vague anxiety, like a slight ache; then gradually, it seemed to him that a dull but violent heat entered into his head via his eyes at each new encounter; then symptoms of vertigo and fever gripped him. In seeking to sustain the glare of the eyes behind the mask, he felt the nervous contractions that one experiences before a copper plate on which sunlight is falling vertically.

"That ended up turning into torture, so, one night, Monsieur de Thurigny resolutely accosted his mute companion and demanded that he explain his strange obsession. The eyes of the mysterious individual seemed to redouble their sparkle. In a hollow voice into which he strove to inject some joviality, he said:

"'Marquis, we poor German debauchees are so stupid, so hampered in our familiarity, that I thought I would permit myself to follow you and study you, as the gentleman most intrepid in his pleasures; but I'm beginning to despair. You excel in all the vices, but I only have one that does me honor.'

"Which one?" asked my father, surprised but fundamentally flattered by that reply.

"'Gambling,' the masked man replied.

"'Damnation!' said my father, with a sigh. 'You're complaining, but you like gambling!'

"'Yes, I confess,' the stranger continued, 'that the rustle of cards is the sweetest of harmonies to my ears, but I'm far from making them talk the sublime language that they have in your hands. If you wish, Monsieur le Marquis, you would render me the happiest of men by agreeing to play a game with me. Don't refuse, I beg you.'

"The final words in a commanding tone that belied them, and the strange man accompanied them with such an energetic glance that Monsieur de Thurigny, felt shaken. He almost fell over, and it seemed to him that a secret and invincible force drove him to accept. He was the man to gamble with Satan himself, and the mystery that enveloped the mask was not calculated to frighten him—quite the reverse.

"'Very well, Monsieur le Ténébreux,' he said, 'I accept. At what game shall we measure ourselves?'

"'At Brelan, if you please, Marquis.'

"'Brelan it is! But that noble game demands, in order to be piquant, at least three rivals, and we are but two.'

"'I have a friend who is always willing to follow me in these enterprises; I'll bring him along.'

"'Agreed,' said my father. 'When shall we meet?'

"'Tomorrow, Monsieur le Marquis—but one word before we separate. Powerful motives, political reasons, force me to adopt a disguise. I will only sit down opposite you with this costume and mask. Later, perhaps I shall be free to make myself entirely known. Until then, I hope that you will respect my incognito?'

"Monsieur de Thurigny bowed courteously. Something irresistible drove him to accede to everything. The time and place of the first meeting were agreed. The stakes were fixed, and the next day, in the noisiest part of a tavern, under the clouds amassed against the ceiling by the smoke of pipes and lamps, the strange game commenced whose prelude was full of mystery and whose denouement was full of terror.

"The three players sat down in silence. The Marquis was not exactly anxious, but he was pricked by a superstitious curiosity. He did not believe in anything, but if he had been converted, his first act of faith would have been for the Devil—with the result that he was not very far from thinking that the mask might hide the sulfurous face of some infernal genius. He was not frightened by that, but the enigma he sensed gave his heart occasion for quivers and contractions that astonished him.

"He felt increasingly penetrated and burned by the unknown man's gaze, and all his audacity remained impotent against that dolorous attraction.

"The masked man was like a specter, except that one could hear the breath passing through the openings in his mask. He shuffled the cards slowly, and apart from the few gestures demanded by the game he maintained a lugubrious immobility. The person the stranger had brought with him played his role mechanically, like an automaton. At first, my father tried to direct a few witty remarks at the two companions, but his gaiety froze, and he no longer brought anything but a serious and exclusive application to the game.

"The ante, to begin with, was only a louis, but it was increased by degrees, and after an hour, the drinkers in the tavern awoke with a start on hearing sums named of which the least never descended below ten thousand livres.

"Monsieur de Thurigny lost, but his ardor was increased in consequence. Nevertheless, he retained the impassivity that was natural to him. In spite of that, a kind of feverish terror attained his heart. No matter how forcefully he stiffened himself against that emotion he felt invaded and subjugated by a malign influence. He understood instinctively that the secret of the game was an abyss, but he went toward it.

"At times, vertigo caused his hair to bristle, and he stopped several times to wipe sweat from his streaming brow. At every pause the masked man said to him: 'Are you backing out, Monsieur le Marquis?' And the Marquis, half-mad and carried away by fury, picked up the cards again, tried to laugh, and found nothing in his throat but a dry croak. The more he sought to get a grip on chance, the more it fled him.

"The game continued until dawn.

"As the first gleams of daylight slid through the thick windows of the tavern, the masked man stood up, threw down the cards and said: 'Enough for today!'

"My father, habitually so impatient and proud, who commanded gamblers and never obeyed them, dared not resist; he submitted to the will of the unknown who was stripping him and murmured: 'Until tomorrow!' Then, staggering like a drunkard, scarcely able to sustain the burden of his head, he went home, debilitated, as if by a poison.

"Apart from the conduct of his two companions, another aspect of the game had troubled my father. Several times during the session he had risked considerable sums on a brelan of kings, and each time he had lost, his adversary holding a superior brelan; either hazard had been responsible for that irony, or the players had a secret and skillful means of forcing fortune. The Marquis, whose eyes, habituated to all trickery, had not discovered anything suspect, was astounded by those singular combinations. Bizarrely enough, the fatal brelan of kings was always the same: the king of hearts, the king of clubs and the king of diamonds.

"The Marquis was more disturbed than he wanted to appear by that circumstance, and in the brief and feverish sleep that he had after that session he saw, in his dreams, the three kings walking at the foot of his bed, passing gravely by in their lampas robes, smiling at him through their blue beards, and letting a rain of gold coins fall from their broad sleeves.

"That nightmare terrified him, and when he found himself facing his mysterious companions the following night, his heart, dulled by debauchery, began to beat violently, as if he were a very young man, full of illusion and ardor, at his first amorous rendezvous.

"That second meeting was similar to the first. The Marquis experienced the same losses, the same emotions, the same fever, subject once again to the fascination of the unknown and feeling powerless against it. Nothing that had disturbed him the previous night was missing, not even the cabalistic brelan, which reappeared three times, always the same and always as fatal.

"Either the two gamblers who were profiting were fleecing him, or he was going mad. The Marquis felt his reason tottering; his seething activity and agility in passion had given way to an insurmountable torpor. He felt crushed by a mysterious pressure, and yielded in a cowardly fashion. As soon as a thought awakened in his head it collapsed; his intelligence was torn apart by a vulture whose wings he felt beating to either side of his head.

"I shall not describe all the phases of that extraordinary torture; suffice it for you to know that for a month, Monsieur de Thurigny went to that gambling-den to surrender himself to the infernal power of the masked man. For a month, he came to defend with the cards, hand by hand, all of his fortune, which drained away with his reason. For a month, by a miracle of sorcery, the immutable brelan of kings came to tempt my father, and every time he bet on it, it hastened his ruin.

"Finally, when, exhausted by that agony, withered and wan, his eyes dilated by terror, pursued by bizarre superstitions—imagining, for example, that he saw floating before him everywhere the mocking phantoms of the king of hearts, the king of clubs and the king of diamonds—he came to sit down at the accursed table at which his entire soul had been staked, it was with the shudder of a weary man falling into bed and the sigh of a dying man turning over to sleep in his shroud that he threw his last louis on to the table and tipped back his

239

seat, murmuring: 'It's over. I no longer have anything to lose. Now let me be.'

"A silence followed that sob. His eyelids lowered, as if he were reflecting, Monsieur de Thurigny allowed himself to be borne away by the whirlwind passing freely through his head. Withdrawn into himself, he waited the denouement: the crisis, whatever it might be, destined to close the drama. If the uneven floor of the tavern had opened beneath his feet to allow sulfur and flame to escape, he would not have been astonished. Evidently, Hell had been too much involved in the game for the Devil not to manifest himself at its conclusion.

"The masked man picked up the Marquis' last louis, and dismissed his acolyte, the third player he had brought to complete the party, henceforth unnecessary, with a gesture. Then he unfastened his mask and threw it behind him.

"Then my father, extracted from his stupor by those abrupt movements, raised his head and recognized before him, in the contracted features of Walter, the sparkling visage of the vengeance that the mask has sheltered for so long. A sudden illumination, like a flash of lightning exposing an abyss, explained everything. He understood that the moment had come for a formidable expiation.

"Something of his gentlemanly irritability made him clench his fists at first and stand up as if to slap that Nemesis and provoke him, but a piercing glance from Walter shoved him rudely back into his seat. He fell back into it, crushed, and remained motionless, bewildered, his hands extended in front of him, petrified by the imposing stare of Elisabeth's remaining friend.

"Walter contemplated him with the pride of an archangel holding his fiery blade before the face of the Devil. Standing up, magnified by wrath, pale, emaciated by the fatigue of his endeavor but transfigured by exaltation, his irises bathed with supernatural light, he savored the Marquis' anguish with a bitter voluptuousness, With a sinister joy, he steeped his gimlet gaze in the sweat flowing down my father's creased brow.

"After a few moments of that triumph, Walter made a commanding gesture and said: 'Listen! I demand it!' And the Marquis, obedient to that sovereign voice, set himself to listen.

"'You have forgotten me,'[32] Walter went on, with a forceful voice. 'On seeing me flee the house in mourning, you said to yourself: *Carl was a madman; that one is a coward.* And you laughed, did you not? But, by the immortal soul of the virgin that you immolated, I did not forget you, and you were insane to think that I might. I did not pick up Carl's sword because it might have broken in my hand; because, even if I had planted it in your heart, that expiation would have seemed insufficient and frivolous. For the crime you have committed, a momentary agony was too little; death would have come too soon. I have avenged myself with my own weapons. I am not a gentleman but a physician; I do not kill with the sword, I dissect with the scalpel. I have waited. I have left you free to act. I trembled lest some new infamy on your part might divert the punishment of your life to the profit of another vengeance, but since Carl and Walter you have only dishonored cowards, and the ignominy of your victims preserved you for me. Arrogant gentleman, cynical debauchee, I have you! You cannot flee. Try! My eyes nail you to the back of that chair more surely than iron spikes. You belong to me now, and forever. Everywhere you walk under the sun, I shall walk in your shadow, until the day when you buckle beneath my knees to enter the tomb. I no longer regret the laborious years that have devoured me, now that the result has been attained. My sweat has germinated; my harvest has commenced.

"'At the time when your infamous caprice was tarnishing the gentlest flower that ever leaned over the Rhine, I consoled myself for Elisabeth's love for you by studying, by stifling my soul beneath science. My thought had pierced the visible

---

[32] It is significant that throughout this speech Walter addresses the Marquis as "tu," not "vous," the intimate form of address that can carry an implication of insult when used by one adult to another.

world and I entered, crawling, the world alongside ours where all the strings that cause our machine to move are labeled and numbered, and can operate at the behest of an audacious man like me. I discovered the mysterious relationships between souls. My initiation was interrupted by Elisabeth's agony and Carl's death. You forced me to return to this world, but I swore that it would not be with impunity.

"'I glimpsed a means of utilizing my work. What I had discovered of the empire of a formidable will over the laws of our being determined me to kill you slowly, with powerful impacts of my soul upon yours. But before attempting that proof, which might exhaust my life, I wanted to have no doubt, to have not a moment's hesitation, and, silencing the roaring of my hated, I went far away from you, to read, to study, to fathom further, to forge in silence the terrible weapons with which I had to return.

"'My vengeance cost me dear; twenty times I despaired; twenty times I was tempted to abandon my experiments, to run at you with a dagger; but something sustained me. I had too much belief in my wrath not to believe in the possibility of its effects.

"In the mystery of my retreat, I sharpened my mind and my gaze; I paid victims of whom I made automata, and when, after years of ardent labor, of sleepless nights, of anguish, I was convinced of my power, I was certain that by means of my will I could caused the effluvia of your thought to boil, I set out on your track, I followed you, I made myself the vigilant dog of your shadow, and every time you turned your head, I plunged my gaze into yours like a red hot iron.

"'You have understood, have you not, that hatred has served me faithfully and that I am finally avenged. Since out first encounter, your reason has tottered; you doubt; all the claws of fear have gripped you; you feel accursed. Well, listen, and know what bitter floods you have still to drink before I permit you to die.

"'You are mine, and not only can you not escape my power, but you cannot even want to. I have ruined you; I have stripped you of everything that prevented your being entirely my victim. My plan for you is this: you shall submit to the punishment of talion. In the monstrosities of your caprice, your poisonous breath injected madness into Elisabeth's veins; well, handsome gentleman with the free and lively spirit, you shall feel in your turn the stifling of unreason; you shall go mad. Your mind, which I hold compressed beneath mine, will struggle vainly; I shall allow it lucid intervals, during which you shall be able to observe and measure your own degeneration, observe your decline; you shall be the witness of your agony; you shall have, until the end, the consciousness of your degradation, and you shall submit to it, by a fatal law. But know this: you shall only reflect on my orders; you shall only remember when I consent to it.

"'Henceforth, I no longer want to be, and must no longer be, so far as you are concerned, Walter, the imprudent friend of Carl. I order you to forget that name. I am your steward, your valet, your necessary man; I shall call myself Frantz, and the jealous affection that we have for one another will prevent us from ever being apart. Marquis, we are going to travel through Germany; I shall pay for you everywhere, and never ask you to verify my accounts; I shall be generous, as you shall see. I shall not tell you how long you will be condemned to live; I shall think about it!'

"Such, Louise, was the conversation between my father and his judge.

"More terrified than one can describe, cringing beneath Walter's gaze, he went forth, escorted by that strange man, through all of Germany, parading his decrepitude through the places where his youth, his wealth and his licentious braggadocio had made his name shine most conspicuously, the slave of a companion who seemed to onlookers only to approach him humbly. Monsieur de Thurigny wandered thus for a long time, besieged by phantoms, devoured by fevers.

"After a year, his torturer brought him to France, to the château of the Marquise de Thurigny, and you know what a lugubrious impression my father's first appearance made on me. There, Frantz—or rather Walter—obstinately pursued his task. Gradually extinguishing the flame that was flickering beneath his breath, he savored the joy of his vengeance to the full; then, when he had full uprooted behind that knitted brow the final branches retaining the Marquis' reason; when he had worn out those dolorous alternatives of lucidity and madness, he completed his work, and with the aid of a fascination achieved by the continual exercise of an immeasurable force, he drove the distraught soul of Monsieur de Thurigny back into the vortex, into darkness, into chaos, forever.

"After the departure of Frantz, and having read his letter, my mother, sad but patient and devoted, had the miserable madman installed beside her, whose guide, sustenance and providence she became henceforth. The château resembled a sepulcher; its previous grave serenity had given way to a lugubrious silence.

"At first, I was afraid of the Marquis, but gradually, counseled by my mother's angelic devotion, I was able to approach him, to look at him without fear; I got used to guiding him, to distracting him, to sharing in the childish things with which he was incessantly preoccupied.

"The only memory permitted to my father was that of the brelan of kings that Walter had caused to intervene in such a bizarre fashion, but it returned with the fantastic dimensions of a nightmare. That combination, always the same, the obstinate appearance of which had been so deadly, was profoundly engraved in his mind. Like the sentence of Belshazzar, it appeared before his eyes flamboyant. The three kings came to stir magic words in his ears, speaking of fabulous riches. In his hallucinations, he saw them live, act and move. Sometimes, in our walks through the park, he stopped, gripped me insistently by the arm, and said: 'Let their majesties pass, Monsieur le Comte.'

"At table, he took care to order three extra places to be set for his three illustrious guests. He dressed himself like each of them in turn. He had their full-length portraits pained and hung in the drawing-room. And he died, after a year of that convulsive life, believing that he could see the three kings at his bedside, whose ironic smiles congealed the marrow in his bones.

"The tomb appeared to have been buried Walter's vengeance with the Marquis' hollow head. We heard no further mention of him.

"I grew up. My mother, whose youth had withered away under those harsh ordeals, blossomed for the first time when I was twenty years old. I had realized her hopes; had taken to heart all the noble ambitions that she had put into it, all the aspirations toward love, all the sentiments of the good and the beautiful. She blessed me, and blessed in me her beloved's future companion; then, one day, she died, as if she were about to begin her life in Heaven, and in her final hour, she seemed to be waking up rather than going to sleep.

"My life, from that day on, you know, Louise. I saw you and fell in love with you. The sad and cold wall that enclosed me collapsed under the sparkling radiance of your love. Smiling reality guided me by the hand of my dream; you descended into my arms from the throne where I adored you; for a year, society has admired without understanding the pure happiness in which we steep our lips; for a year, nothing has wearied our joys, nothing has soured our ecstasies, and in this supreme hour, when I am about to break the cup from which our intoxication poured, it seems to me that I have only just begun to love you.

"My poor love, you are an exceedingly beautiful adornment for this funereal night! You are a beautiful bride for death!

"Louise, I dared not conclude, and yet I must. Why, with the heritage of my accursed name, have I dared to put myself at your knees and offer you my soul? Forgive me! Forgive me! I'm weeping, you see. But what use are my tears? Can they save us? I was a coward last night, during the ball. I should have set fire to those draperies, to your lace, to hug you and die with you in the blaze. I have preferred to savor dolorous tenderness at your feet, the terrible embrace of despair!

"Louise, we are doomed. Don't you understand? Do you know why I have suppressed my fever in telling you the story of the Marquis de Thurigny? Why I have taken it upon myself to expose you coldly, in detail, all the incidents of his debauched life, and all the vicissitudes of Walter's vengeance? Do you know why I have abused your courageous attention to that extent? It is because I wanted you to be convinced, as I am, that nothing can save us. It is because I wanted you to tell me, when I destroy your happiness: 'It's all right; you could not have done otherwise.'

"Now, listen to the sentence of fatality.

"Last night, a German gentleman was introduced to me, the Baron von Rorenstein. That man's first glance pierced me to the entrails like an arrow of fire. He bowed to me, ironically, and I felt myself tremble. He talked to me about my father, whom he had known well in Germany; he talked to me about his madness, his passions and his death. I don't know how, but I found myself led by that unknown guest to sit down opposite him at a brelan table. I thought that I was about to faint. I heard the sound of the orchestra in my head, reverberating with a terrible vibration, and I felt as if droplets of molten lead were flowing through my veins from head to foot. I remembered the impressions of my childhood and I murmured, several times: 'Frantz! Frantz!'

"Baron von Rorenstein smiled, and made me play. I lost, and I lost continuously, not only money, but this house, the château, land…what do I know?…everything that I could think of to offer as a stake. And—a horrible thing!—I lost three times with the same brelan that had killed my father; three times, the king of diamonds, the king of clubs and the king of hearts came to offer themselves to me, as a mockery, as a threat.

"It was a monstrous fatality. My eyes could no longer see; my brain was lifting up my skull; I thought I was going mad—and I uttered a laugh so strange that the people who were with us looked at us with an astonishment mingled with fear.

"The Baron von Rorenstein got up, drew me into the embrasure of a window, and said to me: 'I see that you have recognized me, Marquis. Yes, I was Frantz; yes, I am Walter; yes, I was the torturer of Marquis Gaston de Thurigny; yes, I am the avenger of Elisabeth and Carl, and I have just completed the holocaust due to those pious victims. I did not bury my hatred with your father; it sat down on his tomb and waited for you. My life has been devoted to that task. I swore to pursue the murderer of my fiancée and my friend to the very last drop of his blood. You were condemned at the same time as him. I have only varied the occasion, in order to strike more surely. It has finally come.

"'You are at the apex of happiness; all the intoxications of a husband, all the glories of a gentleman, you have, or you have within your reach, whereas your father destroyed my joys as a lover, my hopes as a man. He prevented me from having a son as handsome as proud as you; he exterminated my family; I shall kill his. That's just, is it not? I shall punish you as God punished the sins of Adam. You host fêtes glittering with women, flowers and gems; you live in an atmosphere of perfumes; and meanwhile, my dear dead are asleep out there in a tiny, cold German cemetery. They are no more deserving of their coffins than you, son of their assassin, are deserving of these joys. If I have come to take them from you, that is also just, is it not?

"'Your father sowed madness, shame and death; it is not equitable that his son should reap happiness, pride and all the prestige of life! So, Monsieur le Marquis, know that I shall settle the family accounts—and yet, hear this! I have been carrying the burden of my vengeance for so long that it seems to weigh less; I have been mourning my friends for so long that my heart has been dulled slightly by the tears; and if oaths made to the dead were not imperious and sacred, perhaps, even though I see you so blessed by heaven, I might have taken back my Hellish thoughts. Perhaps I might even have refrained from torturing, in the name of love, a couple so freshly blossomed in love. But I have sworn, and the dead, underground, insensible to everything else, awaken to weep when one commits a perjury. I cannot, therefore, entirely forgive. Except, Marquis, that I will give you this night; if you love, if you are loved, if you are not a gentleman with impunity, if you dare to liberate yourself from the consequences of a second meeting with me...then adieu, Monsieur de Thurigny! If not, *au revoir!*'

"And the Baron von Rorenstein left me stunned, stupefied, penetrated by horror. Now, do you understand? This morning, perhaps in an hour he will come back—he will come, if I have not put an insurmountable barrier between his infernal power and myself.

"That is the whole of my secret, Louise. What do you say?"

During the whole of that long story, Louise had remained a statue of silence, beautiful and calm. She had not made any movement or gesture to interrupt. She had remained suspended by her gaze on Julien's lips, and when she had finished, raising her arms, she said to him: "You're right, my love; we must flee. We must leave. That abominable man must not see you again."

And Louise clutched him, tremulously, devouring him with convulsive kisses.

But Julien, pale-faced, loosened the charming bond that enlaced him with a terrible gentleness, held the Marquise's hands is his own, and said to her:

"You want to flee? But where? Don't you realize that nature has no obstacles for that man, distance no abysms. His gaze will weigh upon us henceforth; we are welded to one another, and everywhere I go, by virtue of an invincible attraction, I will draw him after me. Since his strange pity left me this night, let us not waste time seeking defenses. There is only one means of sparing myself this torture, this agony. There is only one sure and impenetrable refuge. I did not want to descend into it without your blessing. Forgive me! I swore to make your life beautiful and happy. God is my witness that I would have liked to keep my oath for a longer time…!"

With the radiance of a martyr, the Marquise interrupted Julien. "Did you think of dying without me?" she said to him.

Then she added, emphasizing and punctuating her words with an adorable smile: "Egotist! Ingrate!"

The response was one of those long and energetic kisses whose mute eloquence is untranslatable.

Then, between those two children, frightened of life, transpired one of those sublime scenes before which one drops the pen and the paintbrush to kneel down and admire. Only God, who put so much love into the heart of a man, so much devotion into the soul of a woman, could say what happened in that solemn hour. There were oaths, tears, prayers, adieux, hymns of dolor in a word, in a cry, poems in a glance, infinite ecstasies, despairs mingled with delights—an entire struggle of those two angels on the brink of the tomb…a flutter of their wings before taking flight.

Gradually, as the night came to an end and the dawn rose behind the trees in the grounds of the house, the noise that they made slowly died away, like a harmony that, rising from the earth, is eventually lost in the sky. Then, at the matinal hour when Romeo detached the silken rope from Juliet's balcony, at the last murmur of the nightingale, at the first song of the lark, a long sigh was exhaled, and all was said…

When the apartments of the Marquis and Marquise of Thurigny were entered, they were both found dead on the parquet, pale and blue-tinted by the kiss of death, in a tight embrace, fallen to the ground like two flowers escaped from a broken vase. The poison has respected their last smile. They were buried in one another's arms. Legible on their faces was the joy of dying before the end of their dream, and those charming suicides only seemed to be asleep. God alone knows now when and how they will wake up.

Many conjectures were made regarding that catastrophe, but the Baron von Rorenstein kept his secret. He presented himself at the house at an early hour, and, as he had anticipated the event, he was dressed entirely in black.

He followed the procession of his two victims, saw them descend into the earth, and could not help allowing a tear to fall upon their coffin.

Three days later he returned to Germany and went to pick little blue flowers on Carl and Elisabeth's grave.

SF & FANTASY

Alphonse Allais. *The Adventures of Captain Cap*
Henri Allorge. *The Great Cataclysm*
Guy d'Armen. *Doc Ardan: The City of Gold and Lepers*
G.-J. Arnaud. *The Ice Company*
Charles Asselineau. *The Double Life*
Cyprien Bérard. *The Vampire Lord Ruthwen*
S. Henry Berthoud. *Martyrs of Science*
Aloysius Bertrand. *Gaspard de la Nuit*
Richard Bessière. *The Gardens of the Apocalypse*
Albert Bleunard. *Ever Smaller*
Félix Bodin. *The Novel of the Future*
Louis Boussenard. *Monsieur Synthesis*
Alphonse Brown. *City of Glass; The Conquest of the Air*
Emile Calvet. *In a Thousand Years*
André Caroff. *The Terror of Madame Atomos; Miss Atomos; The Return of Madame Atomos; The Mistake of Madame Atomos; The Monsters of Madame Atomos; The Revenge of Madame Atomos; The Resurrection of Madame Atomos; The Mark of Madame Atomos*
Félicien Champsaur. *The Human Arrow; Ouha, King of the Apes; Pharaoh's Wife*
Didier de Chousy. *Ignis*
Jules Clarétie. *Obsession*
Michel Corday. *The Eternal Flame*
Captain Danrit. *Undersea Odyssey*
C. I. Defontenay. *Star (Psi Cassiopeia)*
Charles Derennes. *The People of the Pole*
Georges Dodds (anthologist). *The Missing Link*
Harry Dickson. *The Heir of Dracula*
Jules Dornay. *Lord Ruthven Begins*
Alfred Driou. *The Adventures of a Parisian Aeronaut*
Sâr Dubnotal *vs. Jack the Ripper*
Alexandre Dumas. *The Return of Lord Ruthven*
Renée Dunan. *Baal*
J.-C. Dunyach. *The Night Orchid; The Thieves of Silence*
Henri Duvernois. *The Man Who Found Himself*
Achille Eyraud. *Voyage to Venus*
Henri Falk. *The Age of Lead*

Paul Féval. *Anne of the Isles; Knightshade; Revenants; Vampire City; The Vampire Countess; The Wandering Jew's Daughter*

Paul Féval, *fils. Felifax, the Tiger-Man*

Charles de Fieux. *Lamékis*

Arnould Galopin. *Doctor Omega; Doctor Omega and the Shadowmen* (anthology)

Judith Gautier. *Isoline and the Serpent-Flower*

Léon Gozlan. *The Vampire of the Val-de-Grâce*

G.L. Gick. *Harry Dickson and the Werewolf of Rutherford Grange*

Edmond Haraucourt. *Illusions of Immortality*

Nathalie Henneberg. *The Green Gods*

V. Hugo, P. Foucher & P. Meurice. *The Hunchback of Notre-Dame*

Romain d'Huissier. *Hexagon: Dark Matter*

Michel Jeury. *Chronolysis*

Gustave Kahn. *The Tale of Gold and Silence*

Gérard Klein. *The Mote in Time's Eye*

Fernand Kolney. *Love in 5000 Years*

Paul Lacroix. *Danse Macabre*

Louis-Guillaume de La Follie. *The Unpretentious Philosopher*

Jean de La Hire. *Enter the Nyctalope; The Nyctalope on Mars; The Nyctalope vs. Lucifer; The Nyctalope Steps In; Night of the Nyctalope; Return of the Nyctalope; The Fiery Wheel*

Etienne-Léon de Lamothe-Langon. *The Virgin Vampire*

André Laurie. *Spiridon*

Gabriel de Lautrec. *The Vengeance of the Oval Portrait*

Alain le Drimeur. *The Future City*

Georges Le Faure & Henri de Graffigny. *The Extraordinary Adventures of a Russian Scientist Across the Solar System* (2 vols.)

Gustave Le Rouge. *The Vampires of Mars; The Dominion of the World* (w/Gustave Guitton) (4 vols.)

Jules Lermina. *Mysteryville; Panic in Paris; To-Ho and the Gold Destroyers; The Secret of Zippelius*

André Lichtenberger. *The Centaurs; The Children of the Crab*

Jean-Marc & Randy Lofficier. *Edgar Allan Poe on Mars; The Katrina Protocol; Pacifica; Robonocchio; Return of the Nyctalope;* (anthologists) *Tales of the Shadowmen 1-9*

Xavier Mauméjean. *The League of Heroes*

Joseph Méry. *The Tower of Destiny*

Hippolyte Mettais. *The Year 5865*

Louise Michel. *The Human Microbes; The New World*

Tony Moilin. *Paris in the Year 2000*

José Moselli. *Illa's End*
John-Antoine Nau. *Enemy Force*
Marie Nizet. *Captain Vampire*
C. Nodier, A. Beraud & Toussaint-Merle. *Frankenstein*
Henri de Parville. *An Inhabitant of the Planet Mars*
Gaston de Pawlowski. *Journey to the Land of the 4th Dimension*
Georges Pellerin. *The World in 2000 Years*
Ernest Pérochon. *The Frenetic People*
Pierre Pelot. *The Child Who Walked on the Sky*
J. Polidori, C. Nodier, E. Scribe. *Lord Ruthven the Vampire*
P.-A. Ponson du Terrail. *The Vampire and the Devil's Son; The Immortal Woman*
Edgar Quinet. *Ahasuerus*
Henri de Régnier. *A Surfeit of Mirrors*
Maurice Renard. *The Blue Peril; Doctor Lerne; The Doctored Man; A Man Among the Microbes; The Master of Light*
Jean Richepin. *The Wing; The Crazy Corner*
Albert Robida. *The Adventures of Saturnin Farandoul; The Clock of the Centuries; Chalet in the Sky; The Electric Life*
J.-H. Rosny Aîné. *Helgvor of the Blue River; The Givreuse Enigma; The Mysterious Force; The Navigators of Space; Vamireh; The World of the Variants; The Young Vampire*
Marcel Rouff. *Journey to the Inverted World*
Han Ryner. *The Superhumans*
Brian Stableford. *The New Faust at the Tragicomique;The Empire of the Necromancers (The Shadow of Frankenstein; Frankenstein and the Vampire Countess; Frankenstein in London); Sherlock Holmes & The Vampires of Eternity; The Stones of Camelot; The Wayward Muse.* (anthologist) *The Germans on Venus; News from the Moon; The Supreme Progress; The World Above the World; Nemoville; Investigations of the Future*
Jacques Spitz. *The Eye of Purgatory*
Kurt Steiner. *Ortog*
Eugène Thébault. *Radio-Terror*
C.-F. Tiphaigne de La Roche. *Amilec*
Louis Ulbach. *Prince Bonifacio*
Théo Varlet. *The Golden Rock. The Xenobiotic Invasion; The Castaways of Eros; Timeslip Troopers* (w/André Blandin); *The Martian Epic* (w/Octave Joncquel)
Paul Vibert. *The Mysterious Fluid*
Villiers de l'Isle-Adam. *The Scaffold; The Vampire Soul*

Philippe Ward. *Artahe*
Philippe Ward & Sylvie Miller. *The Song of Montségur*

MYSTERIES & THRILLERS

M. Allain & P. Souvestre. *The Daughter of Fantômas*
A. Anicet-Bourgeois, Lucien Dabril. *Rocambole*
A. Bernède. *Belphegor*; *Judex* (w/Louis Feuillade); *The Return of Judex* (w/Louis Feuillade); *The Shadow of Judex*
A. Bisson & G. Livet. *Nick Carter vs. Fantômas*
V. Darlay & H. de Gorsse. *Arsène Lupin vs. Sherlock Holmes: The Stage Play*
Séamas Duffy. *Sherlock Holmes in Paris*
Paul Féval. *Gentlemen of the Night; John Devil; The Black Coats ('Salem Street; The Invisible Weapon; The Parisian Jungle; The Companions of the Treasure; Heart of Steel; The Cadet Gang; The Sword-Swallower)*
Emile Gaboriau. *Monsieur Lecoq*
Goron & Emile Gautier. *Spawn of the Penitentiary*
Rick Lai. *Shadows of the Opera: Retribution in Blood; Sisters of the Shadows: The Curse of Cagliostro*
Steve Leadley. *Sherlock Holmes: The Circle of Blood*
Maurice Leblanc. *Arsène Lupin vs. Countess Cagliostro; Arsène Lupin vs. Sherlock Holmes (The Blonde Phantom; The Hollow Needle); The Many Faces of Arsène Lupin*
Gaston Leroux. *Chéri-Bibi; The Phantom of the Opera; Rouletabille & the Mystery of the Yellow Room; Rouletabille at Krupp's*
Richard Marsh. *The Complete Adventures of Judith Lee*
William Patrick Maynard. *The Terror of Fu Manchu; The Destiny of Fu Manchu*
Frank J. Morlock. *Sherlock Holmes: The Grand Horizontals; Sherlock Holmes vs Jack the Ripper*
Antonin Reschal. *The Adventures of Miss Boston*
P. de Wattyne & Y. Walter. *Sherlock Holmes vs. Fantômas*
David White. *Fantômas in America*
Pierre Yrondy. *The Adventures of Thérèse Arnaud*

SCREENPLAYS

Mike Baron. *The Iron Triangle*

Emma Bull & Will Shetterly. *Nightspeeder; War for the Oaks*
Gerry Conway & Roy Thomas. *Doc Dynamo*
Steve Englehart. *Majorca*
James Hudnall. *The Devastator*
Jean-Marc & Randy Lofficier. *Royal Flush*
J.-M. & R. Lofficier & Marc Agapit. *Despair*
J.-M. & R. Lofficier & Joël Houssin. *City*
Andrew Paquette. *Peripheral Vision*
Robert L. Robinson, Jr. *Judex*
R. Thomas, J. Hendler & L. Sprague de Camp. *Rivers of Time*

NON-FICTION

Stephen R. Bissette. *Blur 1-5. Green Mountain Cinema 1; Teen Angels*
Win Scott Eckert. *Crossovers* (2 vols.)
Jean-Marc & Randy Lofficier. *Shadowmen* (2 vols.)
Randy Lofficier. *Over Here*

ART BOOKS

J.-M. Lofficier & D. Taylor. *Tongue*Lash*
Jean-Pierre Normand. *Science Fiction Illustrations*
Raven Okeefe. *Raven's L'il Critters; Rave's Faves*
Randy Lofficier & Raven Okeefe. *If Your Possum Go Daylight...*
Daniele Serra. *Illusions*

HEXAGON COMICS

Franco Frescura & Luciano Bernasconi. *Wampus*
Franco Frescura & Giorgio Trevisan. *CLASH*
L. Bernasconi, J.-M. Lofficier & Juan Roncagliolo Berger. *Phenix*
Claude Legrand, J.-M. Lofficier & L. Bernasconi. *Kabur*
Franco Oneta. *Zembla*
L. Buffolente, Lofficier & J.-J. Dzialowski. *Strangers: Homicron*
Danilo Grossi. *Strangers: Jaydee*
Claude Legrand & Luciano Bernasconi. *Strangers: Starlock*

www.ingramcontent.com/pod-product-compliance
Lightning Source LLC
Chambersburg PA
CBHW060348030726
47497CB00003B/645